Praise for J. H. Wear's *Talnut*

"...The dynamic between Carl and Tanya was fun to watch develop. The interactions between Carl and the other villagers showed how it only takes one person to change an entire world. J.H. Wear has built an intriguing world with a variety of characters ranging from human to dinosaur and everything in between."

~ *Hayley, Fallen Angel Reviews*

"This story is an interesting one and I like the various challenges and dangers this place has to throw at poor Carl and company."

~ *Mrs. Giggles*

Talnut

J. H. Wear

A Samhain Publishing, Ltd. publication.

Samhain Publishing, Ltd.
577 Mulberry Street, Suite 1520
Macon, GA 31201
www.samhainpublishing.com

Talnut
Copyright © 2008 by J. H. Wear
Print ISBN: 978-1-60504-004-2
Digital ISBN: 1-59998-623-X

Editing by Bethany Morgan
Cover by Christine Clavel

First Samhain Publishing, Ltd. electronic publication: January 2008
First Samhain Publishing, Ltd. print publication: November 2008

Dedication

This is my first novel and I would like to dedicate it to a few people who have helped me write it. First, to my wife Laurie, I doubt very much I would have the energy and confidence to try my hand at writing if it wasn't for her. Next, I want to thank Samhain Publishing for taking a chance on my book and to my editor Bethany Morgan. Bethany did a great job on making the manuscript much better than the one I originally sent in. Finally, I would like to mention New Zealand. It was there when I was visiting that wonderfully scenic country I became inspired to write Talnut.

Chapter One:
The Newcomer

Tanya sat on the grass with her legs folded under her, her hands resting on her lap as she slowly breathed out. The hilltop was a place for her to relax and meditate, to wash away the negative feelings. Under the nearly cloudless sky, the afternoon sun warmed her back as she stared at the horizon. The time was near when the two moons Era and Trava would rise. For the past week, the two small moons were close together in the sky, a sign of good fortune. As she slowly closed her eyes, she felt the gentle, intrusive images of the Aura. Initially she wanted to ignore them, but the pattern was strong and interfered with her plans to meditate.

Tanya spent a few minutes analysing the images and then stood up with an annoyed sigh before starting her walk back home. *Why do I have to have this so called gift? Because of it, I don't have any friends and the only thing I have to look forward to is becoming the village Witchdoctor like my mother. Other nineteen-year-old girls have boyfriends. I have the Aura. I wish I could trade.*

She followed the path through tall grass and, from the distance of the hillside, she spotted her mother sitting on the stone steps of their dwelling. Teresa was a bit shorter than her five-foot-nine daughter but heavier. The years didn't show on her, she kept her mostly dark brown hair shoulder length and her face had resisted wrinkles as well. She worked a mixture in a clay pot with a paddle—a task Tanya had decided to duck out of when she observed her mother gathering the cubus roots earlier. The grinding was hard work and Tanya had quietly

7

disappeared before she could be asked for help. It was a strange mix of guilty feelings and resentment as she approached the perimeter of their yard.

Teresa looked up and smiled at her approach.

"Is everything alright, dear? You look..."

Tanya waved her hands in front of her to stop her from speaking. "There's a disturbance coming. Don't you feel it?" She heard the exasperation in her own voice and knew she wasn't being fair. She became annoyed with her mother far too easily and she herself didn't feel the disturbance until she had closed her eyes on the hilltop.

Teresa considered, closing her eyes in concentration. Tanya's powers had now surpassed her own and it took Teresa a few seconds to find the Aura. "Yes, you're right. A change, a strong one is approaching."

Tanya walked into the house, calling out behind her "I'm going to try the trivoli."

One of the rooms was partitioned from the others by a curtain and she retrieved a small leather pouch stored on a shelf there. She carried the bag close against her chest and hurried outside, going to a spot near the edge of the forest. Her mother watched her carefully as she hurried past.

Tanya held the bag to her heart as she sat cross-legged, facing due west, swaying to her own whispered chants. A few minutes later, the bag's contents were spilled on the ground, the small bones, sticks and coloured pebbles scattering about. Tanya used her fingertips to sprinkle soil over the objects and murmured a prayer. She closed her eyes, scooped up the majority of the trivoli objects and rolled them in her hand. She whispered a blessing and tumbled them onto the bare ground, watching the pattern form of the small bones and sticks. Some were straight, while others were bent or curved that allowed for a complex alignment. The pebbles were slightly different sizes and colours and she was at first puzzled by their location, until she tossed the trivoli twice more.

Carefully returning the objects to the bag, she hurried back home.

"Good news?"

Tanya was often surprised how her mother could guess what she was thinking. Maybe it was psychic, or maybe her mother could read her face better than she thought.

"I think so. We are going to have a Newcomer. Someone important."

"Are you certain? We haven't had a Newcomer for several years now, perhaps..."

"I'm sure."

Tanya saw her mother frown. "Sorry. I'm sure. And he'll be important." She paused before she gave more of the interpretations, choosing her words with care. "He will arrive, un...without protection and with a memory of the past."

Her mother cocked her head at the information, started to speak and then said nothing. Sometimes it was better to let things be than to ask for details. She was concerned about her daughter. Teresa suspected Tanya kept her dark hair long to shield her face from the probing eyes of the other villagers. She was also aware how Tanya favoured long dark skirts and leather vests that kept her covered rather than the light colourful cloth that most of young women wore. It was if she was trying to hide from the world.

Teresa hoped her daughter would come out of her self-imposed shell and be more sociable. *Perhaps this Newcomer will help her with that.*

Carl woke up lying face down. His first act of consciousness was that of coughing as he tried to lift himself up. Carl was twenty-one, just over six feet tall on a slim frame. His arms felt weak, and now his mind started to race with the memories of why. He looked frantically around and saw no one, and then lowered his head and coughed some more. When he looked about again in a more studied approach he noted he was at the edge of a beach, a few feet away from some bushes that marked the start of a forest. Behind him the water slid onto the beach.

Waking up on a beach is one thing, but waking up without knowing how you got there is quite another. His last recollection was being examined by strange looking humanoids, memories he would rather not recall. He was certainly glad they had finished with him and then deposited him off at this beach, but where on Earth the beach was he couldn't say. One thing that he suddenly realized was that he was naked and that discovery caused him some concern.

Carl's muscles began to return to life and he pushed his from his forehead and raised himself to his knees. After he accomplished that and didn't feel dizzy, he forced himself to stand up slowly to look around again. He still couldn't see anyone else on the beach, to his relief, noting the beach extended only about thirty feet before water claimed its territory. He hesitated before he stepped towards water and stood halfway on the beach cautiously as he gazed down the shoreline that wandered in a zigzag in both directions before disappearing in the distance. The ocean was calm and though he stared at the blue water, he wasn't able to detect boats or any other sign of human occupation, making him, it seemed, quite alone.

What if I'm marooned on some island? How can I get home if I can't contact anyone? On the other hand, at least there isn't anyone who can see me naked.

He noticed the beach came to a rather abrupt end as the plants, trees and bushes crowded in from a forest. After the smooth surface of the sand, the slope rose quickly covered with the vegetation. Walking over to some of the plants lining the beach he tried to determine if he could use the leaves to cover himself up in some sort of leafy garment. He gave up after a few minutes after finding leaves couldn't be tied together easily and certainly didn't want to stay in place around his hips.

Cautiously he walked into the ocean until the water reached his knees. The water wasn't cold and from his new vantage point, he could see farther up along the coastline. There still wasn't a sign of people or even civilization, and once again, he became apprehensive about his isolation. He felt worn out and now that he stood in the water, realized he was thirsty and perhaps a bit hungry as well.

I guess you aren't supposed to drink seawater. Maybe I better start searching for some fresh water and then some food.

Carl decided to follow the coastline until he came across something that was different from the rest of the forest, plants and coastline. Staying in one spot didn't seem to serve much purpose.

Tanya woke up early that morning. A change has come was her first thought as she sat up in bed. She yawned and headed to the outhouse noticing her mother was already up and preparing breakfast. Teresa was an early riser, unlike her daughter who was able to sleep to noon if her mother would let her.

"Good morning."

Tanya merely nodded at her mother's greeting and plunked herself down at the table. She yawned again and muttered thanks when breakfast was placed in front of her. The Newcomer must have arrived—she could sense that. Where was he? As she slowly ate her scrambled egg and bread she probed with her mind as to where the disturbance was coming from.

"Do you want more to eat? I can make up some cakes as well."

"No, I'm full. I have to check on something." She pushed away from the table and headed outside.

Teresa watched her daughter leave. She closed her eyes and now she felt it too, a change in the patterns. He had arrived, whoever that might be, and Tanya was trying to locate him. She resisted the temptation to go with her, it was time for Tanya to do more, to take on more responsibilities for the village's well being. This was a good time for her to stretch her capabilities a bit more. Besides she sensed her daughter really wanted to find him by herself, and her own presence might be a hindrance.

Tanya headed down one of the forest paths that led towards the ocean. The sense that he was near the southern part was strong, though she felt he might also be moving. That was logical, she thought, he wouldn't very likely stay in one spot. The trail, like most of the paths through the forest, didn't seem to have a singular direction. It wound back and forth between the trees and had a gentle incline towards the western part of the beach.

Carl was getting more than a little anxious as he continued his journey, occasionally washing his face with the ocean water to help get rid of the feeling of thirst.

That sun is getting strong. It's going to get hot. That forest would be cooler, but I wonder what animals live in there, maybe bears or snakes. He looked up at the bright sky, glad his skin was dark enough to resist some of the sun's rays.

He switched from walking on the sand to the shallow water, enjoying the coolness of the water. Small schools of fish darted out of his way as he walked, occasionally a foot-long fish would beat a hasty retreat. The beach was quite coarse and was littered with seashells, giving it a white-patchy appearance. Though the shells looked normal enough, there looked to be an over abundance of the larger type lying scattered about. He eyed the coast again and thought he picked out a movement in the water. It was too far out to see much, as a faint mist obscured any detail, but he was certain it was boat. It didn't appear to have a sail and sat low in the water but he believed he could see two figures sitting down in the vessel. He stopped. His mind began to race with what to do next. He considered running up to them and shouting out to attract their attention. But it also occurred to him that they might be up to no good, may even had something to do with the group that put him there. He decided to walk near the forest and get a closer look at them before they saw him. There was still the delicate matter of being naked, and he wasn't sure what to do about that.

Tanya reached the end of the path and stepped onto the beach. She was south of the harbour where the fishing boats were returning from their morning catch. She turned away from the boats and began her search. She wanted to find him before anyone else did, after all she knew about his arrival first, likely before he even did. In a way, she felt he was hers, not that she owned him or anything like that, but because she saw him first and therefore she should at least get credit for finding him.

Her sense of his presence became stronger, which surprised her a bit. Usually events and not people caused that particular feeling of lightness. In a way he was an event so there was some logic in it. Tanya hadn't told her mother everything she learned from the trivoli, for example, being unprotected was only a partial interpretation. A more accurate definition might be uncovered, which intrigued her, and the curiosity of what the other sex looked like was on her mind. She knew the other girls her age were intimate with boys. There was also a game called "Era and Trava" that the younger girls would play with the boys. She hadn't been invited to those games that were held well away from adults' prying eyes, or most of the social activities of her peers for that matter. The others weren't always openly rude to her but there was always a marked change in the conversation when she chanced upon some of them gathering. She heard some of the whispers referring to her as the witch, or telling each other to close their minds as if she could read them.

Carl was peering at the boats as he walked carefully around the extreme part of the beach. The sand was easier on his bare feet so he decided against trying to find a route among the trees. He was also still leery of the forest, wondering what might be lurking there.

The boats were becoming a bit more defined now and it now appeared there were at least two vessels. One of smaller boats held two people who were sitting down and a larger boat held three, one who was standing up pulling on something. The other boats were too far away to make out anything other than they were some type of man-made objects. Still it pleased him to know there was more than one boat out there, which may mean a hamlet or fishing village.

If it's some sort of village, I should be able to phone Mom and Dad. Maybe I'll be able to steal a pair of pants or something before anyone sees me. I sure could use something to drink, maybe a cold...

She was looking right at him as he stepped past yet another outcropping of bush and trees. He froze for a full second before reacting by diving behind a tree, twisting his ankle on a root in the process.

"Ouch!"

"Are you all right?" She took a step towards him.

Carl was down on one knee, clutching and cursing his ankle. "Keep back! I haven't any clothes on for crying out loud!"

"I noticed." She stopped, surveying where he crouched with cool detachment. "It looks like you need some help though."

"Just stay there!" He looked again at her, gazing at the long black hair framing a pleasant face with full lips. He also took in the black leather vest that was held together by a leather lace and a long wrap that wasn't quite black but was made of a dark cloth that had a design embroidered on the bottom.

Not a bad bod, though she looks a bit like one of those Goth chicks.

"Okay I'll stop. Now what do you want me to do?"

Boy she's a cool one, hasn't even cracked a smile. She doesn't even seem surprised to see me. "I don't know. I need some clothes."

"Where are your clothes? I could get them for you." She made the offer, knowing all Newcomers arrived without clothes.

"I don't know what happened to them! If I did, don't you think I'd be wearing them? Look, I don't even know how I got here. Just stay back while I think of something." He crouched, gripping his ankle as it throbbed. *Damn, I really messed it up. What the hell I'm going to do now? Does she have to keep staring at me like that?*

She apparently was running out of patience for him to figure something out, crossing her arms before she spoke "I have a suggestion. Would you like to hear it?"

She's got a strange accent. Foreign, maybe French. "What is it?"

"Why don't you follow me back to my village? When we get close to it I'll run ahead and get you some clothes."

He was feeling tired, thirsty and now his ankle throbbed. Still, it was better than anything he could come up with. "All right. You lead and I'll follow. Just don't turn around without telling me."

"I won't. I really don't care to see you naked anyway."

She walked back the way she came and heard him shuffle behind her. She tried to feel his presence in her mind as she walked and found she could locate him easily enough but his mind was guarded and didn't reveal any emotions other than being nervous and scared. People in the village suspected she could read minds, and while she didn't deny or confirm that ability, the truth was she could only get a glimpse of emotions. If there were a group of people, she had trouble separating individuals. If one person was angry she would have to look at the faces to tell which one it was. All the same, she could detect the overall emotional withdrawal of her peers when she entered their area, as if they collectively wished she would leave.

Tanya retraced the route back slowly, figuring that he would have trouble keeping a normal pace. It took almost an hour to reach the starting point of the path and she stopped to wait for him. He had gradually lagged behind and Tanya found this made conversation difficult when she had to shout while facing forward. She soon gave up, finding he didn't appear to be in a talkative mood. Once she reached the beginning of the return path, she turned around to call out at him. "How are you doing?" she yelled out to apparent nothingness. The curve of the beach hid his location.

A moment later he responded by shouting. "Okay, I guess."

"I'll wait for you up here. There's a path we have to follow through the trees."

She sat down on the sand cross-legged and waited for him, enjoying the warm sun. It took several minutes but he presently limped into view, not noticing at first that she was sitting down watching him. He wasn't all that close yet, well over a hundred feet, but she could see the startled look on his face as he quickly moved to the bushes for cover.

"Damn it! You weren't supposed to turn around!"

The anger in his voice amused her, as if she was pulling a sneaky trick on him. *Well, maybe I did a bit, but what was I suppose to do while I waited for you to show up? Stare at the ocean?* "Relax, you're too far away to see anything. Besides you're the one that's naked, it's your fault for losing your clothes." She knew those last sentences weren't true. He wasn't so far away that she couldn't see anything and it wasn't likely it was his fault for losing his clothes.

"Look I didn't lose my clothes, they took them away and left me here." He sounded exasperated at her insinuation.

"Who's 'they'?"

There was an indignant silence before he replied. "Never mind. I'll tell you later."

"I'm going up this path. Call out if you are having trouble, okay?"

"All right." He continued to sound irritated.

The path opened like a dark river that rolled down the incline, marked by green leaves and shadows that rippled from the sun and breeze. She led the way up the trail wondering how he would manage as it danced about obstacles, notching along its upward journey, and made footsteps less certain.

Tanya was feeling gratified, she had been the first to find the Newcomer, which the trivoli indicated was to be of some importance. She had also seen him exposed twice, which may now put her on par with some the younger girls and their giggled whispers about boys, and finally, she had him a little off balance. Boys normally made her nervous, causing her to feel uneasy as they made smirks and gestures. Their bravado made her less certain of herself, as if she needed any less confidence about herself. It was nice for the situation to be reversed, for a guy to be the one that was uncomfortable for a change, his certainty challenged. Her coolness this time wasn't just a mask. She was able to look at his body, making him uncomfortable while her composure remained intact. All this put her in a rather pleasant disposition.

The thought of her victories were interrupted by a yell behind her. She turned around and headed back down the path. "Are you hurt?" she called out, not sure how far back he was.

"Yeah, my ankle doesn't like this climbing much." His voice wasn't too distant, but sounded tired, but still with a touch of anger in it.

"I'm coming back down. Hold still." She retraced her steps, wondering how bad his ankle really was. He had made it this far, but climbing put a different stress on leg injuries.

"Stop there. I can see you."

Tanya couldn't see him initially but heard his voice come from a bush at the side of the path. She spotted first his arm before making out his general shape as he hunched over behind the plants.

"I keep hurting my ankle. I'll be okay in a minute or two."

"Maybe I better look at it."

"No! It's just a sprain. I just have to rest it for a bit."

She stood there for a minute watching him. "Why don't you wait here while I go ahead? I'll bring something for your ankle and something for you to wear."

"All right. How long will you be?"

"Not long. Half an hour, maybe a bit more."

"Okay. By that time, I might be able to walk. Are there any bears in these woods?"

"Bares? I don't know what you mean by bares, but there isn't much for you to be worried about here. You'll be safe. I'll see you in a little while."

"Could you also bring me something to drink? I'm getting pretty thirsty."

She hurried up the trail. She could make good time now that she didn't have to wait for the Newcomer.

Carl sat looking at his ankle. It was swollen worse than he had initially thought and was starting to throb with pain. He shivered as he used his hands to reposition himself on the soft ground. It hurt even to move it without putting weight on it, and he wondered how he would be able to make it anywhere when she got back.

At least I don't have to worry about the wildlife here. That was odd she speaks English but doesn't know what a bear is. This is one strange place.

Tanya decided to pick up clothes for him first and made her way down into the village, passing some modest homes that were scattered around the perimeter of the village. The dwellings became larger and more organized in rows as she moved deeper into the village and the grass becoming less prominent and replaced with worn paths made of clay and dirt. As she reached the centre of Sorbit, the paths were replaced by brick walkways.

Tanya said hello to some of the villagers as she hurried by, and soon reached the market quarter. The noise and the smell testified that it was early afternoon when the majority of shoppers came to inspect the merchandise offered. Most of the goods consisted of fruit, vegetables and seafood, with a smaller selection of meat. Some merchants sold pottery, jewellery, tools and a variety of products, including items of clothing. She bypassed the stalls and went straight to the tailors. The front counter was full of various garments on display and rolls of cloth and leather piled on the side. Tanya didn't see anyone as she approached but as soon as she came within a few feet of the display, a man seemed to magically appear.

"Ah, Witchdoctor, how are you doing this fine day?" Desmond grinned, showing off a mouth that was missing a front tooth and then spread out his thick arms. "It is about time you came to purchase some new clothes. A pretty girl like you must dress with a little more flare."

"Don't give her a bad time. She knows she needs to change her look a little." Anna came from the back and pushed aside her husband with her arm. She, like Desmond, was short, heavyset with a dark complexion and shared his joviality when dealing with customers, and as far as Tanya knew, was like that even when not trying to sell clothes.

"Hi." She grinned nervously. "Umm, well, actually I came to pick up something for someone else."

"No problem, whatever you like. Something for your lovely mother perhaps?" He held up a patterned wrap.

"No, it's for a boy." She felt awkward for a moment. "Just a pair of pants. Maybe a vest as well."

"Certainly." Anna went over to a pile of clothes. "Leather? Or just plain cloth?"

She thought about it for a moment. *Maybe he deserves a little better treatment than I've given him so far. Cloth is more for younger boys.* "Leather, I guess."

"And what size? Is he tall? Heavy?"

"About this height." She held her hand a few inches above her head. "He's on the slim side."

Anna picked through an assortment of clothes and produced a pair of pants. "Would these fit?"

"I think so." She held up the leather shorts with a leather tie front. The tailors had put in three bone buttons with cord tie so that there was a choice of waist size as well.

"Good. Then this vest should fit too."

"Yeah, that should be okay. Is it all right if I take these now? I'll work out a payment with you later."

"Sure, no problem." She leaned towards Tanya. "Is this boy special?" Anna smiled knowingly.

"No, no, he's just a boy. Just needs my help, that's all." Tanya hurried away, clutching the garments.

Her mother was working in the backyard, collecting plants, when she saw Tanya hurry into the yard holding something in her arms. She got up and went inside the house, pausing inside.

"Hi, Mother. I found him, but he hurt himself. I'm grabbing some stuff to help him."

"Is he hurt bad? Perhaps I should go..."

"No, no, it's just a sprain."

"All right. You found him quickly. The trivoli must have helped you."

"Umm, yes it did. I'll be back as soon as I can."

"It is best that you bring him here. I doubt if he is ready to meet the whole village yet."

"No, he's not. He acts a little different." Tanya hurried out the door, carrying her supplies.

Teresa watched her hurry down to where one of the paths led to the ocean, and the forest quickly swallowed her up. She noticed Tanya was acting upset. The Newcomer was certainly causing Tanya some concern and making her excited.

Tanya sensed she was close to the location she had left him and called out. It was odd that she had spent most of the morning with him and still didn't know his name, but he certainly didn't seem to want to initiate conversation. She was reduced to calling out "Hello, it's me" a few times before he responded.

"I'm over here."

She approached the sound of his voice until he shouted out for her to stop.

"Okay, I stopped. I have some clothes for you, do you want me to drop them here, or toss them to you? You're making this all rather difficult you know. So what if you are naked, it's not that big a deal."

"Yeah? Then you take off your clothes."

She just stood there looking annoyed at the spot where he was protected by a tree trunk and a few plants.

"Toss them here, if you can."

If I can? What's it with guys that think girls can't do anything right? She rolled the pants and vest together and threw them as hard as she could at where he sat. He stuck out an arm but the garments rolled off his fingers and landed a few feet behind him.

"I said toss them, not to make like you were throwing a fastball." He manoeuvred towards the clothes. "Don't look!"

What's a fastball? Then she guessed a fastball must be something that goes quick and, in a backhanded way, he had given her a compliment.

"Look, I don't have all day to spend rescuing you. Just put your clothes on and then I'll fix your ankle." She had a glimpse of him in the bush retrieving the clothes and then struggle to put on the pants while half crouching.

He hobbled back to the path. It appeared his ankle had become worse since he had rested and he looked like he was feeling rather miserable. She felt a sudden stab of sympathy for him.

"You don't look so good. Sit down somewhere and I'll tend to your ankle."

He looked around and found a fallen log to sit on. She sat cross-legged in front of him and opened up a bag she was carrying. "This looks worse than I thought. Why didn't you say something back on the beach?"

"I dunno. Didn't hurt as much then." He gave a shiver.

She looked up at his face. *He's really pale. He must be in some pain.*

"Well, it would have been better if you hadn't been so stupid back there and let me look at it."

"I didn't have any clothes on for crying out loud!"

"So what? Look what's happened now—your ankle is in really bad shape. But you guys always have to act so damn tough." She passed him a leather sack. "Here's some water if you're thirsty. Now hold still while I work."

The skin around his ankle was warm already, but when she placed her hands around it he felt even more heat from her fingers. He watched her hands work the swollen limb and felt the throbbing increase. She began to squeeze her hands together, causing the heat to increase even more. She sat quietly with her eyes closed, her upper body swaying gently side to side and her lips working silent words. Her breathing became slow and shallow as she concentrated.

He sat quietly and took a drink from the water sack. It was obvious she didn't want to talk while she worked so between drinks of the warm water he stared at her.

She's rather pretty, even kinda sexy if you like that dark look. And those green eyes, they jump right out at you. She seems smart too, but a little too weird for me. And too young.

"How does it feel now?"

He moved his foot. "Better. A lot better. Hardly even hurts now. What did you do?"

She glanced up at him and then picked up something from her bag. "Nothing you would understand." She began applying some pale yellow cream on his ankle. If her hands had been hot, this was the opposite, feeling like ice.

Her retort that he would not understand annoyed him, but he held back his initial reply. After all she was helping him, and not for any reason he could see. As a matter of fact, he had been acting like a bit of a jerk to her the whole time. "Thanks, for everything. Helping me, the clothes, the water and fixing my ankle."

"That's okay."

"Yeah, but you didn't have to, and I was a bit rude..."

"A bit?"

"Sorry. A lot rude then."

She finished massaging the cream on and then started to wrap a cloth around his ankle and foot. "Let me know if this is too tight."

"What's your name? Mine's Carl."

"Tanya."

"What's the name of this place? Where am I exactly?"

"Sorbital. My village is called Sorbit."

"Never heard of it. Where's it located? South Pacific?"

"South Pacific? Look, when we get to my home my mother will try to straighten things out for you. Can you walk now?"

He stood up carefully, resting his hand on her shoulder as he slowly placed weight on his foot. He released his breath and tested his ability to walk gamely. "Not bad. If I move slowly, I should be okay. Thanks again, Tanya."

By the time they got to the village, his ankle was getting sore again. But she did learn he was from some place near Seattle, had two younger brothers and a older sister, wanted to become a pilot, played football and baseball, didn't have a steady girlfriend and wanted to buy a car. He learned she didn't know anything about Seattle, airplanes, football, baseball and cars and didn't have a boyfriend. She also hadn't heard about TVs, radios or phones, let alone computers and the Internet.

"It's like you just type what you want and on the monitor you can see what you're looking for. You can chat with people all over the world..."

She listened to him and her reaction told him she couldn't fathom what he was talking about.

The village looked primitive to him and now he understood why she didn't understand anything about technology. It was strange that she spoke English, maybe with a peculiar accent, though that didn't make much sense if they never heard of a telephone. *Is this some sort of time warp thing? Some primitive tribe in Australia or New Zealand? This is all very strange. How am I supposed to get in contact with anybody? I might have to hike or take a boat to civilization.*

They approached a dwelling where a heavy-boned woman stood nervously by the front door. Her face appeared kind and he could see wisdom in her light brown eyes. The house itself might have belonged in a museum. Carl could see it was constructed with a wood frame from crudely chopped tree trunks that were surrounded by clay bricks. The roof consisted of large plant leaves woven together.

Teresa smiled warmly as the two approached. When they had entered the yard, Tanya had provided the introduction, though she left out her mother's title of Witchdoctor.

Carl followed them inside the house, looking around as he entered. The brick walls had a rustic appearance to them, reminding him of a pioneer home. The furniture inside did not belie that suggestion either as he seated himself at the wooden table. The room seemed to serve a dual role of living room and kitchen, though there were two other rooms curtained off to his side. Teresa prepared an assortment of fruit for him. He gobbled it down and between mouthfuls explained how he came to be on the beach.

"I know you won't believe me, but I was with some of my buddies at an acreage just fooling around with some quads."

Tanya exchanged a look with Teresa. "What are quads?"

"Four-wheel drive buggies, you can drive them over any type of ground."

"Oh, I see." Teresa looked at her daughter who was pursing her lips at Carl's explanation. She thought her daughter, like herself, still didn't understand what a quad was but guessed an acreage was some type of land.

"So it was just before dusk and the three of us were bombing about, there was a nice series of hills and stuff to go over. Rick went around a set of rises one way and I followed Billy another way. Billy stopped on one hill and pointed at something in the distance. I pulled alongside of him and there was some type of glow about a half-mile away. We thought it might be a grass fire or some guys had a campfire going. So we went to investigate and Billy radioed Rick where we were going. I looked back a bit later and saw him following us." He took another long drink of water, and Tanya got up to refill the cup from a pitcher sitting on a modest counter in the kitchen/living room.

"Thanks, I must be really dried out." He took the cup from her. "We reached this hill and there was this flying saucer thing just sitting there a few feet above the ground. It was actually below us in a small valley. We stared at it for a about a minute, not knowing what to do. Then it started to rise and we figured it saw us. We both hit the gas and Billy, he had the bigger quad, took off just like that. I tried to follow him, but I had trouble turning mine around and just when I was able to open her up, the bloody thing stalled. I tried to kick start it, but it must have been flooded so I jumped off and tried to run. I made about ten feet when my legs wouldn't work anymore and soon all my muscles went to sleep. I couldn't even yell for help."

"That must have been very frightening for you." Teresa reached across and touched his arm.

"Yeah, I was some scared. Then these alien creatures were suddenly around me and took me up to this UFO and I found myself on this table. I don't know how long I was lying there, 'cause I suddenly went to sleep. Only it wasn't sleep, I didn't dream or anything. It was like I was knocked out." He took another drink and looked at Tanya and Teresa, but they didn't give any sign they didn't believe him. "I woke up a few times on this table, and they were doing some kind of tests on me. It didn't really hurt too much, more like poking and prodding, though they took some blood and skin. They may have done more while I was knocked out because some parts of me really hurt later."

"What did those aliens look like?" Teresa turned to Tanya. "Tanya, I think it would be good if you redressed his ankle, it may be getting sore again."

Now that she had mentioned it, Carl felt the pain had returned, though it wasn't nearly as bad as it was when he had to stop on the trail. "Well, my eyes didn't focus so good, it was like all of my muscles wouldn't work. I could move my fingers a bit and my lips, but everything else was dead. From what I could tell, these aliens were about five and half feet tall, pale skin, their face was flat, like they hardly had a nose, no hair. Not even eyebrows, though there was a bony ridge above their eyes. Let's see what else...oh, yeah, all of them, there were four, had black eyes. Their eyes were maybe a bit bigger than ours, but the black part was really big compared to ours."

"What about their hands?"

"They were small with skinny fingers, and I think they had an extra finger too."

Tanya pulled a stool to his side. "Give me your foot, I'll redo the bandage."

He shifted his chair around and extended his leg. "That's about it, except I went out again and then I woke up on the beach down there. I still don't know where I am. Tanya told me, but I never heard the name before." He felt the heat of her hands on his ankle and glanced over. She had her eyes closed and moving her lips, the same as before. Once again the pain began to evaporate.

"So you woke up and just started to walk around?"

"Yeah, after my muscles came back to life. I didn't have any clothes either so I was worried someone might see me."

"And how did you hurt your ankle?"

"Well I was walking around, and like I said I didn't have any clothes on, and suddenly I saw Tanya. I was out in the open so I tried to jump behind this tree and hurt my ankle on this root that was sticking out."

Teresa glanced at her daughter who was still concentrating on his injury. "I see. What about your two friends? What happened to them?"

He shrugged his shoulders. "I don't know. I guess they got away, but I don't really know."

"And how are feeling now? Are you still hungry? Tired?"

"I'm all right, I think."

"But you are still hungry then?"

"A little, I guess."

Teresa got up and went to a cupboard, returning a few minutes later with two thick slices of dark bread along with a hunk of cheese. "Here, this should help."

He started on the bread as Tanya began to reapply the cream that caused his flesh to chill. A minute later, she wrapped the cloth around again.

"I'll check on it tomorrow, but it should be all right in a couple of days."

"Thanks." He finished off the first slice of bread. "Can you explain where I am now, and how I can get home, or at least contact my parents?"

Tanya looked at her mother, who gave a tight smile as she looked at him.

"You are not the first to arrive here by aliens. The people on Sorbit are either born here, or are dropped off here by ways similar to what you have described. At one time, we use to have many who have shown up as you did and we referred to them as Newcomers. Gradually there has been less and less, and you are the first in many years. You're one of the very few that has arrived with his memory as well, most Newcomers can speak, but cannot remember their own name sometimes. Where are we you ask? That's a question we cannot answer with any detail. Sorbital is all that we know. Monsters that will not allow us to leave protect the ocean, and to the north is the desert, which is so hot that nothing has survived that has gone out there. This may be a part of Earth that is uncharted or a different planet all together. It makes no difference—we cannot leave and no one has come to look for us."

"You...you mean I'm stuck here!" He stood up. "That can't be!"

"I'm afraid that it is."

"No, this must be on Earth somewhere. I'll get out of here somehow." He walked out the door and gazed around the yard. The village lay to the north and he pondered if he should go there to ask for help. *Someone must know more than what the old lady did.* He felt a warm hand on his arm and he looked to see Tanya standing just behind him.

"Before you run away from here, maybe you should obtain some more information." Her voice had a hint of sarcasm.

"I intend to." He pulled his arm away. "Can anyone show me how to get out of here?"

"Look, your ankle won't hold up for any more walking today, it's soon going to be dark and you don't even have a map. We'll draw one up if you like, but there isn't much you can do right now. Come back inside, tomorrow will come soon enough."

She's right, there's not a whole lot I can do right now. Maybe if she draws a map and I talk to some of the other people in the village I can figure how to get out of here.

"Come on. You haven't finished eating yet." Her voice became a just a shade softer, sounding almost concerned, but then she turned around and went back inside, leaving him alone in his frustration.

Reluctantly he went back inside and plunked down on the table, eating the bread and cheese without thinking. He put both elbows on the table and held up his forearms to isolate himself from Teresa and Tanya. *They're nice to me, but I don't want to deal with them right now. Stupid women, there has to be a way to get out of here. They just haven't figured it out yet.*

How long he was sitting at the table, he wasn't sure, but when Teresa lit a candle and put it on the table, he suddenly looked out the window and noticed it was dark. Tanya sat across from him and looked at him carefully, trying to judge his emotions.

"Are you okay now?" Her voice was almost a whisper, but still insisting on a reply.

"Yeah, I guess so." His voice was flat and he didn't look at her as he replied.

"Come, I want you to see something." She got up and went outside. Slowly he rose and followed her to the doorway and outside.

"What am I suppose to see?"

"The sky. See the stars. See the moons? Can you see those on Earth?"

The stars fluttered above him, but they were in the wrong position. The constellations he remembered back home weren't there. The moon was less than half the size and was darker in appearance with only a few bright areas covering a ragged surface, and he could see a smaller, brighter companion trail it.

"No." His voice was quiet, beaten. *This isn't the sky of home. Maybe the stars are something that's seen south of the equator, but that sure isn't the moon. I'm on another planet.*

"I'm sorry to have to show you, but you had to know."

He stood there gazing at the dwarf moons and squeezed his hands into fists. *Damn. What the hell do I do now?*

"It's time to rest now. Tomorrow we'll try to think of something." She pulled him by the arm to the back of the kitchen/living room where a cot was set up. The surface was made up of branches tied together and covered with leaves, which combined to provide a hard but springy platform. Reluctantly he laid down, not knowing what else to do. She tossed a blanket over to him and disappeared.

She doesn't come across too friendly. That really doesn't matter. I don't think she's going to be much benefit to me anymore.

He began to plan what he was going to do the next day, rise early and head to the village before Tanya and the old lady even woke up. The plan was still forming when he fell asleep, dreaming dreams of shadowy figures chasing him.

Chapter Two:
The Mentor

The whispers invaded his consciousness and gradually became distinct words. Carl slipped out of his sleep and listened while his eyes remained closed. Judging from the direction of the voices, he surmised that the two women were conversing quietly at the kitchen table. Gradually he opened his eyes, noticing by the light in the room it must be already mid-morning and that his plan to sneak away early was gone.

He lay for another minute watching them through his half-open eyes, not wanting to let them to know he was eavesdropping on them. Teresa was facing him as she refilled her cup from the teapot and talked to Tanya.

"...I think the Elders may want to make a decision on where..."

"He's awake."

Teresa focused her eyes on him. "Oh, so he is. Good morning, Carl. How are you feeling? Did you sleep well?"

Carl couldn't figure how Tanya knew he was awake, she couldn't see him and he wasn't making any noise. *She's an odd one.* "Fine, I guess." He sat up on his elbows and then used one hand to push his hair away from his eyes.

"Good. What would you like for breakfast? Eggs? Cakes?"

He carefully tested his ankle before he swung his legs over the bed. Satisfied it hadn't gotten worse during the night he stood up, pleased that it ached only a little. "Anything would be fine."

"You're easy to please for a man." She smiled as she made her way to the kitchen.

He made his way to the outhouse, giving a nod to Tanya as he went past her. She didn't respond, just watching him as he went outside. He returned to the smell of food being prepared, with Tanya still following his movements. He found it more than a little unnerving, as if she were trying to see inside him.

He sat opposite of Tanya at the table and after another moment of intense staring she looked down.

"Tanya, after he eats could you check his ankle again? We'll have to get him some sandals to wear today as well." She changed the subject as Tanya sat hunched over at the table, supporting her head with both hands looking both bored and annoyed. "Carl, we'll have to take you to see the village Elders today. They'll be delighted to meet you."

Teresa placed an empty plate in front of him and two other plates loaded with eggs, pancakes, bread, cheese and meat. He took a few of each on his plate and started to eat, realizing he was hungry and the fare, even if it did taste different, was good.

"Eat as much as you want, we've already eaten."

"Who are the village Elders?" He spoke through a mouthful of bread.

"A group of seven village seniors who have been chosen to make the major decisions for the village. One is appointed Grand Elder and is the spokesman."

"Oh, kind of like a mayor." He shovelled more eggs into his mouth.

He ate quickly and continuously, pausing only to drink the strange milk, as he emptied his plate and then refilled it. Tanya watched him eat, first with an irritated look, then with an amused expression. "Aren't you afraid your stomach is going to burst?"

"Huh? No way. Your mom's a good cook."

"I guess so. I've never seen someone eat so much before." She didn't sound duly impressed.

"Young men are famous for their appetites, dear. Don't worry, Carl, have as much as you want. I can make more if you want."

"Thank you. This is really good." He continued to attack his plate of food and finally finished the last of the food on the table.

Tanya shook her head. "Come on. Let's check your foot."

She unwrapped the cloth and examined the swelling. "Not bad. I suppose I could give it one more treatment to be on the safe side if you like, but it should be okay anyway."

"What do you do with your hands to get them so hot?"

"Nothing. It just happens."

"Weird."

"Look, do you want me to work on your ankle or not?" She knelt on the floor as she looked at him in exasperation. "I don't have all day."

"Tanya, just do one more treatment to be on safe side. We don't want him to be limping when he meets the village Elders, do we?" Teresa swooped down to clean off the table.

With a heavy sigh, Tanya clasped his ankle again, and once again he felt the heat spread inside him. After a short time, she stopped to massage the cream in.

"Thanks, Tanya. It's nice of you do this."

"That's okay." She stood up. "Let me know if it gets worse or you hurt it again."

The trip to the village Elders was fascinating for him. He had been given a pair of sandals to wear and walked with Tanya and Teresa to the village centre. He noticed Tanya and her mother lived on the outskirts of Sorbit. Some of the initial homes were quite small but didn't look to be in bad shape, even if they did have a pioneer appearance. The outside walls of the dwellings all used the same small yellow bricks, suggesting it was an easily obtained building material. The roofs matched each other as well with large leaves woven together to cover the tops. As they continued their walk, the streets became more pronounced and the homes a bit larger, some with coloured bricks instead of the plain yellow used in the earlier structures.

"The homes look bigger as we get more into town. Why's that?"

Tanya looked at him before she spoke. Carl wondered if he had asked a stupid question that didn't need an answer, but she replied, looking straight ahead as she did so. "The closer you get to where the Elders live, the higher the social status."

"Oh." *And Teresa and Tanya live pretty far away. I should've figured that out myself, now I look like an idiot.*

Several of the people he passed stopped to look at him, pointed and called out to others, "Newcomer! Newcomer!" By the time he reached an impressive looking home near the centre of town, there were a number of others following. The home was taller than the others close by, with the exterior covered with white stucco, broken up by windows and a large double door. The home was protected by a yard covered with coloured rocks and potted plants. Teresa led him up to the door where an elderly man, standing slightly stooped on a slim frame, greeted them. Behind him were several other men and women that approached the senior in age and stature.

After Teresa introduced Carl to the Elders, he was invited into the home and led to a large open room a short distance from the entrance. He sat between Tanya and Teresa with the rest of the seven Elders sitting opposite from them. Carl looked around taking in the stone tiled floor, white plastered walls with a high ceiling and the dark wood furniture. The overall effect was of a primitive, Spanish-style architecture, though Carl saw it more as a glorified hut. Still, the house apparently was a symbol of power and elegance in the village. The Elder, who identified himself as Elder Bronwick and had welcomed them at the door, was apparently the leader of the village as well, at least the other Elders seem to defer to him as he took the centre of the group and sat down. He was the main questioner, taking his time to inquire exactly what happened to Carl, what he remembered of his abduction, and then, with the help of the other Elders, what he recalled about Earth. One of the Elders recorded the information on misshapen paper, dipping her pen in brown ink in quick, birdlike movements.

Carl was tired of answering one question after another, and definitely found the slow and precise way they asked questions a bit exasperating. He was tempted to respond to the question before they even finished speaking, anticipating what they were going to ask.

"And now, young man, are you able to tell us approximately how many people presently live on Earth?"

Carl thought the questions could go on forever and he was finding his patience wearing thin. "A few billion, five, six, I don't really know. Can I ask a few questions? Like…"

"There will be plenty of opportunity for your questions later. Did you say five or six billion? Are you quite sure of that number?"

"It's around that. Can you tell me where…"

"What are the major countries on Earth and their populations, if you can recall?"

"Look, I'd like to help, but I'm getting tired of answering all these questions. How much more do you want to know?" Carl was finding even the padded chair uncomfortable and despite his large breakfast was getting a bit hungry again.

"We keep a large library of facts that we have compiled from all Newcomers. There is a danger that you may lose your memory of Earth and therefore we must obtain as much information from you as possible now. So if you don't mind, perhaps we can continue." The Elder stared at him with clear blue eyes that challenged Carl to refuse him.

Fortunately before Carl could make a retort, Teresa broke in. "Please, Elder Bronwick, he must be getting fatigued after his ordeal yesterday. I don't believe he will suffer a sudden loss of memory, so perhaps we can allow him a break in the proceedings."

Bronwick studied her a moment before coming to a decision. "You are quite right, Witchdoctor, he deserves a period to regain his strength." He turned to one of the Elders seated near him. "Elder Harden, please inform the help we will be having lunch now." As Harden disappeared out of the room, Bronwick rose. "Let us retire to the dining room and allow the Newcomer to relax for a while."

Carl turned to Teresa and whispered "Thank you." He stood and followed the rest out of the room.

Tanya turned to him after they were seated at a long dark wood table. "Are you really hungry again?"

"Yeah, aren't you? It's gotta be lunch time."

She shook her head. "I can't figure where you're putting all that food."

It occurred to him that for first time she used a friendly voice on him, perhaps a bit sarcastic, but at least it didn't sound as if she was annoyed with him. But there's something else that was bothering him now, what the Elder said...Witchdoctor. He had called Teresa a Witchdoctor, and if Tanya was her daughter... *She healed me using her hands. Tanya must be some kind of Witchdoctor too. This is spooky. No wonder Tanya dresses weird.*

After a meal that consisted of fruit, bread, cheese and sliced meat, they returned to continue the questioning. At first, Carl was tolerant of the queries about Earth, but eventually began to get bored as one Elder after another pressed for answers and more details.

"Do you recall the principles behind flight? In other words how airplanes or other types of aircraft fly."

Carl had trouble believing they were asking such questions, if they knew of airplanes, then surely didn't they know how they worked? "Not really, I think it has something to do with the wings being curved, like the air is thinner above the wing than below. If you have heard of airplanes, why don't you know how they work?"

Elder Bronwick looked annoyed for moment, then it passed. "I suppose we owe you a bit more of an explanation. You see, when Newcomers normally arrive here, and that includes myself as well, we suffer a peculiar type of memory loss. We can remember how to speak, and names and places to some degree, but have trouble associating them with actual objects. We may recall the name of our spouse, but not the city where we lived. It's a very selective memory. Sometimes we can work out a definition by comparing notes with each other, other times someone will get an inspiration from a dream or a sudden insight. All such knowledge is written down and placed in our library."

"So you can remember words but not what they mean?"

"Essentially correct. The more complicated an object, the more difficult it is to bring up details. One of the reasons we're asking you these seemingly pointless questions is because we have so many gaps in our knowledge. We're also worried that you may start forgetting as well, so we want to ask you before you lose valuable information."

"Okay, but you can't ask me everything I know. Like, that would take forever."

He smiled quickly. "I'm impressed with your knowledge then." He paused a moment, taking a quick look at his colleagues. "You're quite right, we can not, and should not, expect you to answer just any question we come up with. We have been over zealous when we found a Newcomer that could actually remember facts about Earth. Perhaps we can discuss a more suitable arrangement for you at a later date."

Carl was relieved, it appeared he wasn't going to have to sit and answer questions until nightfall. Still, he understood he did have an obligation to help them if he was to stay in the village, and he was under the impression the village was his only real choice he had to live in.

"We do have one more item to work out, Elder Bronwick, and that would be living arrangements for Carl." Teresa looked at Carl quickly before turning her attention to Bronwick. "He needs accommodation that would be beneficial to him, while allowing him the opportunity to help the village with his skills."

"That would be the ideal solution. Are you thinking of one of the more established families?"

Teresa shook her head. "No, not a family, more along the lines of giving him the freedom to explore Sorbital, perhaps to learn a new skill and also the time to do research in our library." *He's too old to be adopted by a family. He needs more of a mentor than a new set of parents. There's intelligence behind those eyes and if we can get him to do work in the library out of his own curiosity, that'll help him and ourselves. And I know just the person to help him.*

Bronwick looked puzzled but then relented. "Very well. Come see me with your solution later. It would appear you have someone in mind but don't wish to reveal it at this time." He fixed his eyes on Carl. "Welcome, Carl, and may you consider Sorbit your home. Talnut."

"Thank you. Umm, it was nice meeting you." Carl stood up. "All of you."

The way back had more people gathering in the narrow streets to catch a look at the stranger. Calls of "Newcomer" could be heard but he didn't respond, keeping his gaze forward as much as possible. The people appeared to be of varied stock, dark-skinned as well as Caucasian. He noticed, for the most part, men wore pants like he did and that the women wore skirts. Most of the younger women wore shorter skirts or wraps and tops that accented their figures, while older women were more conservative in style. An occasional male could also been seen in a loincloth as he held some type of spear. They did reach the home of the Witchdoctor without incident, though Carl realized his presence was causing quite a stir and could understand the reason why. It was unnerving and he hoped Teresa and Tanya could smooth things out for him the next time he had to go to the village.

"Well, you certainly created an impression, Carl." Teresa smiled broadly at him as she sat down at the kitchen table. "Tanya, would you be a dear and make some tea? Perhaps you can put out some cheese and bread as well, I'm sure Carl could eat something, couldn't you?"

As Tanya rolled her eyes and went into the kitchen, Carl sat down at the table. "I suppose so."

"I hope you weren't too frightened by the crowd, everyone was just excited to see a Newcomer." She turned her attention to Tanya who was nosily preparing the tea. "He certainly attracted the attention of all the young ladies, a fine looking young man like that, right Tanya?"

"Right." Her voice was flat and without much conviction as she placed the food on the table. She gave him a quick glance and noticed that he blushed as he reached for the bread.

"Carl, I want you to know that Tanya and I would enjoy having you stay with us, and I don't want you to think you have to leave at all, but we're thinking that perhaps you would enjoy staying in a place that would give you more room and privacy." She watched him carefully, looking for his reaction. "I do have a person in mind, dear, and if you're interested we can invite him over for you to meet him. What do you think?"

"Sure. Like, I know I can't stay here, so I would be glad to meet this guy."

"Excellent. After my tea, I'll go down and talk to him. Perhaps I will invite him for dinner tomorrow, and you can meet him then. How does that sound?"

"Fine. I could go with you, I don't want you to go to too much trouble."

"No trouble at all. You just stay here and relax. I know Tanya will enjoy your company while I'm gone."

Tanya opened her mouth to say something and then closed it as she caught a look from her mother.

After tea, Teresa left for the village leaving Tanya and Carl to sit at the table. An uneasy silence lasted for several minutes.

"Would you like some more tea?" Tanya rose and stepped towards the kitchen.

"Sure. What's it made from?"

She shrugged. "Just some herbs and flavour leaves."

"Oh. All the tea back home comes in these bags you soak in boiling water."

"Bags? We strain the tea as we pour it."

Again, silence dominated the table for several minutes.

"Your mom is really nice."

"Yeah, thanks."

"Umm, you don't have a father, do you? I mean it's none of my business, you don't have to answer or anything."

"No, that's okay. I don't know who my father is or if he is alive. According to some, maybe I don't have a father at all."

"What? You have to have a father, I mean..."

"I know what you mean. But my mother is the Witchdoctor, and some think I was born through magic." She squirmed in her seat.

"That's crazy!"

"How would you know? What if I was?" She barked out her questions to him.

He was silent from her assault for a moment. "Sorry, I don't mean to question what you said or anything. I guess I never heard of..."

"Forget it. I probably do have a father but he's too scared to show his face to me."

Carl was sorry he asked about her father and tried to find a way out of it. "What do you do around here? Do you go to school or something like that?"

She gave a small smile, recognizing his attempt to get out of an uncomfortable discussion. "Sorry I jumped at you like that. It's...it's just a difficult...subject...for me."

He held up his hands. "That's okay. Sorry, I didn't know."

She took a drink of her tea, studying the cup carefully. "We have school here, but I finished last year."

"What did you take?"

"Same as everyone here. Reading, writing, some math, history of Earth, knowledge of Sorbital."

"History of Earth?"

"It's mostly guess work of what Earth looks like, the cities, culture, countries, that type of thing. That's why the Elders were so keen in asking you questions about Earth. Do you go to school?"

"Yeah. I just finished my second year at college."

"Second year? How many years do you have to go? What're you taking?"

"Math, calculus, physics, chemistry, English, pretty much a full load. I've got another three years."

She put down her cup and stared at him. "Are you getting good marks?"

"Yeah, they're pretty good."

"I'll bet. I'll even bet you're getting top marks." She paused, hoping her words didn't sound like resentment. "What else did you do besides school?"

"Not much. I played with games, computers." He ran his hand through his hair. "I didn't have much of a social life."

"How come? You must have had a bunch of friends."

"Well I had a few friends, male friends that is. I didn't get along with girls too much. I liked them but they didn't seem to notice me."

Tanya studied her cup for a moment and then looked at him. "So you're a smart guy who stayed at home."

"I'm far from home now."

"Sorry, I didn't mean it that way."

"That's okay. How about you? Do you have a wild social life? Parties?"

She laughed quickly. "Hardly, I'm the Witchdoctor's daughter. A witch in training. Not too many people want to talk to me, let alone be my friend. And certainly not any boys."

"That's strange. I would have thought you would've had a few boyfriends." He gave a shrug. "You're good-looking, smart and sometimes nice."

"Sometimes nice?" She laughed. "Do you really think I look good?"

"You dress funny but you do look good."

"Thanks." She looked down at the table. "I never thought of myself as good-looking." She looked back up at him. "Are you just saying that?"

"No. You're pretty, at least from my perspective."

She stared at him, another question hung at her lips but stayed silent.

"Look, Tanya. I'm new here, and I don't have much to offer, but if you ever need to talk or need a friend, I'm here for you."

"Thank you." She placed her hand on his for a moment and then withdrew it quickly. "What do you mean that I dress funny?" She gave an indignant look, crossing her arms in the process.

"Just kidding. I noticed the other girls in the village wore shorter skirts, and, well different tops than you do."

"I don't think I look good in short skirts and those tops. I've always worn long skirts."

"Maybe its time for a change. Maybe it'll help you get along with the others if you didn't wear such different clothes. Besides, I think those other clothes would look good on you, give it a try."

"Maybe I will. I need some new clothes anyway." She finished her tea and saw he was done as well. "Would you like some more tea?"

"No, or I'll float out of here."

"Have you ever had your palm read?"

When Teresa returned she could hear her daughter laughing before she reached the door, giving her pause. *That's so good to hear. I get worried about her, being an outcast like that. It doesn't have to be that bad, she puts up so many barriers to others. This Newcomer is good for her, and it's unfortunate that I don't have room to let him stay here. Hopefully he'll keep in touch with her.*

As she entered the door, she heard him talking, and then noticed he was holding her hand as he studied her palm.

"...this line means you will have to climb a hill to get water everyday. This one tells me you have a bad temper and..."

"I do not!" She laughed and then heard her mother come in and pulled her hand away. "Hi, how did it go?"

"Fine. I had a nice talk with him and he'll be coming over for dinner tomorrow."

∞

It had been an odd feeling, a sense of déjà vu. When she had entered the door, Malcolm almost felt like he had been through that experience before. But that was impossible because she had never been to his home before—that he would have remembered without a doubt. Still, it had bothered him how she acted so calmly when she sat in the living room, her gaze roaming around the walls, pausing at the open bedroom door before she returned her attention to him.

"Malcolm," he remembered her saying. "I was wondering if I could talk to you for a while" causing him another shiver of déjà vu. She sat quietly as he poured her a drink of spiced tea and then discussed the matter of the Newcomer. He had been happy to accept the stranger, though he agreed it would be best if they met before making a commitment. He had seen her to the door, breathing in a fragrance of earth, mint and flowers that came from her. Déjà vu, again.

He went to bed that night feeling troubled, sleeping a series of recurring dreams that he had thought had gone away years ago.

ಐ

When Carl woke up the following morning, he realized that he had to find better accommodation, if only for his back alone. The bed wasn't bad at first, but it was beginning to take a toll on his spine. He didn't fall asleep at first as he struggled to get comfortable. He eventually did drop off to a deep sleep, becoming conscious of the outside world when it was already midmorning.

"Good morning." Tanya gave him a smile. "How did you sleep?"

"Fine, just fine. I seemed to have slept in again."

"That's okay. My mother's out in her garden, so I thought I'd be quiet and let you sleep. You've been through a lot lately and probably needed the sleep. Would you like breakfast?"

"Well..."

"Of course, you're always hungry. Wash up and I'll make something."

As he waved to Teresa working in the garden, Carl reflected how friendly Tanya was being to him.

She's actually being nice to me, and though that's a pleasant change from her earlier disposition towards me that verged on contempt, I don't know if I want to get into a relationship with a person who thinks of herself as a witch. Undoubtedly she's joking, but she still acted a little too different for my taste, maybe because she's a couple of years younger than myself. She seems to like me but this really isn't the time or place to start a romance. Perhaps having her as a friend would be good. Certainly both of us could use more friends.

"So has the whole place been explored?" Carl followed Tanya down a slope. The vegetation was sparse, consisting largely of ferns and other leafy plants. The soil was too weak in some areas to support trees, as witnessed by the overturned logs rotting in the undergrowth. They had been walking for the better part of an hour, not following any particular path for long before jumping to another that criss-crossed in front.

"Pretty much. All this area anyway. To the north is Ghoul Desert, which no one goes."

"Why not? Has anyone tried to see how far it goes?"

"I think some have tried, but it gets way too hot. It gets hotter the further you go, after only a couple of miles it's too hot to go any further."

"So no one knows how far it goes?"

"No, I guess not. It's one of the barriers that keeps us locked on Sorbital. Sea monsters in the water and an impassable desert by land."

He thought about the desert to the north as he walked. It seemed that it would have to lead somewhere, and if Tanya was right that no one had managed to travel very far into the desert, perhaps it was hiding secrets.

She took a sharp turn, waited for him so he could see where she headed, and plunged into bush. He pushed plants away from his face and found her sitting on the rocky edge of a plateau.

"Careful, some of the rocks may be loose."

Gingerly he made his way to her, nervous about the height but at the same time taken by the view. The ocean moved in slow waves onto a sandy beach, which in turn was surrounded by various shades of green.

"Wow, this is great."

"Yeah, it's one of my favourite spots. I don't know if too many others know about it, at least I've never seen anyone here." They sat looking at the view for another minute, looking up and down the coast. "There's another reason I wanted to bring you here."

He looked at her quickly, wondering if she had some romantic notion, but she was looking the other way.

"You were asking if Sorbital was all we knew. That wasn't quite true." She pointed with her hand out towards the horizon. "If you look carefully, you can see a dark grey smudge at the edge of the water."

He followed her direction and then saw a blob of dark land. "An island?"

"Silent Land. They think it is an island, or a tip of a larger land. Some have watched it for days on end, hoping to see something. Occasionally someone will claim to see something move on it, but generally nothing happens there."

"Hence the name Silent Land?"

"Right. To the south is a small island called Rhume Island. There's not much there but plants and some small animals." She turned to him. "Now you know all there is that surrounds Sorbital. Sad isn't it?"

"It does shorten the learning curve. You said something about sea monsters. Are there really sea monsters out there?"

"For sure. They leave you alone when you're close to shore, but if anyone goes out too far they appear. If you don't get back quickly, they attack."

"Has anyone ever killed one of them?"

"No, they're too powerful to be killed."

That sounds like a fable. "Tell me, why was the desert called Ghoul Desert. Rather an ominous name, isn't it?"

"It's an old name. Some think it comes from those that tried to venture into the desert and returned looking half-dead. Others say it is because ghouls live in the desert, that they enjoy the heat of the desert, or even created it. Others say that if you don't live a good life, you're sent to the desert to live as a ghoul."

"Do you believe that?"

"No...but." She paused, trying to pick her words. "Sometime go to the library and look up *Days of the Future*. It is a book written from the words of Witchdoctor Mariah, when she was in her dual-states. Like she would be in a trance and speak words that others would copy down. She predicated the future, as well as some of the secrets about Sorbital."

"She wrote about ghouls?"

"No, she spoke about them and others wrote what she said. The part about ghouls is 'They act when not seen, watching their work unfold. Hiding north of the great heat of their own choosing, the ghouls add to their experiment.' There's more about ghouls elsewhere in the text, but some of it is hard to interpret. For example, '...great heat of their own choosing' can mean they choose to hide in the heat of the desert or that they created the heat of the desert to hide."

"But you also said 'north of the desert'. Doesn't that imply that there is something past the desert?"

"I suppose so. It depends on how accurately they wrote what she said."

"Ghouls. You know I can still have this vision of those aliens that put me here. They did look ghoul-like with their pale skin and strange looking faces. I wonder if they're the same ghouls she described."

"Could be. There's a lot more to it than that. You really should read it yourself."

They walked back to the Witchdoctor's home, continuing to chat. Tanya divulged more information about Sorbit when he asked how many people lived there.

"A couple of thousand or so. We tend to think of it as an island but it may actually be a peninsula with the far south of the Ghoul Desert reaching into the mainland. The north part of Sorbit reaches into a bay of the Serpent Sea. The middle part of Sorbit is the widest part. It's fairly high compared to rest of Sorbit and is used as farmland."

"Farmland? What do you grow there?"

"Just about anything. Grain, fruit, vegetables and animals."

"No shortage of food then."

"No, the climate and soil makes it easy to grow things. Most people have fruit trees in their yards. I guess it's almost ideal here except we can't leave."

"What kind of animals do you raise here?"

"Goats, pigs and kytle are raised."

"Kytles?"

"Kytles are about twice the size of a pig and have a double set of horns on their head. They also have this long, thick tail with a small, bony club on the end. They live in herds and eat grass all day long. Their meat is good and their hide is used for stuff as well. The only problem with them is they have a nasty temper. The ranchers have to watch out for both the horns and the tail. You can buy their meat, hide, horns and tail club at the market so they're pretty valuable to raise."

ℰℴ

Malcolm chatted with the others during the meal. As he expected, Teresa made a delicious meal and he ate as much as could. The conversation jumped around to different topics then slowly stopped. Carl saw that both Teresa and Tanya were observing Malcolm and himself, seeing if the two of them could be friends.

"Well, young fella, I reckon these women folk are waiting to see if we can get along, so let's cut to the chase. As far as I'm concerned, you're all right, though a mite wet behind the ears. I think we can get along just fine. How about you? What's your take on this?"

"Umm, if you have room for me, I would be happy to stay with you." Carl took in the friendly face, well tanned with sharp features. Malcolm looked to be in his mid-forties with black hair spotted with strands of white. His hands and arms showed signs he worked hard and he was average in both height and weight.

"Super. I'm glad that's settled. You can tell me all about Earth, and I'll teach you about Sorbital. I can also tell you some things only a man is meant to know." He gave Carl a wink.

"Puleeze. 'Some things only a man is meant to know.' What would that be? How to eat like a glutton?" Tanya reacted quickly to Malcolm's barb.

"Tanya! He was just joking. Don't take him so seriously, dear."

Malcolm laughed. "Sorry, didn't mean to get you upset. I was just kidding there."

Tanya gave one final glare, and then listened as the conversation jumped around to topics that were more pleasant.

Malcolm informed Carl he worked with wood, usually making furniture, though also the odd weapon and tool. He also enjoyed tromping around Sorbital, exploring and studying plants and wildlife.

Carl said goodbye to Teresa and Tanya. Teresa stepped forward at the doorway and gave him a hug.

"Talnut, Carl. Make sure you come by often to visit." Teresa stood to the side and now he faced Tanya.

"Umm, thanks Tanya for helping me." He stood awkwardly, looking at her.

She smiled and stepped forward. "You're welcome." She hugged him quickly. "Come see me some time, Earthboy."

"Sure. I'll have you over at my new digs sometime."

Malcolm led the way, chatting with his nervous companion. "I have a fair-sized place, not huge, but I have a couple of extra rooms and I've converted one for your bedroom."

"Thanks. Can you tell me what 'talnut' means? I have heard the word a couple of times and haven't a clue what it means. Is it some sort of greeting?"

"I suppose so. Talnut is a name of a tree and the large nuts it provides, about the size of your fist. The wood is a dark hardwood, naturally resistant to insects and rot. It's often used in home construction as part of the foundation. The nut is edible, though a bit bitter, but can also be made into oil for cooking and also to help preserve wood. When a person says 'talnut' as a greeting, they mean the use of the tree into making a home's foundation that's strong, resistant to sickness. In other words, a place to go to that is strong and safe. Often one will say 'talnut' when another is going home."

"Oh."

"Clear as mud?"

Carl laughed. "No, I think I understand."

"Good, 'cause the other explanation is they're calling you a nut." This time Malcolm laughed with Carl.

Chapter Three:
Mandy

After a few days of staying at Malcolm's home, Carl worked to establish a routine that was more in-sync with the rest of Sorbit, including eating and sleeping on a more reasonable schedule.

"It sure took me long enough to wake up and sleep the same time as everyone else here. I went to Germany once and it didn't take me that long to get into a regular sleep pattern."

"Yeah, but did you consider that Earth and Sorbital may have a different length of day?"

"No, not until now. How long is the day here?"

"Well, some crazy American long ago insisted on using a twenty-four hour day like on Earth, including sixty minutes in an hour. Except that we didn't know how long an hour is here compared to Earth. My guess is that the day is slightly shorter here, but I could just as easily be wrong."

Nothing's easy about this place. Everything is a mystery here, sea monsters, a desert you can't cross, mythical writings. They just haven't applied proper science to these things. Maybe that's the way out of here. I'll use scientific principles to find a route out of Sorbital. "Malcolm, how long have people lived here?"

"In Sorbit itself? I would reckon a few hundred years. Maybe a few thousand. Could be more. No one has really kept track."

"How is that more things haven't been done yet, like inventions? For example, motors, electric lights and stuff like that."

"I don't know for sure, but I can hazard a guess if you like. When people are transported here as Newcomers, they lose much of their memories, you're the rare exception. They also seem to lose their ability to think deeply. They're okay initially in working out a problem, but I guess the ability to reason out complex issues relies on parts of our memory, memory that was wiped clean on them. The other group of people that were born here don't have that memory problem, but they'd never heard of electric lights or motors before. So maybe they aren't inclined to invent those either. But the real hold up to those inventions is need. We have lots of food here, a warm climate and not much danger from wildlife. So it comes down to we have what we want, why do extra work?"

"Yeah, but new stuff can make life easier and maybe help find a way out of here."

Malcolm tilted his head and grinned. "I can tell you're a real go-getter. Try to remember the culture of Sorbit is made up of people from all over Earth, you can see the different races here, and some of these people are very content the way things are. Not everyone wants to change the world."

"I don't want to change the world. I just want to find my way home."

"Talnut, Carl." He put his arm around Carl's shoulder. "C'mon, let's go to the workshop. I'm going to show you how to make wood dance."

Carl didn't have much experience using tools on Earth, preferring video games to saws and hammers. Still, he was impressed with what Malcolm was able to create out of some rather crude tools and a pile of lumber. He examined the various hammers, chisels and saws plus a few other objects of unknown use.

"You have some metal tools here. I haven't seen much metal anywhere on Sorbit. Is it hard to make?"

"Mineral and metal deposits on Sorbital are not easy to get out, and we have some difficulty working with it. Fortunately I know someone who has a bit of knack for smelting, and he'll make some tools for me when the mood strikes him."

A small table on a workbench caught Carl's attention. "Wow, this is a great looking table. It looks like something made in a factory."

"Thanks, I do my best. How'd you like to make something?"

"I don't know how to make anything out of wood."

"The best way to learn is by doing. What would you like to try first?"

He was glad of one thing, the novelty of being a Newcomer had gradually gone away over time and Carl was able to socialize without feeling everyone's eyes were on him. Malcolm had noticed Carl had been reluctant to venture out of the house by himself. After a few weeks, Malcolm decided to help Carl's initiation with others in Sorbit by suggesting that he join him in going to church.

Carl and Malcolm approached the rather plain wood and brick hall that served as a gathering place for the church service. The hall quickly filled up with people who talked and yelled out greetings to one another as they arrived, which certainly wasn't like any service he was used to. Malcolm positioned himself in the middle of the hall, right behind the backless benches. Carl joined him, observing the older and less capable village members sat on the benches while others crowded in the rear portion in the hall in a rather unorganized fashion and stood. All told, Carl guessed there had to be nearly a hundred and fifty people jammed inside. The church service itself was noisy and was led by both a man and a woman who took turns speaking. Carl noticed they both had strong voices, which helped carry over the constant talking from those around him. There were many shouts from the congregation during the sermon, which did not seem to be overly serious with plenty of laughter spliced in. As far as Carl could tell, they preached about several different gods and demons, including the desert ghouls. After the service people grouped around outside to talk and that provided an opportunity for Carl to meet others, in particular those within his own age group.

After supper with Malcolm, Carl helped with some cleaning up and then headed towards the centre of the town. A couple of weeks ago he had been introduced to a group of new friends that met near the market in the evenings. Carl was happy to find others near his own age and Malcolm encouraged him to join them.

He followed narrow brick walkways that took unexpected turns around the market shops. The air had lost the smell of various foods as the merchants had shut up their stores, closing wooden shutters over the open front. A few taverns and bistros were still open as he made his way to edge of the market and then suddenly he was in behind the market place, in a street that led to a small park.

"Hey, Carl, how's the woodwork going?" Benny was leaning on a wall with Valerie, Mandy and Kyle. Benny looked oriental, a bit on the heavy side on his five foot seven frame. Valerie and Mandy were almost as tall as Benny was but were on the slim side.

"Slow. It's harder than I thought."

Mandy moved closer to Carl, flipping her blonde hair back in the process. "Are you still getting slivers?"

"Yeah, not as much, but I sliced my finger with a chisel this morning." He held up a finger wrapped in a cloth.

"Ohhh, that must of hurt." She touched his hand, looking sympathetic.

"A bit, bled more than anything else. Kyle, how's things with you?" Carl was feeling a bit uncomfortable with Mandy's attention, he had thought she was going out with Benny, but after she had turned her attention to him Benny didn't act concerned. Carl had a feeling he just didn't understand how the social structure worked on Sorbit. Although, he reflected, he was not up on social behaviour back on Earth either some of the time.

Three more members of the group joined them and then they trooped off to a park a few blocks away. The park contained an artesian well that was used by various people of the village, and provided a rest area for people to sit after shopping in the market. During the evening, it was usually empty save for groups like the one Carl had associated himself with.

"We should have a beach party next week guys. I can get some wine, maybe someone can bring some food." Valerie sat leaning against Kyle as she played with her long dark hair.

"Sounds good. We should invite a few others and make it a decent party." Benny was lying on his back as he spoke. "Everyone should invite at least one other person."

There was a general chorus of agreement.

"Could we invite Tanya to come?" Carl decided to suggest something that had been in his thoughts every time he met this new group.

Valerie sat up straight. "That witch? Are you kidding?"

Angie chimed in "She is so strange. I've seen her sit by herself under this tree like she was in some sort of spell."

"Yeah, she can read minds, you know." Mandy then laughed. "Not that she would get much from the guys here."

"Seriously, did you know she came about from a union between her mother and the devil?" Jules spoke in a whisper. "She knows spells that can turn you inside out."

Katrina tossed her long, blonde hair back and then leaned forward. "You know she practices the dark arts don't you? You have to be careful around her."

"That's right. Remember when Lizzy called her a bitch and she overheard? A week later, Lizzy was sick to her stomach for days." Angie looked right at Valeria as she spoke. "So you do have to watch what you say when she might hear you."

"Are you all mad? She's just a girl for crying out loud." Carl found himself getting angry.

"Hey, you don't know her like we do. Sometimes when she practices magic I've seen her use this bag with little objects in it." Olivia wiggled her fingers at the others.

"She and her mother heal people."

"Maybe, but that doesn't mean she doesn't practice black magic as well. She and her mother are always making up these potions. Who knows what they are all for?" Katrina watched Carl as she spoke.

"You're all crazy." He stood up. "See ya later."

Mandy reached for his hand but he turned away.

Valerie watched him stomp off. "Wow, he must really like her."

"Maybe she put a spell on him." Katrina laughed as she watched him disappear.

Carl was upset, angry at their superstition nonsense, and even more annoyed how he had handled the whole situation. *I should've said that I stayed at her place and I know...no, that wouldn't have gone too well either.* He walked slowly back home, muttering to himself, what he could have done?

As he smoked his pipe, Malcolm whittled a piece of wood. The room was a bit on the dark side with most of the light given by a torch attached to a nearby wall, aided by an open window on the west side. Despite the poor light, Malcolm could tell Carl was upset as he slumped against the wall after coming in early. Malcolm waited until Carl had gone into his room, had walked out again and then dropped into chair. Without much coaxing, he related the events of the evening including how he had left his friends in a huff.

"It's just unfair how they treat her. She isn't a witch like they claim, but they are too ignorant to find out."

"Hmm. Well, I suppose it depends partly on how you define witch. She does seem to possess special powers, doesn't she?"

"Yeah, but that doesn't make her a witch."

"No, I suppose not, though they may be looking at things differently." Malcolm took a drag from his pipe. "Let's try to see it from their perspective. Tanya has always kept to herself, even as a young child. That may have come about from living away from the village or just because she preferred it that way. The difficulty is that your friends may not see her as you do, and they may see something you don't."

"But she really is nice if they would give her a chance."

"What did you think of her the first time you met her? Did you think she was nice then?"

"Well, maybe not."

"Look, I don't want to sway your opinion of her, but if your friends all get along except her, is it possible Tanya is the one who might be, shall we say, difficult?"

"Gee, Malcolm, I don't know. I guess I just wanted them all to get along."

"I have a suggestion, if you would like to hear it."

"Sure, anything has to be better than what I've done so far. Looks like all I've done is get caught between them."

Malcolm chuckled. "Don't be so hard on yourself. Why don't you invite Tanya to join you occasionally when you are going to hang out with just a few of your buddies? To have her at a big party right now probably wouldn't work too well, a large group would be rather intimidating for her and could make matters worse."

"You mean to slowly let them get to know her?"

"Patience is a virtue."

Carl figured it would take some time before his friends would accept him easily again. He felt he had overreacted to their comments about Tanya and would have to act with a little more restraint in the future. He walked to the library after breakfast a few days later, remembering his promise to check the written information in their books and manuscripts on a regular basis and had let that slide a bit lately. The paper used in the library was usually yellow in colour, not just from age but also due to the way paper was produced. It was stiff and had to be handled carefully, especially after a few years. A regular task for some of the volunteer staff was to rewrite some of the older works before the paper became too brittle.

The librarian recognized him from the last time he was there and gave him a warm smile. The middle-aged woman asked him if he was going to work in any particular section, offering to help him. Carl declined remembering her help last time prevented him from getting almost anything done. He did find more errors in the books and manuscripts—pointing out unicorns didn't actually exist, and that dinosaurs died out long ago and were no longer a danger on Earth. Carl thought it was unfortunate that the people of the village, at least the ones that arrived from Earth, had trouble remembering what their fragmented recollection of Earth meant. It became more complicated when they tried to supplement their memories from dreams. The books became a strange mixture of truth and fantasy.

The library had been converted from a home and contained two main rooms and two closet-sized rooms that served as storage areas. Carl sat at one of the four tables away from the four people doing work in the rooms and leafed through a manuscript titled *Cities of Europe and Earth*, written by Terry Eggleton sometime in the year 456. Carl wondered if Eggleton really thought Europe and Earth were two different places. He was also curious about the year. Obviously, the year 456 was counter from some event that happened on Sorbital, and that was something he would have to check out.

Cities of Europe and Earth was primarily about the cities of Europe, making up well over half the cities and towns mentioned. As far as Carl could tell it was reasonably accurate, although the map of Europe itself looked odd and he decided to pencil an "X" next to Atlantis and wrote "fable" next to it.

Carl decided he would go through a half-dozen books before he would stop, knowing there were a lot of books on both the shelves and the storage rooms.

After he finished his task he wandered about the library and found what he was looking for, a map of Sorbital. It was on a large sheet of paper and he carefully unfolded it on a table and studied it. Sorbital appeared to be bigger than he thought, and he tried to locate where he had originally landed.

He jumped when the librarian came up behind him as he concentrated on the map.

"If you find that map useful, you may have it. It's a copy of an original we keep stored away and I can have one of the staff make another easily."

"Are you sure it would be okay?"

"It is the least we can do for your work here. If you want anything else, just ask."

He carefully refolded the map and went back home.

Malcolm was sitting in the living room working on a drawing for a spearhead when Carl burst through the door, looking quite excited as he waved his map. Malcolm inspected his map and commented it looked fairly accurate. "Of course, it's hard to make a perfect map if you are restricted to only ground and water travel. Maybe you can improve on the map when you do some exploring."

"I doubt it, I'm not very good at directions." He paused as he folded up the map. "By the way I saw a reference to the year 456. What does that mean? What year is it now?"

"The year is 598, and that means it is 598 years after one of the largest groups to arrive at Sorbital. Something like two hundred newcomers arrived within a few days of each other, partly, I suppose, to replenish the sixty villagers who died from some flu epidemic."

"What's the population of Sorbital now?"

"I reckon it's around twenty-one hundred or so. That's about as high as it has ever been. According to records, when the population dropped below about five hundred, we used to get an influx of Newcomers to restore the population base."

"I noticed on the map there seems to be other villages besides Sorbit."

"There are a couple of very small villages, maybe about fifty people in each one. One is not even a half-day's walk north along the west coast, called Tribute. The other town, Colburg, is in the interior and sits by Tolge River. I suppose it would be almost a day's walk due north."

Malcolm pointed at the folded map in Carl's hand. "If you look where the Ghoul Desert begins there's a town called Terral and has a few hundred people. There are also a few isolationists—families that prefer to live away from others. There was even a group that lived on Rhume Island, but they didn't stay in any particular spot and sort of wandered around. They might still be there but they haven't been seen for a few years."

"Rhume Island? Where's that? Tanya mentioned it earlier."

"Sorry, I didn't mean to keep you in the dark about that. Rhume Island is separated from the main land by a channel, maybe by a couple of hundred yards at best. It's not a big island, and it looks like it was a part of Sorbital at one time."

Carl filed the information for later, and went into the workshop. "I'm going to work on that bowl."

"I'll call you for dinner later."

Malcolm answered the quiet knock on the door, opening to two nervous young women that stood away from the entrance.

"Is Carl in?" Mandy tentatively asked twisting her fingers together as she spoke.

"Sure, come on in. He's in the workshop out back." Malcolm stood aside for Valerie and Mandy.

"Thanks. Would you rather we went around outside to the back?"

"No, this way is just fine."

Mandy had gotten Valerie's support on her visit to Carl's. The group was reluctant to accept her suggestion on allowing him to invite Tanya to their party, but she pointed out it may be already too late to stop him. Besides, he had added some excitement to the group and there was some risk that they may have alienated him. One final point she made was that Tanya wasn't likely to go to one of their parties anyway, so they could take the high road and tell him to invite her if he wanted and she would probably turn him down. The guys weren't convinced that asking him to rejoin the group was the best move, after all he was the one who had walked out on them and should be the one who asked to come back. The women were of a different mind and all wanted to find a way for him to return. Mandy quickly volunteered to the task.

"Hi, Carl, whatcha doing?"

He jumped at the sound of her voice. "Oh, hi, Mandy. Hi, Val. Just making a bowl." He pointed with a chisel at the wood block he had sitting on a spindle that slowly came to a halt as he stopped pedalling on the lathe.

"Interesting, so that's how it's done."

"This is the rough part. The last part is to smooth out the wood with a sand and oil mixture."

They chatted about the making of the bowl before Val nudged Mandy with her elbow. Mandy then mentioned how the group was sorry if they had appeared rude but if he wanted to invite Tanya, she was welcome to come to the party.

"That's really nice of you, but I think it'd be difficult for both Tanya and the group for her to show up at the party. I was thinking that maybe it would be best if I slowly introduced her, you know, just small meetings."

"Sure, that would be fine too."

Mandy touched his arm. "I would like to keep you as a friend. Sorry if we got you upset." She played her fingers on his arm, noticing he didn't pull away this time. "Are you, like, really close to her? Like boyfriend and girlfriend?"

"No, no. We're just friends. She's not really my type."

"Oh. Show me around the workshop."

He pointed out various tools and materials while Mandy casually slipped her arm through his. He showed completed tables, chairs and other items that needed to be oiled before being sent out, and other pieces half completed. By the time they had completed the modest tour, she was holding his hand. Val was patient with her friend's effort to get Carl as her boyfriend, though she did find woodworking a bit boring.

"This is really interesting, isn't it, Val?"

"Yeah, right." She looked around in an endeavour to appear interested. "What are those?" She pointed a finger in the direction of some long poles.

"Oh, spears. Or rather, they will be when we put the heads on them. Malcolm designs the head according to what each person wants and then puts it on the spear body. I'm not sure why each design is so particular, he spends a fair bit of time on each head but I guess it must be something special."

"Carl, didn't anyone tell you about the Quest?" Mandy looked at him with a smile that bordered on a full grin.

"No. What is 'the Quest'?"

"Quest is something all the guys go on, that is if they are able. It's kinda like a rite of manhood or something like that. When a guy gets to a certain age he is supposed to journey to Rhume Island, survive there for twenty-one days and then return safely, hopefully with a trophy of some poor creature's head."

"Is this spear what he carries as a weapon to this island?"

"Right. The head of the spear is supposed to be a symbol of something special to the spear holder, like a serpent head or something like that."

Carl thought about what she said. The ritual sounded a bit ridiculous. "Is that all? Sounds rather an absurd way to prove manhood." He gave a second thought to what he just said. "I'm sorry. I don't mean to jump on someone's customs as being crazy. We sure have enough of those back on Earth."

"You may be right, but it is a very old custom here. There are a couple of other details." She picked up a partly carved head of a spear. "The men, they would be your age when they go their first time, carry only the spear and wear only a gartez."

"A gartez?"

"It's just two pieces of cloth you wear around your waist to cover your front and back."

He remembered seeing a young man with paint on his skin, holding a spear and wearing a loincloth. "Do they also paint their bodies?"

"Yeah, you must of seen one who was preparing to leave."

He fingered the spearhead in his hand, looking at the intricate design.

Valerie watched him look at the carving as if for the first time. "So when are you going on your Quest?"

"Huh? I don't think so."

"All guys do. Talk to Malcolm about it. You're of age."

Carl looked dubious. "I was raised in a city, I don't know anything about living in the wilderness."

Mandy laughed. "You'd be fine. Food is easy to find there, so is water. You just walk around and sleep there for a few days. Besides, I think you would look great in a gartez. Wouldn't he, Val?"

"Oh, I think so too." Val giggled with Mandy.

Carl found himself feeling uncomfortable. "I'll talk to Malcolm about this Quest. I don't know if it's for me though."

"It started out long ago as a rite of manhood. This was generations ago, probably a carryover from one Earth tribe or another. At one time, a young warrior was to go to Rhume

58

Island without clothing or a weapon. He was then to make a spear or a weapon and use it to kill one of the beasts there, maybe a mountain lion or a highcroc and return with its head as a trophy. This was supposed to have proved his manhood and he was given a gartez to wear during a ceremony of some sort.

"Nowadays the warrior starts out with a gartez, a spear and a bit of body paint to scare off the demons, though the odd one goes naked as respect to the old customs. The object is only to survive for one passage of the moons on Rhume Island, not really a difficult proposition."

"What about the mountain lion and, what did you call it? A highcroc?"

"Oh, they found they were killing off the lions too fast, so that was stopped. They're rather small cats actually and avoid people. The highcroc, now that is a rather ugly thing. It's a giant lizard, about as long as a man is tall, that walks with its legs straight, not splayed out like those small lizards. They can run fast and usually are found on the beach looking for easy game. It's best to avoid them by staying in the forest and high ground, though I don't recall the last time anyone got killed by one."

"Doesn't sound too bad."

"It's not, unless you listen to stories of the men who have just completed the Quest. Some men go several times as a way to become one with nature. I go to Rhume Island now and then just to explore it, though I usually only go for a few days at a time."

"Do women ever go there?"

"No, fortunately, or they would know what a crock this whole Quest business is." He laughed. "I suppose there's nothing to stop them other than custom."

"So you think I should go on this Quest?"

"Well, it won't likely hurt you none and probably help you learn a few things. If you don't, some of the other guys and women, may not see you as reaching full manhood. Again, a crock, but that's how people think here."

"Do I have to wear a gartez? Can't I wear what I have on now?"

"I suppose you could. Not a big deal. One thing we'll have to do is make you a spear, and design a spearhead."

"Those are usually of some animal, aren't they?"

"Yeah, give it some thought which one you want."

Carl finished the bowl he was working on and Malcolm showed him how to make an armlet out of a short length of a wood core. Carl polished and rubbed both, until they became dark and gleaming. At Malcolm's suggestion, he took both to the Witchdoctor's home.

Teresa gushed over the bowl, while Tanya held the armlet carefully in her hands, turning it over and over.

"You didn't have to bring us anything, that was so generous of you. Come in. I have just made tea and biscuits."

Tanya eventually found her voice and, after putting the armlet on, asked him how he was doing. She acted unusually quiet, and her normal sarcastic tongue was held in check.

Carl ended his visit with a promise to stay in touch and walked back home feeling pleased they appreciated the gifts he had made under Malcolm's supervision.

Carl had some time to kill before he was to meet with the others so he took a long route back to the village. The path wound around a small hill and he enjoyed the sight of the lush green growth around him. Feeling a bit adventurous he decided to climb the hill, wondering if there was anything special to see up there. The top wasn't much different than what he expected, though there were less trees and more low-lying grass. Carl looked around, spotting part of the village to the east and, to the south, he saw the Witchdoctor's home. He was about to head back down when a figure caught his eye. The blonde-haired girl was sitting against a tree and facing south as she gently rocked back and forth. Carl was going to go over to say hello, but the way she acted reminded him of Tanya when she was healing his ankle.

Maybe she's meditating or something. I better not disturb her.

Carl quietly left, looking one more time at the girl in the blue wrap and white top. She looked familiar but he couldn't be certain without seeing her face and went down the hill.

The market was busier than normal as Carl made his way to the usual gathering place. His friends apparently hadn't made their way yet, and he waited while leaning against a wall. They arrived by ones and twos and greeted him warmly. Carl was glad there was no sign of any lingering anger from the argument a few days previous.

Mandy kept close to him, sometimes holding his hand and making sure everyone, including Carl, understood that they were going together. Carl wasn't sure how to react, and while he enjoyed her being close, wasn't use to being pursued by a woman.

Kyle tried to stay near Valerie, but she was ignoring his advances.

"Hey, Carl, have you decided to go on a Quest yet?" Valerie called out to him.

"Maybe. I'm talking it over with Malcolm."

"Good. Do you need help picking out a gartez?" Valerie grinned at him.

"No. Malcolm said wearing one wasn't necessary, I can wear these shorts."

"Oh, come on. That wouldn't be any fun for the rest of us." She laughed.

The group collectively went to the park and sat on the grass, exchanging stories. After awhile, Katrina joined them and sat close to Carl and Mandy. He looked over at her and noticed her blue wrap.

"Hey, Katrina. Were you up on a small hill earlier today meditating?"

Her eyes focused on him and her mouth opened a second before words came out. "No, that wasn't me. I was home all day."

"But I thought..."

"I said it wasn't me."

"Oh, sorry." The subject was quickly changed by the others leaving Carl to wonder why she had lied about being on the hill.

Tanya made her way to the village. She picked up a few items for the household, paying with good luck charms and herbs instead of the usual metal rods used as currency by some of the merchants. She was largely ignored by most of the crowd, though a few acknowledged with a quick nod or smile. The tailor shouted a greeting, trying to entice her to buy some new clothes. She waved back and carried on. She did make one more stop, and that was at Malcolm's home.

"Hello, Tanya, Carl isn't home right now. He should be back for dinner if you want to wait."

"Oh, no. I didn't come to see him." She touched her armlet. "I...that is my mom and I...want to invite you and Carl for dinner tomorrow evening."

"Well, that is awfully nice of you two. We would be delighted to. Is there any special occasion?"

"No, no. Just because, well, Carl brought over a bowl and my armlet." She touched it again.

"Well, that wasn't necessary to have us over, but it sure would be nice. Your mother is a wonderful cook." He touched the armlet. "Carl made both the bowl and the armlet. It looks like he did a fine job on his first try."

Tanya froze her arm in place, his touch causing an odd feeling of disorientation.

"Uh, yeah he did. I gotta get going." She quickly said goodbye and made her way home, not knowing what to make out of what just happened.

∞

The meal was delicious and once again, Carl elicited comments on how much he ate.

"Gee, young fella, you act as if I never cooked a meal for you."

"Uh, you cook fine, but not like this."

"Save room for dessert, Earthboy. Mom made berrycake."

After dinner, Tanya and Carl sat outside by themselves near the garden, engaging in small conversation.

"So, what are you nervous about?"

"What do you mean, what am I nervous about?"

"I can sense that you are nervous about something. It hasn't affected your appetite, but there's something. What is it?"

He shook his head. *How does she do that? Maybe she does read minds.* "A Quest. I'm suppose to go on this Quest, and I don't know what to expect."

"All the guys do it. It really can't be that difficult."

"Maybe not. I was raised in a city. No jungles, forests, wild animals but a food store on every corner."

"Put on a gartez, wear some war paint to scare off demons, wave a spear around and hide in a forest for a few weeks. You can do that."

"I guess so. Anyway Malcolm said I can wear these shorts and not have to wear a gartez."

She looked at him with a bit of amusement. "Want some advice?"

"Sure."

She kicked at his foot with her own. "Okay, two, no make that three things. One—the bottoms of your feet are too soft. Go barefoot and toughen them up a bit before you go on your Quest. Two—don't fear the unknown. The unknown is usually a lot worse than the truth. Seek it out and you will be safe in its knowledge. That is an old saying, not mine, but it's true. Three—wear a gartez. It'll make you feel that part of the Quest better, and wearing shorts is silly. People will be watching you. Better still, go nude."

He looked at her shocked.

"I've seen you. You've got nothing to be ashamed about."

Carl turned red.

She laughed. "Okay, wear a gartez, but not the shorts."

Carl followed her advice and tried walking around barefoot. Initially his feet were sore, but after a few days, they toughened up and he was able to go about without wincing every time he stepped on a sharp rock.

He continued to see his friends and in particular Mandy during the evenings when the group got together. Mandy commented that he appeared to have lost his sandals but he replied he was following Tanya's suggestion to prepare for the Quest.

"Are you still keeping company with her?"

"She's a friend."

"Just keep it that way."

∾

A few days later, Carl walked to the Witchdoctor's house in the afternoon and convinced Tanya to go to the market with him to walk around.

"You're feeling good about yourself."

"I guess so."

"Girlfriend?"

"Yeah, we're kind of seeing each other."

Tanya didn't say anything for a long time. Finally. "Is she pretty? She must be. What's her name?"

"Mandy."

"Oh, her." Tanya looked withdrawn for a moment, but quickly recovered and started to joke with Carl again.

They looked at various goods in the market square, making jokes and just making a nuisance of themselves to shoppers and merchants.

"Hey, look at these pots, don't they look like..." He realized she wasn't paying attention to him, staring across the market. He followed her gaze, and saw Mandy. His heart stopped.

Mandy made her way smiling towards them. Tanya had a calm face on, though there was fire in her eyes.

"Hello, what are you guys doing here?"

"We were just..." He didn't get a chance to finish.

"Shopping. The *two* of us were shopping. Together. By ourselves."

It was an icy conversation, and Carl hadn't a clue on what to do to calm the situation.

Mandy turned to him. "Carl, would you be a sweetheart and find Kyle? He's somewhere by the corner."

"Uh, sure." He left, and while he was relieved to leave the conversation, he was even more anxious about what was going on while he was gone.

"Tanya, he's your friend, and I'm not going to stick around during your little shopping trip with him. But he's my boyfriend. I just don't want to make a big deal about it, okay?" *Don't put a hex on me either.*

"Your boyfriend? Big deal, I saw him before you." Mandy heard the anger in Tanya's voice and knew she was ready to battle her. *Gee, this is turning ugly. I better change this conversation quick, if Carl see us fighting like this he probably dump both of us.* "True. But I'm more his age, wait...this is getting us nowhere." She gave a forced smile. "He's just a guy we both know. Let's try to act a little less..."

"Desperate?"

"Yeah, desperate. He talks a lot about you, you know. He wants us to get to know you better."

Tanya's voice softened. "He does? What does he say?"

Carl came back. "I can't find him anywhere. Are you sure...?"

"Oh, that's right, he went home." She put her hand on his hip. "Say, Tanya and I want to do a bit of shopping. Why don't you come back here in an hour or so?"

"But, Tanya and I were..."

Tanya looked at him. "It's okay. Come back in a while. Mandy and I have some things to discuss."

Carl watched them disappear. He felt glad they appeared to be getting along but still felt troubled.

"Tanya, I think I know what you are going through. A couple of years ago I had a big crush on Thomas..."

"Thomas Hule? The fisherman?"

"Yeah, one and the same. I don't know what I saw in him, but he wouldn't give me a second look at the time. I felt so mad at him and his girlfriend. Now that he's married, he leers at me, the creep."

"So you think I only just have a crush on him?"

"No, I think he's more than that to you. He's also a friend to you, and unlike Thomas, he's not a creep. But, Tanya he's a lot older than you. You're eighteen?"

"Nineteen."

"Well, he's got to be at least twenty-two, maybe twenty-three. Which might make him feel a bit old for you, though we both know how immature guys are."

"I know what you're saying, but I still..." She fingered her armlet again.

"Look, things may change in the future. You do know how many girls want to go out with him, don't you? The tall, mysterious stranger from Earth is getting lots of attention. Attention he seems to be oblivious of most of the time. He'll probably go through a few girlfriends before he settles down, and if I were you I would plan to be his last girlfriend, not his first." Mandy hoped her argument sounded convincing, though in fact she planned to be his first and last girlfriend. In Sorbit, eighteen wasn't considered too young for marriage.

Tanya sighed. "I suppose you're right."

"Hey, are you thirsty? There's a kiosk that sells a nice fruit drink, I'll get you one."

"Sure, thanks."

"By the way, were you the one who convinced him to go barefoot?"

"Yeah, to toughen up his feet for the Quest."

"It may do that, but his feet sure stay dirty." Mandy passed a drink in a clay cup over to Tanya. "Let's sit over there and talk some more."

Carl continued to shop with Tanya later that afternoon. Mandy disappeared after giving him a quick kiss and making him promise to see her later that evening. He was happy Tanya and Mandy had seemed to patch up their differences, not sure what he would do if they hadn't.

"Hey, Carl, here's a shop that'll sell you a gartez." She pulled on his arm. "Come on, you'll need one."

"I haven't decided if I'm going on a Quest, let alone be wearing one of those."

"You know you're going on a Quest, and don't you dare embarrass your friends by wearing those shorts instead. It's either the gartez or nothing. Understand?"

"Oh, all right." He picked up one of the leather garments.

"No, get one with a design on it." She picked through the items on the counter. "This one looks good."

"Okay. How much is it?"

"Don't you want to model it for me first to see if it fits?"

"No."

She laughed. "You're no fun."

He paid with the odd-looking metal rolls and then challenged her. "Look, I bought something. I think it's your turn now. You need some new clothes."

"Maybe another time."

"Either you buy some new clothes or I'll return this gartez."

After looking at clothes at a few kiosks, they heard Desmond and Anna shouting out a greeting to call them over.

Tanya looked through their selection and with Desmond, Anna and now Carl pressuring her, she finally relented and chose a new top and two skirts. The skirts were quite short to her, though not any shorter than skirts worn by girls her age. Her top was loose and had short sleeves, a change from her usual plain vests. The biggest difference was that her new garments had colour, a radical change from the basic black she normally wore.

"So is this nice young man your boyfriend?" Anna smiled broadly as she folded up the clothes. "A good choice. He is tall, handsome and very polite."

Tanya looked surprised for a moment. "Oh no. Believe me I'm the last girlfriend he would want to have." She then laughed at her own joke with Anna.

Carl shrugged his shoulders. He had given up trying to understand half of the things going on around him. This was one of them.

Chapter Four:
Rhume Island

The weeks changed into months and Carl was feeling more comfortable living on Sorbital. That was until he was pressured by his friends to make the journey to Rhume Island. He eventually made the commitment and set a date to travel to the island.

The boat, shaped more like a rough dugout than a streamlined craft, bounced along the water. Carl paddled quickly, not out of a hurry to see his destination, but to just get out of the choppy water as soon as possible. He tried not to look panicky and put on a nonchalant attitude since there were several of his supporters on the shore behind him. The send-off went well. The night before he was the centre of attention at a beach party, enjoying the celebration but now felt the result of excessive drink. He had decided to ask Tanya to join him at the party after securing the group's permission that she could attend. She didn't act out of place during the revelry, being quiet and polite for the most part, though he wondered what happened after he fell asleep. She never seemed to be far from making one of her smart comments or losing her temper. He was certainly grateful for the potion she delivered this morning to Malcolm's home. He gulped down the harsh tasting liquid and felt better a half-hour later.

The next ordeal was when Val, Mandy and Tanya had all decided they would help him paint his chest and back to ward off evil spirits. He might have even enjoyed the women applying paint on him if Malcolm wasn't there laughing at their efforts. He noted that Tanya and Mandy at least were getting along, although there seemed to be a bit of rivalry of who could be the best artist. The other difficulty was when he first stepped out of his bedroom wearing his gartez and blushed to the comments of his friends.

Now he was approaching Rhume Island, feeling apprehensive and alone as he slid through the waters. The boat grounded just short of the shore and he dragged it the rest of the way onto the rocky beach. He secured the boat by a length of rope to a dead tree still rooted desperately to the earth with its branches bleached white by the sun and water. He waved at the small figures across the channel and then ventured into the bush with his spear, which had a figure of an American bald eagle on its head.

There wasn't much of a path. It appeared the landing he chose was common for those on a Quest but the visits were infrequent enough that a path hadn't been formed. He followed the easiest route he could, but still had to endure branches and brush that hindered his steps. His attempt to use his spear to push some of them away wasn't effective, and he ended with several cuts and scrapes on his legs, chest and arms. His feet were better conditioned for his adventure thanks to Tanya's suggestion to walk around barefoot, but he still felt the rocks and roots as he lumbered on.

The climb was uphill and with the earlier exertion from taking the boat across was making him thirsty. He remembered Tanya telling him if he needed to drink, the green fruit of the surute tree was good. "Of course the fruit is fairly high up, so you would have to climb up the trunk until you reach the limbs where you can crawl across to reach the fruit. Fortunately one thing guys can do well is climb trees—you should be okay." As usual, Tanya's comments about men involved a subtle put down. He had stopped wondering why, just accepted it as part of her personality.

As he made his way through the forest, he looked up to spot any fruit, in particular green ones. He was actually surprised to come across a surute tree a short time later. The two-foot diameter trunk had a smooth surface save for circular bumps approximately every foot. This made climbing easy and Carl quickly was able to reach the branches where the fruit was stored. He perched himself on the fork where the branch met the tree trunk and carefully extended his arm to the green softball size fruit. The taste was close to that of watermelon and it did quench his thirst. He grabbed a few more and after realizing he was not going to be able to climb down without using his hands, gingerly dropped the fruit to the ground. Even without the fruit, the climb down was harder than the climb up and he was grateful he made it down with only minor scrapes on his legs.

The first few nights were nerve-racking. He found the ground to be home to several types of insects, various rodents and, as he found during his second night, snakes. After a bit of trial and error, he discovered a tree that had two branches that ran close to each other and could provide enough support for him to sleep on above the ground.

He thought about the changes in his life over the past several months making Earth seem like a distant memory. He wished he could let his parents know he was all right but there wasn't much he could do about that. He missed them, his friends, TV, the Internet, pizza, baseball...he found the list too long to finish.

So far, his diet consisted of various fruit and berries. He wasn't sure about the mushrooms and decided to leave them alone. Catching small animals would be difficult and he wasn't keen on how he would have to prepare them for consumption. Eggs were a possibility, except he wasn't able to find any nests. If he wanted a change in diet, the only option was fish. Carl figured he could use his spear to catch and clean them. He would have to start a fire, but he felt he should be able to start one by using the method Malcolm had showed him, rubbing two sticks together by using a length of cord.

The journey to the beach meant he would have to wind his way through the forest, but as long as he went in a downward direction, he should find the open water. Like Sorbital, Rhume Island did seem to sport some wildlife. Besides the birds that were prevalent in both areas, he also saw racoon-like animals scurrying about and small deer. The miniature deer stood only to his chest and stayed together in groups. They were wary of his presence, watching him carefully as he made his way by. There was also a badger-size animal that sported the animal's temper. He encountered one while he walked about, and the creature made so much noise that he made a circle around it even though it didn't seem to pose much danger.

The thought of cooked fish was appealing to him more and more and he ignored thinking of the difficulties in accomplishing his goal. It took longer than he thought, but he reached the beach and for a minute enjoyed the sight of the water as it washed up on the golden sand.

The art of catching a fish with a spear was difficult, and despite several large fish swimming by his feet, he missed repeatedly. He recalled from his science classes that the water caused objects below the surface appeared to be in a different place when viewed above.

Index of refraction or something like that. Maybe I have to aim where the fish isn't.

He tried to shoot a few inches off to either side and to his surprise speared a fish. He quickly hauled his wiggling prize out of the water, wading out of the water as fast as he could in case the fish managed to free itself.

Making a fire was as difficult as catching the fish, and Carl was frustrated at the effort it took to even get the wood sticks to the point of smoking, which still didn't equate to a fire. He was glad Malcolm had given him a small length of cord to wrap around his spear, giving the appearance of providing a better grip on the shaft. Malcolm had assured him it was easy to make a cord from small vines, but he had decided he didn't want another challenge on his Quest. After several false starts he managed to get a fire started and using a long stick proceeded to cook his dinner. Cleaning a fish with a spearhead wasn't without problems either, but that was one task he was going to finish.

The meal was the best he had had in days and he resolved he was going to eat fish more often. Carl sat on a washed up log and picked at the last of the fish, feeling better than he had since he arrived on the island.

Perhaps it's not going to be so hard to live here for the duration after all. There's food, I can find places to sleep and the temperature is like Sorbital—warm during the day and a bit cooler at night.

He relaxed under the sun, gazed at the blue sky and saw a semi-circle of a thin, very faint white line that hung in the air above. It was hard to determine the height, and therefore the size, of the object. It seemed to be a bit below the height of clouds, if there were any, but it looked rather high.

Has it been there all along and I've just now noticed it? Or, has it just suddenly appeared? It can't be natural. It has to be manmade, or at least artificial. What the hell can it be or represent?

Carl watched it for several minutes but it didn't appear to change or move. His neck was starting to complain as he stared at the white line, and he decided it was not going to change soon. He went back into the forest to find more fruit, a suitable tree to sleep in and to work on the latest puzzle.

The following morning he made his way back to the beach after attempting to check the sky, and finding that the tree canopy obscured his vision. He was curious if the white semi-circle would be present again today and decided the beach would be the best place to look. He also was eager to try his hand at fishing again, though he thought he would start a fire first this time.

The half-ring was visible again, though it appeared to be orientated in a different part of the sky from yesterday afternoon. He watched it to see if it moved at all but it appeared to be fixed, or if it did move, it was rather slow.

The fire started a bit easier this time and a few minutes later he was up to his knees in water watching the fish swim past his spear. He noticed the empty seashells on the beach, including shells that looked like they used to belong to giant mollusks, but he wasn't sure how he would cook them even if he was able to find them. He watched another fish glide by his missed spear and he poised for another shot. He glanced quickly back at his fire and then back to the water.

A movement in his peripheral vision caused him to jump, noisily tumbling backwards towards the shore before he fell down short of the shoreline. The four-foot shark-like creature lunged at him, his mouth wide open. It missed Carl on its first try. It quickly turned and charged at him as he sat and watched the row of sharp teeth aim for his leg. He knew using his spear was his only chance to save himself from serious injury, and to his surprise found himself hurling the spear the length of his arm even before he finished the thought. Blood coloured the water a moment after he felt the thud of the spearhead driving into the open mouth. The creature tried to swim back again but he held fast on the spear shaft, finding himself being pulled up from the water as he dug in his heels.

"Oh no you don't, you son of a bitch! You started this and now let's see how you like it."

For a moment, the whole shark-like body floated out of the water as it squirmed on the end of the shaft. He took advantage of the lack of power and pulled it towards the beach, almost falling backwards again as his arms were pulled side-to-side. But he had it caught in the shallowest of water and he dragged the flopping creature onto the dry sand. It was very much alive but getting weaker, the loss of blood out of its mouth slowing down. He could see where his spear went, entering at the side of the mouth before going right through its throat where the spearhead protruded underneath. The spasms were getting less strong now and he was able to pull the beast closer to where his fire was. With one hand, he grabbed a large stick he was going to use for the fire and instead, used it as a club against the beast's head. Exhausted but feeling triumphant he stood puffing over his adversary.

"Thought you were going to use me for a meal, did ya? Well, guess who's dinner now?"

It took some effort to extract his spear, and he was annoyed at some of the gashes along the wood from the creature's teeth. It did look like a shark, though this one had black stripes along the length of the body, and the top of the fish had a type of fin that ran the length of it.

Probably not a shark but something a lot like it. Sure put up a fight.

Feeling immensely proud of himself, he decided to run a stick through the main part of the body and use that to support it over the fire. The head of the fish was outside of the fire and the tail was a bit on the high side to cook fast, but he managed to have it cook enough by propping it up using several sticks. He was worried the sticks themselves would start to burn, but they held up and soon he was able to relax.

He pictured himself as a warrior, standing over his kill while holding his spear by his side. A moment later, he laughed at himself.

The smell of the cooking fish stimulated his appetite and he hungrily hacked chucks of cooked white flesh off and stuck them on a stick, blowing on them as he nibbled. He managed to eat a good portion of one side of the fish before he began to feel full, though he didn't stop then, continuing to eat until his stomach began to complain. He wandered away to the water, washing his hands and face, as the rest of the fish kept warm over the slumbering fire.

A grunting, growling sound attracted his attention to what at first looked like an ugly dog running down the beach, then a few seconds later the vision clarified. The six-foot body's front legs were shorter than the back ones, with a tail making up almost half of its length. A crest ran from the tail to a crocodile shaped head.

It was still some distance away as it lumbered towards him, but it seemed to be moving fast, perhaps as fast as Carl could run. With that realization, he bolted towards the forest, thinking the creature would not be able to climb a tree to get at him. He underestimated its speed, though he still managed to climb a decent sized tree with a minute to spare. Whatever it was, and he presumed this was the highcroc Malcolm warned him about, it didn't give up easy. It stood on its high legs as it clawed at the tree trunk with its three-clawed front paws, the large mouth drooling and working the jaw in anticipation of a meal. His yelling at it didn't have much effect but presently the highcroc got bored and returned to the beach. Carl found his heart was pounding and his hands wet from his ordeal as he clung to the tree limb he was sitting on.

From his vantage point, he could watch the creature attack the remains of his fish, finishing it off in a few large bites while yelping from the pain of the low fire. The highcroc then disappeared down the beach. Carl wasn't anxious to return to the ground quite yet, there had been a few too many surprises already this morning and he felt a bit safer in the tree. He knew he had to get down eventually and glumly prepared to face whatever was waiting for him below.

The beach was empty of life and little remained of his fire or of the shark. Fortunately he wasn't hungry, just annoyed that it was stolen. He walked down the beach, occasionally going into the water and checking behind him in case another beast wanted him for lunch. He remembered on how when he first arrived at Sorbital he was walking along a beach, very much alone and wondering what was going to happen next. It seemed so long ago that he was on Earth having fun with his friends without much of a care in his world. Now...well at least he had a girlfriend and, come to think of it, a lot of girls were rather friendly towards him. He looked up at the sky and noticed that some clouds had blocked the sun and gave some relief from the heat. Then he noticed the half-circle was gone and he puzzled over its disappearance.

He returned to the forest with his mind racing about what had happened to him today.

The following week he returned to the beach to catch more fish. He encountered the highcroc again and found he could outrun the reptile if he had to, the creature normally just walked up and down the beach. It was more of a scavenger than a hunter, though it would try to take deer or anything else by surprise if it could. The time it chased him was its sprint mode, which was fast but it couldn't sustain it long. He also noticed the odd shark-like fish occasionally and managed to avoid them, poking at them with his spear a couple of times. He did come across some of the odd slug-like creatures with a shell, this time alive in the shallow water, and he felt he had seen them somewhere before. The half-circle in the sky continued to appear and then disappear, moving to a different part of the sky when he finally began to notice a pattern. When the sky was clear the white line appeared but would vanish when the clouds obscured the sun. It was interesting, though he still hadn't figured out what it was.

It was during that same week that he came across the best hunter of Rhume Island. One of the small deer that inhabited the island lay dead in a bit of a clearing, its head twisted back at an odd angle. Carl slowly approached it, when a second creature that was hidden by the bulk of the deer appeared from behind it. He made eye contact with it and then cautiously backed away. The hunter was a cat, a small one not much bigger than a house cat but without much of a tail. What really caught his attention were its teeth, specifically the front ones. The small feline was a sabre-toothed cat. Instinctively he lowered his spear towards it and he heard a hissing sound in response to his presence. He kept his eyes on it as he backed up, not wanting to be caught by a surprise attack from behind.

After he covered a good distance from the clearing, he climbed a tree to relax on a branch. One of the skills he had improved on was climbing trees and he had lost his fear of falling. His proficiency at using a spear had increased as well, learning how to balance the shaft between the head and the round weight at the other end. The weight he knew came from the bony club of a tail from a kytle. He could easily spear fish and carry it like the weapon it was.

As he munched on a fruit, he recalled the miniature sabre-toothed cat, the highcroc and the odd slug-like crab. The cat could be a relic from the time of prehistoric man, and he thought, the highcroc might be an ancestor of the dinosaurs. Maybe, besides people, the aliens also collected other forms of life from Earth. That would mean the aliens had been doing this a long time. He thought about the crab-like creature with the elongated body and a name suddenly popped into his head.

Trilobite.

He remembered reading how trilobites were an extremely successful species that suddenly died, along with ninety percent of all life during one geological timeframe or another. It made sense, the aliens must have collected them and other species to study, or perhaps just to make humans feel like home in a natural habitant. If Sorbital was a giant zoo, then there had to be a way out.

Carl had only a few days left before he left Rhume Island and went back to Sorbital. He was glad he had gone on his Quest now, learning much about Sorbital and himself. He felt confident as he walked down towards the beach, no longer noticing the constant brushing of plants and branches or worrying about creatures hiding in the shadows.

He arrived at the beach before lunchtime but was feeling hungry and decided to eat early. As usual, he glanced at the sky to see if the white ring was present and to his mild surprise almost three-quarters of the ring was complete. Fascinated, he watched the sky more frequently as he went to fish. The white line grew larger in the following minutes and he stopped his fishing after catching only one small fish and went ashore. He stuck a stick as close as he could to the vertical and noticed by the meagre shadow that it was now close to noon. The faint line now had formed an almost complete circle and a few minutes later, the ring became complete. More minutes passed and now the opposite side of the ring began to evaporate.

It's a hole in the sky. The sun's rays are catching the edge of a giant glass bowl. Sorbital is in a glass-caged zoo with the ring as an opening at the top!

It seemed more logical as he thought about it, but knew he would have trouble convincing anyone else of his discovery, let alone getting anyone to act on it. Regardless it was a start towards what he perceived to be the secrets of Sorbital.

෨

Carl paddled the boat back to Sorbital, and though he was glad to be going back, he was thankful for the time he spent on Rhume Island. It might be his imagination but he thought he was able to paddle the boat more smoothly than when he left. Halfway to the far shore, he noticed one or two individuals had walked down to the beach where he had left, and then several more joined them.

Tanya, Malcolm, Mandy, Tanya's mom...Val...Benny, there's a whole group of them.

He tried to stop himself from grinning as he approached the last few yards to the beach. Several of his friends waded out to help pull the boat ashore and fired questions at him faster than he could hope to respond, so he didn't even try.

Mandy gave him a hug and kiss as he stepped out of the boat and he almost fell on top of her. He shook hands with the guys and several of the girls gave him a kiss. He made eye contact with Tanya and she gave a fleeting smile, took a hesitant step forward and then froze. He broke through his circle of greeters and moved towards her, placing his hands on her hips. She still acted nervously, hesitated and then suddenly kissed him hard on his lips as she wrapped her arms around his neck, broke free, muttered "Talnut, Carl" and walked quickly to where her mother watched.

Carl had expected, or at least hoped for, a small kiss from her. The passion behind her kiss surprised him and when she walked away, he felt unable to move at first. He looked around, saw that Mandy was watching closely, Teresa was frowning and the rest of the group was looking. He felt awkward about the situation and wondered what to do next.

"Well, young fella, let's get some grub into you and you can tell me all about your Quest." Malcolm came up from behind him and slapped him on his back.

Feeling a bit dazed he followed Malcolm up the beach with Mandy hurrying to catch up to him.

Chapter Five:
The Sea Serpent

The food was great. He had forgotten how good meat, potatoes, turnips and bread could taste. He stuffed food into his mouth as he told Malcolm and Mandy about his adventure. Malcolm took his story in stride but Mandy reacted with alarm at nearly every part of his Quest. She refilled his plate for him and sat next to him at the table. Carl felt a little uncomfortable with her attention but Malcolm didn't appear to care. He also mentioned his observation about the white ring and his theory about what it represents.

Mandy was impressed by his deduction but Malcolm acted less certain.

"Possible. The ring is called Mary's necklace and it's known that the sun's position affects it. Your theory that it's a hole in a barrier of some sort is interesting and has some merit. I'll have to give it some thought. In the meantime, I had better clean up in here. We're having a party here tonight in your honour."

The party, as far as Carl could determine, was a smashing success. There wasn't any music other than someone attempting to play a stringed instrument accompanied by some rather interesting flute playing, but there was still a lot of noise generated by people talking and laughing. He couldn't tell how many people were there. The partiers had overflowed the house and covered the surrounding property. People were dressed a bit different than normal, and several of the women sported painted designs on themselves. Flowers on cheeks reminded him of photos he had seen from the sixties, though some of the other designs were quite different. Carl was introduced to many new people during the evening but had given up trying to remember their names. Mandy divided her time between him and talking to her friends, which gave him opportunity to talk to new people and wander about. He also found that he was drinking perhaps a bit too much as he stumbled outside to get a breath of fresh air. A tree became a convenient leaning post for him as he tried to act nonchalant while people mingled, talked and laughed around him. A few tried to strike up a conversation with him but most soon realized he wasn't able to respond very quickly to their questions and let him rest against the tree.

"Hi."

He looked at the source of the new voice, wondering where the dark-haired girl came from. She was on the short side but possessed a well-curved figure along with a beaming smile.

"Uh, hi."

"You must be Carl, I'm Terri."

"Oh, hi Terri." *That was lame. Now please go away and come back when I'm not so drunk.*

"Congratulations on your Quest."

"Uh, thanks."

"Are you feeling okay? You don't look so good. Too much to drink?"

"A little."

"You must have started early. Come on—let's go for a walk. It'll make you feel better."

Carl really didn't want to walk anywhere, but lacked the energy to argue and followed her as she went down the dirt path that led towards the village.

She chatted continuously as they made their way past other homes and people, saying hello to a few of them without breaking her conversation with him. He wasn't doing much talking himself and stopped listening to most of what she said.

"...that is where Andy and his sister Carline live, they were the ones rowing that boat I told you about. And here's where

Chelsea lives—she's the one, well you must have seen her at your party, she's tall with red hair..."

How does she even breathe? She has been talking non-stop since I met her. "Can we stop for a minute? I'm not feeling too good."

"Sure. Do you feel like throwing up?"

"No." *At least not till you asked.* "I just feel kind of hot."

"Yeah, your forehead is all sweaty. Why don't you take off your shirt? That might make you feel better."

With clumsy fingers, he managed to take off his shirt. He didn't feel much better from the effort and a moment later leaned on tree for support. She picked up the shirt he dropped on the ground and watched him struggle with his stomach.

"Wait here. I'll get you some water."

She disappeared before he could answer and with a sigh, he sat down on the ground. *Damn, I do feel like throwing up now. Shit, I'm never going to drink this much again.*

His stomach did a final rebellion and turned itself a knot before it erupted with his dinner.

Terri returned to see him coming from behind a tree. "You okay? Did you get sick?"

"I'm...I'm fine now."

"Here, I got you some juice. I live over there and I ran back to the house for you."

"Thanks, uh..."

"Terri."

"Terri. Thanks." He drank the juice and a few minutes later felt a lot better. The headache was still there, but now his stomach wasn't having a civil war anymore. "Let's head back to the party now."

"Sure." She pointed at a house. "I live there. Drop by for tea sometime."

The walk back was better and he was able to break her monolog with a few questions. Overall, he was in much better shape than when he left, and for that he was grateful to Terri.

Mandy didn't look pleased when he returned with Terri. "Carl, where did you go off to? I was looking all over for you." She gazed at Terri. "How come she has your shirt?"

"Oh, sorry, he was getting really hot and left it on the ground, so I picked it up for him."

"How nice of you." She turned and walked away.

"Mandy, wait. You got it all wrong. I just went for a walk." He found himself talking to an empty space. "Hell, how did that happen?"

"Sorry, Carl, I guess she misinterpreted what happened. Did you want me to talk to her? I don't mind. Oh, here's your shirt."

"Thanks. That's okay, I'll explain things to her later."

"Is there anything I can do to make you feel better?" She leaned into him a bit, her knee touching his leg.

He was tempted by her apparent proposition, but figured he had gotten in enough trouble without doing anything wrong. "Thanks, but I just need to wander around a bit and think."

"Okay, I'll check with you later. And make sure you remember to come by my house for tea sometime. Okay?"

"Okay."

"Promise?"

"Scout's honour."

"Scout's honour?"

"Never mind. I promise."

Carl walked around outside for a few more minutes before going back into the house. He knew he was still under the influence of too much drink, but his headache had pretty much disappeared. Feeling that he could now explain things to Mandy, he stepped around people in the living room looking for her. He noticed Katrina standing next to an older woman, the resemblance close enough that he surmised they were mother and daughter. Katrina did smile while nudging her mother and he smiled back as he headed towards the food and drink table. A waving hand caught his attention and he spotted Teresa smiling and signalling him to come over, though he didn't see Tanya with her and looked around quickly to see if she was around. A girl with short black hair wearing a blue pattern blouse stood with her back towards him then turned quickly as he approached. The short hair and colourful blouse had disguised Tanya until she faced him. The flash of her nervous smile almost caused him to stumble as he fixed his eyes on her.

She's gorgeous. Why haven't I noticed that before?

Carl stammered out hello and riveted his gaze on her. Her hair was cut quite short and for the first time he had known her, she had put on some makeup, accenting her eyes and lips. The blouse and the short skirt displayed her figure much better than her usual long skirt and vest.

It was an awkward conversation. He felt tongue tied and nervous, though Teresa and Tanya didn't act as if they noticed his loss of words. He was relieved when Malcolm came up to join them and spared him the need to think past Tanya. He stared at her too much, he knew, but couldn't avert his eyes.

"Maybe you better close your jaw for a minute, young fella, you're starting to drool." Malcolm whispered quickly to Carl before starting in a dialog with the others.

The party carried on long into the night, though Carl was unaware exactly when it ended. He consumed a few more drinks after Tanya and Teresa left early, and then fell asleep on a chair. Mandy said a cold goodbye to him and disappeared early as well.

"You sure attracted a lot of attention last night Tanya, your new hair style really suits you. Though I still think your skirt was a bit on the short side. When I was your age..."

"I know, Mother, but it wasn't shorter than any of the other girls." She watched her mother as she chopped various ingredients to add to a stew. "You told me I should dress, as you so carefully put it, less hidden. I thought you'd be happy that I made some friends last night."

"I am, though most of those new friends seemed to be boys." Teresa paused, trying to sound casual as she added another comment. "Carl certainly reacted favourably to your new look, didn't he?"

When Tanya didn't answer, Teresa stopped her cutting and turned to face her. Her daughter stood there with her arms crossed, a trace of a smile on her face.

"I can tell what you really want to ask—you're practically shouting out your thoughts." As was Carl last night, though his were more of a physical need. Recalling his thoughts caused her to feel bit excited, a warm glow tingled at her cheeks.

Teresa sighed. Her daughter continued her own progress of reading emotions and now could interpret those thoughts with more accuracy, not just the base emotions of anger, fear or happiness. "So why don't you just tell me what I want to know. A daughter shouldn't keep too many secrets from her mother."

"Carl and I are just friends. Nothing more."

"I saw how he was looking at you last night. That was not just a friend's stare."

"He was drunk."

"That he was, but he still was looking at you with lust. Feelings I know he'll have when he's sober again."

"Maybe, but that doesn't mean I have any of those feelings for him."

That wasn't exactly a denial, but Teresa knew that was all she was going to get from Tanya this time. "Tanya, I believe it's time we had a serious discussion on what is expected of you. Let's sit down."

"...like all of your ancestors, including great Witchdoctor Mariah, you will have one child, a daughter..."

"Only a daughter?"

"Yes, each Witchdoctor has one daughter, and only one."

"You could have more than one, couldn't you?"

"No, it weakens the mother's power and reduces the time spent teaching her daughter the craft."

"But what if a son is born?"

"No, no males are born."

"You also said something about there wasn't a father."

"There is, but this is what I must talk to you about. Choose your man carefully—you have to make sure he has all the right qualities you want to pass on to your child." She got up and retrieved a small container from the cupboard. "The time you decide to make love to him, you must get him to consume this powder in a drink. In the morning he will remember nothing of that night, and you will be able to raise your daughter without the negative energy of a man."

Tanya listened to what Teresa said and held the small vial of grey powder. "Who was my father?"

"I...I cannot tell you that. It might cause you to lose some of your powers. It is best to think of him as dead. I never found out who my father was and you must live without the knowledge of who your father was."

"Please, I need to know."

"No, you don't. I cannot tell you, period. Let me tell you more about the powder and how to use it."

§?

Carl was not certain how he was feeling, his disposition had improved but a conflict of emotions was eating away at him. Several days had passed since the party and he had tried to make amends to Mandy. She still acted cool towards him, and he accepted that as part of his punishment. She, of course, was still upset that he had taken a stroll with Terri. Terri apparently had a bit of a reputation and Mandy was under the mistaken assumption he had done more than just walk with her. That wasn't true, though when Carl had decided to visit Terri, who lived with her two sisters and mother, she made it quite clear she was available to him when he felt the need. Carl did have guilty feelings when he saw Mandy, though it had nothing to do with Terri. Rather it was with his feelings about Tanya. She was constantly in his thoughts and wouldn't go away. He didn't know how to react to Mandy when she accused him of wanting to have other women.

All of this did not slow down his appetite, and he realized that in the time he was in Sorbital he had gained weight and grown taller. Certainly, the work he had to do around the workshop had increased his strength as well. The combination of his increased size, strength, confidence and being a stranger with an accent had made him the target of many females in Sorbit. That explained part of Mandy's jealousy, but did not explain why he wanted the one girl who often acted like she couldn't care less if he was in the same room with her. Maybe that was part of the attraction of Tanya, but he wasn't buying it as he kicked a rock down a street.

"Carl!"

He turned towards the caller. Rog was walking up behind him and gave him a wave. Rog normally hung out with a different group of friends, but they had met at a party and struck a friendship. The tall, dark-skinned man had a quick and easy laugh and had made it easy for Carl to fit in the first time he met the new group.

"Hey, Rog. How's it going?"

"The going is good my friend, the going is good. And you, has that hangover finally disappeared or should I keep my voice down?" He laughed as he approached, his white teeth filling a large mouth. Rog was as tall as Carl and, though thinner, his muscles were visible as twisted ropes under his skin.

They walked together talking about a multitude of subjects. Carl found himself feeling better as they talked, and soon was laughing with Rog.

"...I tell you it was one of the funniest things I ever saw, big ol' Marla trying to push Bennie up that muddy hill. I laughed so hard tears were running down my cheeks."

Carl laughed with him, the vision of what Rog described painted an image so outlandish he had trouble believing it. "God, where was I when this all happened?"

"Oh, you wasn't here yet. But don't worry, if you hang around with me funny things always happen." He stopped a moment and considered. "Hey, have you seen the sea monster yet?"

"No, I haven't. Why?"

"Because that sea monster is something to see. Come on, we're near the pier, let's get a boat and give you your first look."

Carl wasn't all that anxious to see the sea monster at first hand, but he didn't want to appear to be a coward, so he tagged along with Rog and watched as he negotiated the use of a small boat at the dock.

Rog, of course laughed at Carl's attempt to use the paddles. "Man, if you don't start rowing proper we'll be going around in circles. Lift, then dig in like you're shovelling dirt."

The rowing was erratic but eventually they reached a fair distance from Sorbital, to the point where the shoreline was a grey outline.

"Are you sure this sea monster won't try to kill us?"

"No, unless we are dumb enough to keep going. We'll be fine, the monster is strange looking but it doesn't want to eat us." He laughed. "We must taste sour to him like Jake's liquor."

"Is this close to the spot he shows up?"

"Yeah, though it really isn't so much a spot as a distance. If you draw a huge circle around Sorbital, kind of like a boundary, anything that crosses that line gets in trouble. The sea monster warns you first. If you ignore it, then it'll kill you. Or least that's what I've been told."

"You've been told!"

"Hey, I never stick around to see if the second part is true."

The sea monster didn't just rise out of the water like Carl expected with a lot of noise and commotion—rather it suddenly appeared in front and above them. The green and black serpent rose thirty feet in the air, ending in a dragon-like head. Water poured off the huge body as yellow eyes peered down on them, its sharp teeth gleaming as the mouth opened and closed. A low growl emanated from above them.

"There, now how's that for a sea monster, Carl? Isn't she something?" Rog laughed.

For a moment, Carl was scared out of his wits. Then as Rog and he started to row backwards, he took a closer look at the sea monster. There was something wrong about it as it hovered above them. It certainly looked frightening enough, but it also had a surreal appearance. Carl was puzzled at the sight.

It looks almost artificial, like the same amount of water keeps pouring off its head, and those eyes are too big to be real. Damn, if the neck is so long, how big is the rest of the body?

When the small boat had retreated approximately fifty feet from the sea monster it disappeared. It didn't merely drop back into the water, but rather it faded away.

"Did you see that? How it just disappeared like that?"

"Yeah, she always does that."

"What happens if we go forward again?"

"It reappears, but I heard the second time the warning is more severe, like people get burned, sometimes their boats sink. But if you're game, and you can swim, we can try to get close again."

"No, I'll take your word for it."

Carl was silent as they rowed back, the sea monster turning around in his mind.

"Rog, that monster isn't real. It can't be."

"You saw it didn't you? What's the matter, that drink you had still affecting you?"

"No, but look, you said it always shows up the same distance no matter which direction you go. The water keeps pouring off it throughout its appearance like it just rose from the sea. But in fact it doesn't come out of the water. It just suddenly shows up, and then suddenly disappears."

"So if it isn't real, then what is it? Carl, you're not making much sense here."

That sea monster is too artificial looking, like it was some movie monster made up to scare people. It's probably a giant...

"Hologram. It's just a hologram."

Rog gave him a strange look. "I can't argue with you there. You're probably right. It's just a hologram. Now, what's a hologram?"

As Rog laughed at him, Carl tried to explain but gave up and laughed with him too.

Carl believed he was right. He turned over the idea a few times looking for other possibilities, and there were others. In his heart, he felt he was right. There were a few other details to work out. Like the growling noise they heard, though he thought that might have been accomplished by hidden speakers somewhere. The injuries, and the rare deaths people sustained could have been done by lasers he supposed, or perhaps by some other power beam. There were still too many questions before he advanced his theory to others, and so far, only Rog knew of his hologram idea. He still puzzled about one other problem, namely what triggered the sea monster's appearance? But he did have a plan brewing to unlock that secret.

∞

Teresa opened her copy of Witchdoctor Mariah's book *Days of the Future*, glancing at the memorized lines.

The Newcomer came from a home of a thin tower, not losing his past.

He seeks his way back, not knowing how long the road winds.

Travelling to the home of the ghouls, he will break the barrier to Sorbital.

Challenging monsters, both pretend and real, as he meets a hundred deaths.

She jumped ahead a few pages, landing on familiar text.

He waited for the dark one, the one who he will stay with. The one who would break the chain.

Together they will change the world and Sorbital will be the one home no more.

The words were still vague, and since they didn't reveal the time in which the Newcomer existed, there wasn't any reason to believe he was on Sorbital now. When any Newcomer arrived, Teresa decided to check the words of *Days of the Future* to see if he qualified as the one written about. Carl was a possibility. He retained his memory of Earth. The line of not losing his past may have meant having a memory of his past.

She hesitated a few more seconds and hurried out the door, heading towards the village.

As she approached Malcolm's home, she slowed her pace and tried to give herself a calm appearance. Her visit at Malcolm's wasn't helpful. Carl wasn't in and she gave a quick excuse why she had dropped by and then hurried on.

She found him in the market area with Mandy, though they didn't look like a couple. She pretended to bump into them and struck up a quick conversation, leading up to the question that caused her to leave her house.

"I was wondering about the buildings back on Earth. Where you came from, were there tall buildings?"

"Oh, sure. Some were pretty big I guess." Carl thought the conversation was a bit odd, but Teresa was always friendly towards Malcolm and himself and he wasn't going to act like he wanted to be somewhere else as she chatted. Besides it was a nice diversion from the awkward silence Mandy and he were enduring as they walked about. Mandy was good enough to join in the conversation as well, though she had admitted to Carl previously that the old lady caused her to feel nervous.

Teresa wasn't quite satisfied with his answer and moved the conversation back to more details. "So were all the buildings big in both height and width?"

"Yeah, I suppose so. Except for the Space Needle. It was just a tall, thin building with a restaurant on top. I guess it's Seattle's best known building, it was built for a world fair."

Teresa had trouble containing herself. She hid her excitement the best she could and hurried home. *He is the one! He came from a place of a thin tower, and didn't forget his past.*

Teresa didn't know exactly what to do with her knowledge. There was a part of her that thought she may have jumped to conclusions and Carl was not the one who was being referred to in the book. She decided to watch for other clues, though it was hard to get definite statements from *Days of the Future* that would either prove or disprove her theory.

The one thing she was sure of was that she didn't want Tanya to get too close to Carl, especially if he was going to the home of the ghouls and lead his followers to their death. Besides, he was going to stay with the dark one, and though she didn't know who the dark one represented, it certainly sounded ominous.

Chapter Six:
The Way In

Carl carefully carved the edge of the table leg. The furniture was being made for one of the Elders, which meant extra attention to detail. The cut was purely decorative and it took Carl's patience to hold the knife steady. Malcolm had watched him start the first leg and then disappeared into the kitchen, leaving Carl alone to finish. Carl had noticed that Malcolm was leaving him alone on work projects more often and his advice was getting less frequent.

"Time for chow, young fella."

Carl was glad for the call, his stomach had started to growl twenty minutes ago. He carefully put down the knife and hurried into the kitchen. He was amused Malcolm still called him "young fella" after a year and a half on Sorbital.

Malcolm dished the stew into two bowls and then sat down. "I was thinking of taking some time off and do some exploring. Think you'd be okay by yourself?"

"Sure."

"It'll just be for a few days and there isn't much to do here but that table and that doesn't have to be finished for a couple of weeks. You can take it easy as well."

Carl was pleased by the show of confidence, and decided not to take it easy but finish the table before Malcolm got back. The next day Malcolm left after breakfast and Carl immediately went to the workshop.

Carl finished carving the last table leg and washed up before heading to the library. He stopped by Terri's house and chatted with her for a few minutes, inviting her over for tea that evening. He then continued on to the library and became immersed in a book that the author claimed to have met the desert ghouls. Most of the book described his journey into the desert itself, and his meeting with the ghouls seemed more like the hallucinations of a mad man. In the end, he decided it was more a work of fiction and he put the book away.

He also tried to read the book *Days of the Future* again, but the vague way in which the script was written left him confused about its meaning. It did reinforce his opinion that there was something beyond the Ghoul Desert.

He left the library after looking through a few more books, getting a bit frustrated how the authors could not tell the difference between facts and fables. He was impressed by one book that gave accurate sketches and designs of bridges, including angles and dimensions. Unfortunately, the author did not provide much detail on how he did the calculations, and Carl believed they were from an earlier memory. The other problem was that there wasn't a need for bridges in Sorbit and thus would likely never be built.

The book did inspire Carl to check out the math taught in schools, and the librarian on duty showed him the textbook used in the final season of schooling. He was disappointed in the simplicity of the math, perhaps around the equivalent of grade nine or ten level on Earth.

"Excuse me for bothering you again..."

"Oh that's alright." The elderly, heavyweight librarian almost jumped out of her chair as he approached. He had hoped his presence in the library would become less of a novelty as time went on.

"I was wondering if I could have some blank paper? I want to write out some higher levels of math for those who might be interested."

"That would be so kind of you. How much would you like?"

Carl spent the remainder of the afternoon putting down what he recalled from high school math classes, and then realized it was going to take more than just an afternoon to describe differential equations and calculus. Gathering the papers into a stack, he took them home to work on them later.

He took a long route back, cutting through the market area before ending up in front of a medium-sized home. Two young girls, perhaps around thirteen, were sitting on the front steps. Carl recognized one of them as Rog's sister.

"Hi, Charlene. Is Rog in?"

"Yeah, he's in." She turned her head to the open door, yelling. "Rog. Carl's here."

When Rog appeared Carl sparred verbally with his friend before asking a favour.

"Are you game for another trip to the bay to catch the sea monster?"

Rog laughed. "I thought you had enough the first time. Sure, why not?"

Carl outlined his plan to understand what the sea monster actually was, causing Rog to laugh some more. "You see when I was a kid I use to make toy sailboats. Since I had some free time I made a small boat to see, well, if the sea monster would attack it."

"You're crazy. But come on inside, you can stay for dinner."

Carl appreciated the meal and the time with Rog's family. Besides Rog's parents, there were four siblings plus Charlene's friend crowded around the table. The whole family joked during the meal and Carl laughed with them.

Since Carl had returned from his Quest at Rhume Island, Rog had become his best friend and the two spent much of their free time together, especially since neither kept a steady girlfriend. Mandy still could be seen with Carl, though she was no longer his exclusive girlfriend. He had also spent some time with Terri, after he managed to persuade her that they didn't have to talk every second they were together. Val also enjoyed his company and overall, though he certainly wasn't complaining, he found the women in Sorbit a bit promiscuous. In fact, he found most of the women he met flirted with him openly. He felt if he made the effort to respond, he could have his choice, not that he was conceited. His previous social status on Earth prevented him from getting too much of a swelled head and he was happy for the opportunities that suddenly fell onto his lap. The one opportunity that kept eluding him was Tanya, and try as he might, she just wouldn't let him be more than an acquaintance. There were times when he saw something in the way she looked at him or she did something that made him feel she wanted something more from him, but such moments were fleeting and despite his efforts she kept her distance.

The rest of the evening he spent with Terri, the tea eventually giving way to glasses of wine. The following morning he walked Terri back to her home. He said a quick goodbye and then went over to meet Rog at the docks.

"If nothing else, Carl you're learning how to row better with these visits to the sea monster. Just don't get in a race with anybody."

"Thanks. But I'll bet no one can row faster backwards than you when that monster shows up."

"I have to, I've got to row for two men."

When the beast from the sea did make its appearance, Carl pushed out the small sailboat before the two men rowed back. The small boat went straight ahead and headed towards where the monster stood high above them. The creature didn't look at the new boat but kept its huge yellow eyes on the rowboat before disappearing.

The sailboat made its slow journey with Rog and Carl watching it.

"Well the sea beast doesn't seem to be concerned about it. I would have guessed it would have sunk it by now for sure."

"I think the sea monster appears when some sensors detect people, maybe infrared or object recognition software."

"What? All this time you been on Sorbital and you still talk about stuff that nobody has a clue what you're on about."

"Sorry, I was kind of thinking out loud."

"Try thinking before you speak then or give me a translation."

Carl tried to describe what sensors and computers were, but Rog shook his head.

"Sorry, I'm sure you're right, just that I have trouble getting a good picture of those things."

They watched the sailboat as it bobbed along the waves. After about half an hour, it turned sideways.

"Look at that, your boat just made a turn."

"Yeah, but how? Look at it, it's like it has hit an invisible wall and is running along the side of it."

The boat continued its journey, now heading north.

"Damn, Carl, I think you're right. It's sure as hell following something."

"It looks like even if we could get past the sea monsters there is still a barrier to cross. Something wants to keep us penned up on Sorbital."

ॐ

Tanya hesitated a long time before she decided to make the party that Val was having. When Val found out her parents were going out for the evening she decided to have a small party. The invitation was extended to Tanya in the market yesterday afternoon, and though it was given to her by Mandy, it appeared to be sincere. She knew she should make a bit of an effort to be sociable. Enough people had told her she was always putting a shield around herself and this was a safe enough way to extend herself to others. A small party and she could leave when she wanted without getting anyone upset.

Tanya allowed herself one drink that contained a small amount of alcohol and nervously chatted with Terri and Val. She saw Carl looking at her as soon as she came into the medium-sized house but ignored him after giving him a small wave.

The conversation went well enough with Terri and Val, allowing her to relax enough that she talked to Kyle next. She sensed uneasiness, though whether that was due to talking to her in particular or girls in general was hard to say. Outwardly, he acted collected, so she gave him the benefit of the doubt.

Rog was a different matter. When she went over to where Carl and Rog were talking, his eyes squinted at her and she felt his annoyance at her intrusion. Carl was the opposite of course. His smile and emotions were just as easy to interpret.

"Tanya, it's great that you made it. You look good—doesn't she, Rog?"

Rog gave him a quick look before looking back at her. "Yeah. Hi, Tanya."

"Easy on the enthusiasm, Rog, nice to see you too." Satisfied with the reaction she saw on Rog's face, she turned towards Carl. "What have you been up to lately besides chasing sea monsters?"

His eyes widened slightly, and he started to ask a question, but then changed his mind. "Lots of stuff, making furniture, the library, hanging out with Rog."

She chatted a bit longer with them before moving around the room to talk to Val again, making small talk before she left. It was early to leave the party but she felt a bit stressed talking to the others who obviously weren't entirely comfortable with her presence.

Might as well leave now. I've made some inroads socially, except for Rog. He sure doesn't like me. Can't win them all. Carl's too busy talking to Mandy to see me go. Oh well, at least he likes me.

She slipped out the door to the fresh air and slowly walked home. A few minutes later, she heard the sound of someone running behind her, not surprised to see Carl calling out for her to wait.

"You don't need to walk me home, I'm fine by myself."

"I know. I felt like leaving early too and just wanted to talk to you."

Oh, is that all? I thought it might be because I'm the only girl in the room you hadn't taken yet. "Okay, so what do you want to talk about?"

"You. Why did you have to leave the party early?"

"I was bored."

"So you have something more exciting to do?"

"Yeah, I think."

"What do you think about?"

"How glad I am that I left the party."

He didn't have a retort for the last comment and walked in silence with her for a few minutes. "Are you going to the beach party tomorrow?"

"No, I don't think so."

"Come on, it'll be a blast."

"A blast? Never mind, I can guess what that means. No, I know what happens at some of those beach parties, too much drink and then people ending up taking off their clothes and playing in the water."

"So what's wrong with that? I'll be there and maybe we can play in the water together."

She laughed. "That's not too subtle. Sorry, you're not going to get to see me naked." *At least not that way.* "Besides, I've already seen you nude. I can last a bit longer without the privilege of seeing you without clothes again."

"Look, that's not what I meant. I like you and want to...well...spend more time with you. Get to know you better."

"Fine, but you have lots of other girls to keep you busy. I'm not ready for that type of relationship."

"What type of a relationship are you ready for then?"

"The one we have right now. If that's not good enough for you, there's not much we can do about that."

She felt his emotional withdrawal, a moment of resentment and prepared herself for a verbal backlash.

Instead, he sighed. "All right, if that's what you want."

"You surprise me sometimes." She slowed as she approached her house. "Hey, are you hungry? Mom made some fresh fruit bread today."

"Sure, especially for her bread. Malcolm's always turns out too heavy and flat."

She had a slice herself and talked with him as they sat outside so that they didn't disturb her mother, though Tanya knew she was lying awake in bed until her safe return from the party.

"What type of food did you eat back on Earth?"

"All kinds of stuff. What was called junk food, not really good for you but tasted delicious. My favourite was pizza." He described the round bread used and the various ingredients placed in it. He also told her about potato chips, burgers, hotdogs and submarine sandwiches.

"It sounds like you miss the food."

"That and everything else about Earth." He shrugged. "Maybe I'll get back somehow."

She felt sorry for him for a moment. "If anyone can get back to Earth, it'll be you. Thanks for walking me home, but my mom will get up soon if I don't go inside."

They stood up and then on impulse she gave him a quick kiss on his cheek before retreating inside, leaving him as confused as ever how she felt about him.

Her mother called out to her as she quietly made her way to her bed. "Was that Carl you were talking with outside?" The answer was not required, Teresa had recognized his voice immediately but this gave her a chance to talk with Tanya.

"Yes, sorry if I woke you."

"That's okay, I was still awake." She paused as she worked out the right words. "Please be careful when you're with him—you know what the book *Days of the Future* said."

"Yes, but that might not be him the book speaks of."

"The trivoli you used indicated he was of special powers."

"He causes things to happen. He doesn't have special powers himself."

"All the same..."

"I know, I know. A Witchdoctor cannot allow strong emotional ties to anyone save her own daughter." What she didn't say was she had to work to keep herself from getting too close. Somewhere in the back of her mind, she played with the idea that Carl was to be the father of her daughter.

The other information she was reluctant to admit was that the trivoli indicated that Carl and she were following a common path. She had chosen to read the small objects differently, trying to interpret the rolls to mean something else.

℅

Sorbit contained the majority of the population on Sorbital, but as Carl noted on the map there were a few other small villages. One, Terral, was located on the northern boundaries of human occupation, right next to the Ghoul Desert. Terral had a warmer climate than the rest of Sorbital thanks in part to being closer to the equator and next to the hot air that would blow from the desert. Their main trade item with the rest of Sorbital was the unique fish that lived in the warmer waters.

The journey between Sorbit and Terral was by a footpath, kept open mainly by the travellers themselves. Occasionally pieces of sandstone soaked in talnut oil were spread along the path to help discourage plant growth and once a year a group of workers went along the path with machetes to cut back the advancing green leaves.

The journey, providing the weather was clear, normally took about twelve hours. Late starters and rainy season travellers could rest for the night at a covered shelter just off the pathway called, appropriately enough, the halfway house.

Rog and Carl were getting tired as they walked the final distance to Terral, preferring to do the journey in one day. That meant getting up early and keeping a steady pace throughout the day.

Carl had been getting bored sitting around the house. Malcolm hadn't returned and as a result, there wasn't much he could do around the shop. Rog, of course, laughed when Carl had asked him to accompany him to the Ghoul Desert and then agreed.

The small village was the last stop before they reached the desert. Despite its proximity to the desert, the weather wasn't that different than the rest of Sorbital and the evidence of a rain shower two days ago left the tail end of the path muddy.

The two friends stayed overnight in Terral. After dinner they joined with the locals to drink and share stories. Rog in particular made friends with his quick wit. Carl had persuaded

Rog to join him for company and now his chatter and jokes helped make new friends.

The desert started rather abruptly, the sand appearing between the blades of grass after the brush and trees had disappeared. Soon, within a span of a hundred yards the sand took over completely. The sand was warm to the touch, and Carl noted that it actually seemed to be warmer than the air itself. They continued into the desert where the temperature rose rapidly.

"See, I told you. It gets hot fast."

"Yeah, but that doesn't make much sense. I mean the sun is supposed to be really hot to make a desert, but the heat is coming from the ground, not the air."

"Maybe. In a little while it will be too hot to walk. It just gets hotter and hotter. Some people have tried to see how far they can go, but most don't get very far before they have to turn back."

Carl was sweating enough to know Rog was telling the truth.

"What about the coast where the desert and sea meet? Is it just as hot there?"

"Pretty much. If you try to stay in the shallow end of the water, eventually the ol' sea monster makes another appearance. Something really doesn't want us to travel too far in that direction, that's for sure."

They made their way back to Terral, the walk back taking only a few hours. By that time, Carl had thought of a plan to determine why the desert was so hot. Despite the objections from Rog that it was too hot to do any work, the two returned the following day with two men from the village and shovels.

"Carl, how much are we going to dig? So far all we have is this big hole that just keeps getting bigger, like my thirst for beer."

"I don't know. We're only down about five feet. Take a break if you want, but let's hold off on the beer until we finish."

The four men dug slowly but deliberately, tossing the sand out of the ever-increasing pit. Roy and Shawn, the two teenaged boys that had decided to help them because they were bored, looked like they were starting to regret their decision.

"Hey! We hit something!" One of the helpers tapped on the bottom with his shovel.

Carl moved over and pushed more sand away from the area where the shovel had reached the hard surface. The smooth ceramic-like material was hot to the touch, and ran unbroken as far as he could push the sand away.

"There. That's the source for the heat of the desert, underground heating. Someone, or something, has planted this plate under the sand to make it hot."

Rog considered. "Maybe you're right. But what good does that do us? Does it mean we can now have a beer?"

The four headed back to the village. Rog's question was a decent one. So what if he knew that the desert was artificially created.

How is that going to help me? Carl considered the problem. *It doesn't matter if I can't figure it out right now—it's just another clue. When I get enough clues, I'll be able to put it all together. Hopefully.*

The trip back to Sorbit was uneventful for most of the journey. Rog kept up with his usual bag of humorous stories while Carl tried to be more serious and urged him to relate any information he had on Sorbital's past. Rog did ask him about his relationship with Tanya.

"Are you still hot about that witchbitch?"

"She is not a bitch." Carl snapped at him.

"Okay, okay, sorry. Are you still hot about a girl with a sharp tongue, who ignores everyone when she feels like it, insults every guy who ever approached her and does what she wants when she wants to? Oh yeah, she's also a witch."

"Witchdoctor."

"Same thing."

Carl clenched his fists and then tried to relax. *Getting into a fight over her would be stupid. Especially with Rog. He's right about her, she can act like a bitch at times.* "I still like her, she has her good points."

Rog did a side-glance at him as they walked, sizing up what he was going to say next. "Look, I'll give you she's good-looking, especially since she decided to wear something other than those long black skirts. But man she can talk mean."

"It's just a front. She's scared what others think of her."

"Well, I've known her a long time, we all went to school together. She never seemed particularly concerned what others thought about her."

"I've got a question for you. Tanya is a couple of years younger than you and the rest, how come she went to the same classes?"

"Easy. She's smart, very smart. She may have been younger but she just breezed through. Some thought she read the teacher's mind to get all the right answers, but I think she was just too damn clever. Remembered everything."

"No one made friends with her?"

"You got it. I'm not saying the others didn't tease her about being a witch, but she seemed to enjoy proving it. Sorry, I know you're seeing something in her I don't. But with all the other good-looking, friendly women around, why do you chase her? Did she put a spell on you or something?"

"No, that's silly. But maybe you're right, there are lots of other girls to hook up with."

Rog laughed. "You just like a challenge, that's all. Put Tanya out of your mind for a while. She'll still be free later, I can guarantee that."

By the time they made it back home Carl was more determined than ever to work on the clues he had, feeling he was missing only a bit more information to find out what Sorbital really was and how he could get out.

Malcolm was glad to see he made it back okay. Those who ventured too deep into the desert didn't always make it back out. Carl told him about the ceramic plate he found under the sand and that triggered Malcolm's memory about some travellers long ago who had dug into the sand looking for water and found only the hard, flat rock-like surface. It didn't occur to the travellers that the hard surface was the source of the heat but they did find the ceramic layer extended for miles under the sand.

Carl spent more time at the library, looking for bits of data that may help him. A lot of the material consisted of rumours, fables and third hand accounts of events. All the same, he plodded on, searching for something.

He stumbled on a book called *First Appearances*, almost ignoring the text because of the title. He assumed it was about how to present oneself to strangers since the book was next to a volume called *Fortunate are the Elders*.

First Appearances had a roughly drawn but accurate map with several pages of handwriting that described the author's investigation of where Newcomers were first discovered or where they thought they had arrived. The author carefully explained that the exact location was sometimes hard to determine but made every attempt to be accurate. Almost everyone first landed on the coast, and the area where over ninety percent of the small x's that were so carefully marked was right where Carl himself had landed.

There's got to be something in that area, some sort of drop off zone. Maybe I'll poke around there next week sometime.

The next week was filled with work in the wood shop. Malcolm put him to work the following day making a set of chairs and a table. After taking time to go to the desert, Carl didn't want to ask Malcolm for more days off, even though Malcolm would not have objected.

℁

Though the furniture was done, there were a few other minor repair pieces that had to be taken care of before Carl could go back to where he first landed. The time had passed quickly since he had first arrived, and his memory was vague where he had first appeared on Sorbital. He decided he should ask Tanya for the exact location on the beach where he first met her, and from there he would be able to backtrack to where he first arrived.

As he walked to her house, he realized that he had changed considerably since he first arrived and so had she. Tanya was much easier to talk to, at least to him, not acting like she was angry all the time. She had also changed her appearance, wearing her hair short with clothes that matched what the other girls wore.

"Right about here." She pointed with a finger on the map. "The map isn't perfect, but that spot has some high cliffs around it."

"Do you want to show me personally?"

"Can't. I've to do some work in the garden that I can't put off." She looked away from him and crossed her arms, giving him a thought that there was more to her refusal than just the gardening.

"Okay. Thanks for your help."

"Are you going to be there all day?"

"Yeah, probably."

"Come into the house then. I'll make something for you to eat later." She walked into the house, not waiting for his reply. "Don't you guys ever plan ahead? Like where your next meal is coming from?"

Carl walked up and down the beach, spotting the cliffs easily enough and then finding the location where he first arrived. The search took longer than he thought and he wondered if he was just dropped there because of its isolation from Sorbit and most of the population. It made sense, the aliens had taken care to avoid detection and make the human population believe they were hemmed in by natural forces, such as the sea monsters and a desert.

He strolled along the beach munching on a sandwich, looking for something that might be out of place. An hour of looking in the shallow water and the beach area took him to another cliff that jutted out of the sand, exposing a reddish brown rock that stood a dozen feet in the air in a semicircular arc.

That looks a bit odd, like it's a bit away from the other cliffs and formations. The shape is a little too rounded.

Curious he walked up to the rocky surface, feeling the rough texture. It felt like a natural rock layer, but it was almost too flat, like a rocklike texture had been sprayed on the surface. He inspected a bit more closely and saw several vertical lines that may be natural, but might be artificial, perhaps giving evidence of a hidden doorway.

He found a fist-sized rock in the sand and tried to use it like a hammer. Bits of the red-brown layer broke off and finally revealed a white coloured metal underneath. It appeared the rocky surface was just a camouflage for what lay beneath. He tried hitting the metal with the rock but without any effect.

Malcolm was amused by Carl's excitement. Every time Carl made a discovery, or thought he had, he engaged Malcolm to listen to his theory. Sometimes he had something, sometimes nothing. What he said this time was at least worth checking out.

The following day Malcolm, Rog and Carl headed back, lugging the crude, heavy sledge hammers with them which were little more than a blob of cast iron on a piece of wood.

Primitive as they were, they were effective. Each of the three men took turns hitting the rocky side of the cliff. A few blows later, several areas of the reddish brown stone covering came off to reveal more of the white metal underneath. Other than some mild scratches and a bit of a minor depression, the metal was unaffected by their efforts.

"Damn! I know this has to be an entrance of some sort. How can we break in?" Carl took another swing at the metal and then glared at it.

"Maybe that's not the only way in."

The three men turned around at the sound of the voice.

"Tanya, what are you doing here?" Carl dropped his hammer and walked down the small slope where she stood.

She stood there, crossing her arms. "I wanted to find out what exactly you were doing. You do know you can't break down that barrier, don't you?" She didn't want to explain how she felt a disturbance, and after using the trivoli, decided to investigate herself.

"I do now. What do you mean that's not the only way in?"

"If that's a doorway, or a wall, it stands to reason there has to be another side to whatever room it's protecting."

It was an obvious conclusion once she pointed it out and they started looking around for another part of the structure. The cliff behind them dropped away, not leaving room for a structure behind it.

Malcolm stood, leaning on a tree after walking around with the others. "Anyone have a suggestion where else to look?"

Rog shrugged. "Maybe that cliff was all there was to it."

"I know." Carl looked among the others. "It's a tunnel. The cliff is just the exit, and the tunnel drops under the ground. I'll bet if we dig here we will find the top to the tunnel." He pointed at the ground that was behind the small rise where the cliff rose.

Malcolm looked over at Rog and they exchanged questioning looks. "What do you think, Rog? Do you think there might be a tunnel down there?"

"Maybe, but it sure will take a lot of digging to find out, and then what?"

Tanya walked over to where Carl had indicated and sat down.

Carl watched her as she closed her eyes, her arms limp by her sides, looking like she was about to fall asleep. Her lips whispered soundless words and she slowly rocked back and forth.

Rog did a quick assessment of the others and glanced back at her. "Boy, I sure find that spooky when she does that." He whispered the comment from the side of his mouth to Malcolm who gave a bit of a chuckle.

"Don't be worried, she's just checking some things out. But be careful, she's got very good hearing."

The expression on Rog's face caused Malcolm to laugh louder.

Tanya suddenly opened her eyes and stood up. "Carl's actually right. There's a structure underneath us. It could be a tunnel, maybe something else, but there's definitely something below us. And it's not natural, just very old."

Carl was pleased by her support but wondered how she could be so certain. He was just guessing about the tunnel himself from conjecture. "How do you know that?"

She hardly smiled but her amusement stole into her voice. "The air told me."

"The air told you?"

"Yes. I've learned how to listen to something other than sounds." She looked at Rog. "I also hear voices very well."

The next day Malcolm managed to enlist several of his friends to join the ones Rog and Carl had solicited to help dig where the tunnel hid under the earth. With eight people digging in the sand, rocks and soil, it wasn't long before a large pit developed. By midday, someone shouted he had found a barrier.

Carl and the others hurried over to look at the grey barrier that gently curved away from where it was exposed. It lay ten feet below the surface, looking like an old dinosaur bone brought to light for the first time in millions of years. For several minutes they just stared at it in awe, waiting for something to happen.

"Congratulations, young fella, you were right." Malcolm put his hand on Carl's shoulder. "Now what?"

The "now what?" turned out to be using the sledgehammers again on the newly exposed wall. The barrier turned out to be fairly resilient and resisted efforts to break it. But small chips of the grey material broke away after the strongest men took their turns swinging at it. It wasn't until the next day that cracks actually formed on the surface before the larger pieces came loose. Towards sunset the grey wall finally gave in and a hole in the three-inch thick material appeared.

The third day of work made the small hole larger, and eventually large enough that a person could fit into it, assuming someone wanted to drop into the dark hole with an unknown bottom.

"Tomorrow I'll bring a rope and lower myself into there and find out where it leads to. Does anyone want to join me?"

One of the men holding a sledgehammer stared at him. "You must be crazy. Demons live down there. Maybe ghouls too. They'll eat you alive."

Another helper stepped forward. "We should ask the Elders first if we should go inside. Maybe we shouldn't have broken inside that wall in the first place."

"We should set up guards until the Elders get here."

Carl couldn't believe his ears. "What's the matter with you people? There aren't any demons down there. It's a tunnel, nothing more."

The argument went back and forth with voices rising. Carl was being outgunned and out-shouted until Malcolm stepped in.

"Hold it, hold it!" He held up his hands. "Does anyone really expect the Elders to walk all the way down here to look at a hole in the ground? Come on folks, Sorbital has never stopped anyone from going on a Quest, or any adventure they choose. If the young fella wants to do some exploring, let him. We all know the ghouls live in the desert where it's hot, and this is too cool for them for us to be concerned."

There was more talking back and forth, but it became apparent no one was going to oppose Carl in climbing down.

"Thanks, Malcolm."

"That's alright, son. Just be careful."

Carl glanced around at the departing men, and then noticed Tanya observing from the beach. Their eyes met for a moment before she turned and disappeared into the bush.

The drop into the tunnel wasn't difficult, both Carl and the reluctant Rog slid down twenty feet to the floor easily. The inside looked much like the outside as far as the walls were concerned, grey and smooth, though the inside was coated with clear plastic-like coating. The two men used torches to light up the surrounding area, the flickering light showing bulges, pipes and odd rectangular objects sitting randomly along the curved walls. The floor was flat, approximately twenty feet wide, matched by the ceiling a dozen feet above.

"Which way do we go?"

"That way, I guess." Carl pointed down the tunnel, though Rog was looking the other direction. "It's towards where the tunnel ends at the beach."

They walked slowly, allowing their torches pick out details along the sides of the tunnel. The ceiling was flat except for a single two-inch white tube that ran the length of the tunnel. After a half-dozen steps, they were suddenly bathed in a yellow light, the source apparently belonging to the entire wall and ceiling. Rog dropped his torched, crouched down and held his spear in a defensive position. His eyes flicked around looking for a possible attack.

Carl reacted more slowly, lowering his torch as he gazed about. "It's okay, Rog. I think these lights came on automatically, maybe by a motion detector."

"I haven't a clue what you just said. Are you saying there's no danger? I'm not convinced of that."

"There might be danger, but not from these lights." After a minute of watching Rog looking around in all directions, Carl started to walk again, bringing a round of protests from Rog.

As they walked, their footsteps disturbed a very thin layer of dust on the floor, though everything else looked new. More lights came on as they walked with the lights matching their movement. They also came across a six-foot section of the wall that was dark. Carl examined the area carefully and concluded it didn't signify anything special other than that the technology that had made the walls glow had failed. It was comforting to know that those who made the tunnel were not perfect after all. Another half-hour passed before they reached the end of the tunnel and a pair of large metal doors. A seam ran in the middle of the ten-foot doors, but the surface was smooth and devoid of any handles or controls.

Carl investigated the doors carefully and then the sides of the tunnel at the end. One side had a black device the size of a shoebox that had a number of finger size depressions on it. Coloured symbols were imprinted on each one, though their meaning was not clear. Above the black box was a transparent screen, approximately two-foot square and less than an eighth of an inch thick.

"What're you poking at that thing for, Carl? Something might happen."

"That's what I'm trying to do."

"I meant something bad might happen. Maybe wake up some ghouls."

That caused Carl to pause for a second and then he resumed his efforts. "If they're here then they know about us already. This has to be a control unit or keyboard of some sort."

Carl wasn't sure which symbol, or combination of several of them, caused the screen to burst in to life. It took Carl several seconds to recognize the image. It was Sorbit from a view from high above. Various symbols were also present on the screen and Carl tried touching them, causing the image to zoom in. Another symbol caused the image to zoom out, but the rest of the symbols did not have any apparent effect.

Carl tried the control unit again, depressing a combination of the symbols. He tried to be systematic in his approach, though after a few minutes he began pushing buttons at random. It was at a moment when he was not paying attention to what he was pressing that one of the doors opened. The left hand door quietly slid forward and then the inside edge swung inward, causing the sunlight to spill into the tunnel.

"Wow, you did it!" Rog stepped out onto the beach. "You are smarter than you look."

Rog and Carl surprised the others by coming up behind them as they waited by the break in the tunnel wall. Following the barrage of questions, Carl and Rog described what they found and soon after everyone headed back to where the tunnel door had opened.

The group stared at the open doors in wonder, with Malcolm one of the few to nervously step just inside. "So what the devil are you going to do now, young fella?"

"I want to see where the other part of the tunnel goes."

Rog groaned. "I knew it. He wasn't satisfied with getting out alive once from the tunnel. He wants to roll the dice again."

Most of the people around the tunnel entrance shook their head at the thought of venturing into the unknown. A few thought the Elders should be asked for their advice, but the general consensus was that if someone wanted to risk their neck on exploring such a place, that was his business.

Carl felt a pressure at the back of his head and quickly looked around. Tanya was standing behind the main group of onlookers watching him. When he made eye contact with her, she stepped between the others, stopping in front of him.

"Have you considered how far the tunnel goes?"

"No. Only one way to find out."

She squinted her eyes. "Don't be stupid. Use your head for a moment. The tunnel has to go somewhere—probably just beyond Sorbital."

"So? That could be anywhere."

"Not anywhere. Somewhere." An edge came out in her voice.

"Okay, suppose you tell me where that somewhere is."

"Where the ghouls live—the desert."

Carl looked at her. She sounded very sure of herself, and he began to think she was right as he stood in front of the open tunnel door. "Is that what your trivoli told you?"

"Maybe." She acted a little upset, as if he had guessed her source of information about the tunnel. "But you better carry some food and water, it's going to be a long hike." She turned and hurried away.

The following morning the entrance to the tunnel was dark. Rog and Carl each carried food and water as they approached the open door, holding their spears in front of them. After they had taken a cautious step into the entrance, the lights along the walls lit up, exposing the long tunnel beyond. They turned around and gave a wave with their spears at Malcolm, Tanya, Teresa and a few others who came out of concern or curiosity to see them off. A few shouted out "talnut" as they walked away. Carl and Rog disappeared a few minutes later as the tunnel began a slow curve down and to the side. Without any obvious reason the tunnel made continuous turns and twists, sometimes rising gently before sinking again.

At first, they were quiet in their movements, not speaking except in low tones and walking with light steps. Gradually they increased their pace and soon Rog was telling another of his stories. They passed the hole they had made in the tunnel the previous day and carried on, looking for possible changes in the tunnel itself. More lights had occasionally burnt out and there were small cracks on the floor of the tunnel. A small breeze blew behind them, causing the fine layer of dust that covered most of the tunnel floor to scatter as they stepped forward. Other than the dust, the tunnel did not give the appearance of being neglected, at least not entirely. Most of the lights were still working and the walls and ceiling were intact.

The men stopped to eat and drink some water occasionally, not sure exactly how far they had travelled, nor how long they had been walking. The tunnel did not have much change in it from one curved section to another, though occasionally there was an additional box or object in the ceiling or the wall. Two of the boxes had small yellow lights that blinked off and on in a slow pattern and exhibited three buttons with graphics imprinted on them. Rog refused to allow Carl to try to see if the buttons had any obvious effect.

It occurred to Carl that if they didn't see an end soon, then they might have to consider turning back. It was difficult to guess where the mid-point might be, even assuming Tanya was correct that eventually it would end at the Ghoul Desert.

Let's see, we must have been walking for five, maybe six hours. If we're walking at three miles an hour, that's about eighteen miles. That's not very far. Maybe we're walking faster, maybe four miles an hour, then we would have gone twenty-four miles. Where would that put us?

"Rog, do you figure we are probably somewhere near Terral by now?"

"Hmm, well, we're making better time than if we were walking above ground, but I don't think we would have reached Terral yet. A couple more hours of walking maybe." He stopped and moved his head back and forth slightly. "I think we are slightly east from where Terral lies, we might be under the water or close to the shoreline."

"Your built-in compass?"

"Yeah, it never fails me." He looked down. "My feet are getting sore from this hard floor."

"Mine too. Let's stop for a break."

A few hours later, after more walking, Carl and Rog decided to catch some sleep, not certain what time it was or how far it was to the end of the tunnel. After lying down for a few minutes, the lights went out, causing Rog to jump up in the pitch-black darkness. The lights suddenly went back on and Carl tried to explain that the motion detectors were causing the lights to flicker on and off. Eventually Rog settled down long enough for the lamps to stay off.

When they woke, the lights came back on as they stirred, and they had to make a decision on whether or not to continue their journey. Carl pointed out they didn't know how far the tunnel went and they didn't know what was going to be there when they arrived. Their water was getting low, but fortunately, the air was not dry nor was the temperature uncomfortable.

"What do you think, Rog, carry on or turn back?"

Rog was thoughtful for moment, thinking. "I don't wanna go back now. What do we tell the others, that we went only halfway? Let's go for it. There'll probably be water and food at the end, likely another door to a beach or something. Besides they'll probably send a rescue party for us in a day or two anyway."

Carl saw many holes in his argument but he desperately wanted to see where the tunnel ended. He did wonder if his friend answered him not out of his own desire to see the end of the tunnel but because Carl wanted to go ahead.

They continued the walk down the corridor, not seeing much variance in the pipes and objects that ran along the ceiling. Carl was wondering how much longer they would have to travel when Rog spoke up excitedly.

"Carl, the floor, its starting to rise again rather sharply."

Carl looked behind him then ahead. He was right. The floor had begun a quick ascent.

Fifteen minutes later, they arrived at a door that covered most of the tunnel. There weren't any knobs, buttons or any devices that could be seen, just a large grey metallic door surrounded by an equally grey metallic frame. Carl banged on the door first with the palm of his hand, then with his fist and finally with the blunt end of his spear.

"Kind of hard to break in, Carl. There has to be some hidden control to open the door."

"You would think that whoever made this door would have been smart enough to put a door knob on the damn door. Idiots!"

Rog laughed. "Maybe we are the idiots for trying to break in."

Carl paced the length of the door. "There has to be a way in." He continued to slap at the door with his hand, reaching its end when his hand hit the frame itself. The door pivoted near its middle, swinging outward.

"Hey it looks like you found the door handle, Carl!" Rog laughed as Carl jumped back.

Carl and Rog stepped through the door, revealing a room thirty-feet deep and forty-feet long with a ten-foot ceiling after the lights came on automatically. The ceiling and walls were curved and gave a gentle shape to the rectangular room. The walls, pale yellow in colour, had a texture to them rather than being smooth and supported a few low-lying counters. They looked at the various objects that were lying about the floor including some wheeled carts.

Rog took a deep breath of air, closed his eyes and took another breath. "Carl, notice anything in the air?"

Carl was examining the devices lying on the counter. He sniffed the air. "No, why?"

"The air, it's humid, but doesn't have a smell."

"Hmm. Like it's been sanitized. The room does have a vacant feel to it, like no one had been here for years." Carl went over to examine the carts that were of different lengths but each had two small front seats with a single control in the centre. Rog wasn't happy to see Carl sit down and touch the control, though nothing happened despite his efforts. Carl decided to try another cart, and touched the central control. The round control reacted to his touch by giving off a soft glow. When he nudged the control forward the cart responded by rolling ahead, stopping when he released it. Carl drove it around the room—

the single control allowed him to move it left or right and back up.

"Carl, you may be having fun, but I'm getting more nervous by the second. Stop that thing and let's see what else might be here, namely water."

"Sorry, I got carried away. There's another door over there. Want to see if it opens?"

The door opened the same way as the last, touching any part of the doorframe caused it to open by pivoting near its centre. Carl and Rog walked down the hallway, stopping to investigate the floor itself. The floor was of different material than the tunnel, still hard but compressed when it was stepped on.

"This stuff is easier to walk on. Why didn't they put it in the tunnel and that first room as well?"

"I dunno, Rog. Maybe because the wheels on the carts would have damaged it."

Rog looked at him, a silent question hanging at his lips.

"It was just a guess. Probably a wrong one."

"No, you may be right. I don't know how you put things together in your head, that's all. You can be so damn smart at times."

"Thanks."

"Except in women. There you're as dumb as a post."

The hall didn't stay straight very long, twisting sharply to the right before branching out in a fork. One rose slightly to the right but the left side dipped down and curved to the left.

"Looks like a maze." Carl muttered to himself, wondering if Rog was going to challenge him on the meaning of maze. They took the left tunnel, following it as it went past another door, this one marked with green symbols.

"What do you think those mean? A warning?"

"Come on, Rog. Probably just a janitor closet." He touched the doorframe causing the door to swing open like the previous doors.

"Janitor closet?"

"Uh, a storage room for cleaning stuff."

The room was shaped like an inflated square box, about fifteen feet along each side. One wall held an array of equipment, but the room was dominated by a huge white cylinder in the middle of the room that not only nearly reached the ceiling but also disappeared below the floor. A rail went around the eight-foot diameter cylinder where Carl peered down, the bottom vanishing in the darkness.

"Don't get too close to that thing, you don't know what it does."

"It's okay, I'm not touching nothing." Carl was tempted to touch the white cylinder, but was worried if something might happen. He could feel a vibration in the rail, something like the sixty hertz that was common around power plants but a bit higher in frequency. "You know, I think this thing must generate power for this place. There sure is a hell of a lot of power around this thing."

To Rog's relief after a brief look at the equipment Carl agreed to leave it alone and continue their investigation.

The room was the last along the short hallway and they suddenly stepped into a large foyer. The rectangular shaped room was almost thirty feet wide but only a dozen feet deep with the walls and ceiling also curved like the other rooms. The walls were empty as well as the floor save for a spiral ramp in the centre of the room that twisted around one and a half times before it disappeared into the ceiling. The ramp was about four feet wide and appeared to be made of the same material of the floor, slightly spongy on top but hard underneath and on the half-inch sides. A single white rail ran along the outside of the ramp about three feet above the surface and was attached at six-foot intervals by posts that joined it to the ramp's surface. Behind the ramp and standing out from a corner was a four-foot square, open platform attached to the wall by a metal lever. A small groove ran from the platform and up through the square hole in the ceiling. At the opposite corner another combination platform and lever stood, but both the platform and the outlet in the ceiling were much larger, approaching a ten-foot square. Carl walked over to the smaller one, examining the simple controls on the small control pad supported on the platform by a small rod.

"You're not going to touch anything there are you?"

"Relax, I think it's just an open elevator or something like that. See, it goes up through the hole in the ceiling." Carl pointed to the opening above him. "Just a couple of buttons here, one has to be up, the other down."

Rog looked but appeared dubious. "Maybe, whatever an elevator is. How about we go and check out that ramp there? That looks a lot safer."

Carl sighed and went over with him to the ramp. The ramp had a slow incline that took them to a larger room on the next level. The room was different than the lower one in several ways, the ceiling was higher, approaching ten feet, the walls and floor were a pale blue colour and there were windows. The windows were round, almost two feet in diameter, and spaced at regular intervals about nine feet apart. The room also featured a slightly curved floor that partially mimicked the curvature of the ceiling below.

Rog reached the windows first, tapping the surface with his fingers.

"Whatcha matter with you? Haven't you ever seen a window before?"

"Yeah, but this stuff is thin and doesn't distort the outside view."

Carl looked at the glass-like surface. It was thinner than the windows he remembered from Earth, and certainly there was no comparison to the coloured, thick glass they used in Sorbit. "I guess so. The plants outside don't look much different, do they?"

"Same as back home, green."

They continued their journey around the floor, finding a curved hollow in a wall that contained a grey ceramic sink. Rog placed his hand above the sink cautiously. Almost immediately, a small faucet within the sink's side began to dispense water. Rog jerked his hand away initially before moving it back to examine the cool fluid. Excited, he called Carl over and they refilled their water sacks after sampling the water directly from the faucet, which was warm and had a strong metallic taste to it.

The next room was entered through an opening behind a curved wall that became part of a short hallway. The room, contained laboratory equipment as well as half a dozen metal-framed beds that lay along a single row. Behind each stood a stack of equipment with various cords and hoses attached to them. That made Carl and Rog nervous enough, but along the opposite wall stood a number of transparent cylinders containing the bodies of a man, a woman and several creatures floating lifeless in a clear liquid.

"Do you recognize either one of them, Rog?"

"No, thank God. Let's get out of here. This is too creepy."

"That thing must be a sabre-tooth cat. Do you know what that reptile thing is?"

"Uh, just a big lizard, they used to be common on Sorbital, kind of rare now. I think they were called claw-tooths."

Carl ignored the other creatures in the vats and turned his attention to the equipment by the beds. It didn't look user friendly and Carl couldn't guess how it worked. *Just as well. These don't look pleasant when used on people. I wonder how many people from Sorbital were placed on these beds?*

The next room contained multiple thin-screen monitors, each with their own control panel at the base. The monitors were all black, and Carl wanted to play with the controls to see what he could do to make them work, but Rog had other thoughts.

"Look, Carl, we found the end of the tunnel. I don't know about you but I'm tired and hungry. Let's call a halt to our exploring while we're still alone here and head back."

"I suppose you're right." Reluctantly he turned and followed Rog. Behind him were several more rooms he wanted to explore, but he understood Rog's concern and couldn't ask his friend for more time. The whole building reminded him of an abandoned laboratory, but what exactly was its purpose and why it was vacated puzzled him.

The carts were irresistible to Carl and he convinced Rog to hop on with him. Carl drove the cart out the doors and back down the tunnel. He slowly picked up speed as he became more comfortable with the cart. To his surprise Rog didn't act concerned at all, even enjoying the ride. Apparently, his earlier nervousness was vanishing as he headed back home. It took only a few hours to drive back to the tunnel's entrance, and would have been less if Rog didn't try to drive part of the way, banging into the tunnel's sides twice before he surrendered the controls back to Carl.

They left the cart at the entrance, walking onto the beach. At first they saw no one and then spotted Tanya sitting on a rock watching them.

"Hey, your lady witch is waiting for you."

Carl shot him a look but held back a retort. "Hi, Tanya."

She had a mixture of annoyance and relief on her face. "About time you two made it back. We were ready to send out a search team. Did you two manage to get lost in the tunnel?"

Carl didn't see who the "we" were—Tanya was by herself. He also decided to ignore her jab about their direction capabilities. "We were okay. Just exploring a little. We made quite a discovery."

"Like what?"

"We'll tell you all about it later. Right now we're starving."

Tanya gave him an annoyed look. "Fine, keep your secrets." She got up and walked away, heading down the beach.

Rog shrugged his shoulders and laughed. "I'm just glad to say she's your girlfriend and not mine."

Tanya turned her head back towards them. Carl thought she was too far to hear them, but she did seem to react to his comment.

"Rog, one of these days your mouth is going to get you into too much trouble."

"I know, I know. But it also makes me unforgettable too." He laughed. "And I can usually talk myself out of trouble after I get in it."

Malcolm listen to their story over dinner, but didn't act overly excited as they talked. His calmness as they related their tale caused them both to relax and provide more detail as they went on.

"That's an impressive journey you two took." He took a drink from his wine. He seemed to enjoy the taste but Carl found the dark red fluid a bit bitter. "It also showed a fair bit of courage to go there and look around. Not many here would want to do that."

"If I want to make it back to Earth, then it was something I had to do."

"I agree." He looked over at Rog. "But not everyone in Sorbit is so keen to go to Earth."

Carl reacted with surprise. "What? I thought everyone wanted to make it back to Earth. At least that's what the Elders told me."

"Carl, if the Elders said that, no one would contradict them out of respect. But Rog here was born on Sorbital and he doesn't know Earth other than from his schooling. At one time most of the population was made up of Newcomers, and all of them wanted to get back to Earth in the worst way. But gradually, as more and more people were born in Sorbit, there was less of a desire to return to Earth."

Carl was surprised. After his initial interview by the Elders, he assumed everyone was desperate to return to Earth. The fact he himself was anxious to find a way back clouded his judgement of what the others wanted. "So, Rog, is it true you don't want to find a way to Earth?"

Rog shrugged his shoulders. "I wouldn't mind taking a look at it, or visiting it. But this is where I live. Earth, from what I have learned about it, is too strange for me."

"What about you, Malcolm? Weren't you a Newcomer?"

"I was, but I was also an infant. To tell you the truth, I doubt that I, or most people on Sorbital could survive on Earth."

Carl looked crestfallen. "You mean no one wants to go back to Earth but the Elders?"

Rog watched as his friend went from showing the exhilaration of a great discovery to the depths of being alone in his search for his home. "My friend, don't despair. I, and others, will do whatever it takes to help you find a way back to Earth. I promise."

"Thanks, Rog, but I don't want to put anyone else in danger just for something I want."

Malcolm refilled the mugs with wine. "I would think the proper thing to do next is to report your discovery to the Elders and let them decide what we're to do next. They may tell us to close up the tunnel or they will ask you to continue with your work. The thing is Carl, you have literally opened the door to another part of Sorbital. In your pursuit of finding your way back to Earth, you may lead us to discover more of our own world."

They continued to sit and drink, the wine becoming less bitter as its effect began to seep in. Carl was feeling better after the support he received from Rog and Malcolm. Under encouragement from Malcolm, he started to tell more about his life on Earth.

"...actually my grandparents on my dad's side came from Germany, but on my mother's, well...let's see, there was French, Spanish and Native blood."

"Native?" Rog looked puzzled.

"Native American, Indian." Carl didn't usually mention that part of his heritage to others, feeling there was an underlying negative attitude to such admission. Now as he spoke about his Native heritage, it was with a touch of pride.

Carl continued with a description of the college he went to. Rog and Malcolm were impressed by the size of the classes and the buildings. The social aspects of the college also intrigued them, such as the nearby bars, when there was a knock on the door.

Malcolm got up. "Wonder who that might be? Not many know you two are back yet." Though it wasn't too late for visitors, Malcolm didn't normally receive many in the evening and most of the callers were for Carl.

He opened the door. "Oh, it's you. Come on in."

Carl turned and watched as Tanya entered the room carrying a cloth-covered plate.

"Hi, Tanya. What do you have there?"

She pulled off the cloth and turned the plate towards him. "Pizza. Or at least that's what I tried to make from your description."

The pizza, made with sweet tasting bread, goat cheese, sliced meat, vegetables and tomato paste was the oddest pizza he had ever eaten. It was also one of the best pizzas he had ever eaten, though hunger was clouding his judgement. Tanya was in a good mood, joking and asking questions.

Tanya tried the pizza herself. "Well, it's okay I guess. Must be something you have to get use to." She considered her own answer for a moment. "I didn't make this quite right did I?" She giggled.

"Close enough. Wrong type of cheese, uh, the pizza sauce is usually spicier and well... Oh, hell, it's still good. No such thing as a bad pizza."

Rog wasn't as kind. "This is weird food. Edible if you're hungry, but not exactly my first choice. What do you say, Malcolm?"

"It's food, a darn sight better than the grub I usually have. Tanya, you did a fine job making this from any obscure directions Carl may have given you."

A few hours later Tanya headed home and Rog soon followed suit, declining the offer to crash the night. "My mom will kill me as it is for not coming home straight away."

"Okay. Thanks for coming along with me."

"That's what friends do. By the way, I still say that pizza was strange."

"Yeah, but she tried."

"Sure, but did you notice how mad she was at us earlier and then suddenly she shows up with food? Women are hard to figure out but she wins the prize there."

"Yeah, well, I guess you have a point."

Carl sat down to finish the last of the wine, knowing a hangover was a real possibility in the morning.

Malcolm watched him for a moment, trying to decide if he should venture into Carl's thoughts. "Problem, Carl?"

"No...yes. I can't quite figure out Tanya."

"Some people are mysteries. What troubles you about her?"

"What doesn't trouble me about her? She keeps giving me mixed signals. One time nice, another time cold. Rog thinks I'm wasting my time with her. Maybe he's right—there's lots of other fish in the sea."

"Fish in the sea? Interesting expression." He rubbed his chin. "For what it's worth, I can give my take on this." He waited until Carl nodded before continuing. "First, Tanya is a Witchdoctor. That means she's not supposed to have any romantic interests. Her training to be a Witchdoctor is to be her life and emotional distractions are not permitted. I would reckon she feels torn between having a social life and her duty to be a Witchdoctor. That would make most people rather moody."

"You have a point there. Still, I don't know if I shouldn't just go after someone who isn't so much trouble. Tanya could be just a friend."

"Perhaps." Malcolm opened another jug of wine and poured more wine into the mugs. "Have you ever gone down to the fishing docks in the evening?"

"A couple of times. Some rather unkempt drinking holes there."

"That they are. But if you were to spend an evening there and listen to some of the fishermen talk, you'd notice something rather interesting."

"What's that?"

"Well, first they'll talk about what they caught that day. As the drinks catch up to them, they spew forth stories about the big catches they had in the past. They're pretty noisy then, laughing, exaggerating and insulting each other, each trying to outdo the other. But then a strange thing happens." Malcolm's voice dropped in volume, and leaned across the table. "The noise level drops and now the fishermen talk about what really grips their hearts. The funny thing is, what they really reminiscence about isn't the easy catch they made, but the one that got away. Carl, don't settle for anything but what you really want. When you get to my age, you don't want to be thinking about the one that got away."

Carl looked at Malcolm. It explained a lot about the man who lived alone, who poured too much of himself into his work.

Carl took a drink to help cover up his loss of words.

After that, they drank quietly. Later, Carl had trouble falling asleep despite the wine.

Chapter Seven:
The Return to the Tunnel

Carl woke up and immediately covered his eyes with his arm because of the morning sun. He did anticipate the headache though it wasn't as bad as he expected. Malcolm had already been up and was busy in the workshop and Carl wandered in to help him.

"That's okay, boy. You look like shit. Get yourself something to eat and drink. You and Rog are going to see the Elders today and you want to look your best. Or at least close to it."

A few hours later, he made it over to where Rog lived and together they went to see the Elders at the town meeting hall. Malcolm had gone earlier to the Elders to request a meeting at the hall and was waiting when they arrived. The hall was actually an open bowl with table and chairs at the front where the Elders sat while the audience sat on benches in the circular structure. The Elders sat under a cover to protect them from the sun or rain but the rest of the bowl was open to the sky. Elder Bronwick sat in the centre of the long table and was the one who held a small gavel and ran the proceedings. The back was filled with onlookers, while at the side of the table stood Malcolm, Teresa, Tanya and several other advisors and higher ranking village people.

Rog and Carl told their story, enduring numerous interruptions from questions from the Elders. It was obvious they were fascinated by what was being revealed, though it was also true some of them didn't understand there wasn't anything supernatural or magical about it.

"That is a very intriguing tale. What do you propose we do about this tunnel? Seal it off?" Elder Bronwick decided on who was to ask questions by pointing at the individual, but more often than not, it was himself making the inquiry.

"I'd like to continue to explore the building and whatever is beyond it. There's still a lot of information to be gained."

The Elders conferred among each other, most of them nodding their heads at what Elder Bronwick said.

"Very well, you have permission to return to the tunnel and the alien building. Please report any new findings. You have done well, Newcomer Carl."

"Thank you." *Done well, Newcomer Carl? How lame is that? And what's this "you have permission" bit? As if I needed that to go back.*

The meeting broke up and Tanya was the first to meet up with them. "Carl, I want to go with you two when you go back into the tunnel. You need someone who can read inanimate objects." She spoke quickly, in a rush to ask him before Malcolm and Teresa reached them. "Well? What do you say?"

Carl looked over at Rog who was slowly shaking his head in small movements. "Umm, well, I better check with Rog first."

She turned her attention on Rog, who in turn suddenly turned around to greet Malcolm and Teresa.

"Excuse us, I need to talk to Rog for just a minute." She grabbed his arm and tugged him away.

Rog reluctantly followed her a few feet away. "Look, Tanya let's discuss this later."

"No, I'm not letting you put me off just because you don't like me or think I'm not good enough for your friend."

"Who says I don't like you?"

"Come on, Rog, this is the witch you're talking to. Don't you know I can read minds?"

"No, you can't." He locked eyes with her and it became obvious she wasn't going to drop her request easily. "For crying out loud, Tanya, I'll talk it over with Carl. But later, not now."

Rog rejoined the others, relieved to have skirted the answer about her joining them and annoyed at her attempt to force her way in. He wondered if the pizza she brought over the previous night was a way to soften them up for her request.

"Rog, good news. Teresa has invited us to her place for dinner." Malcolm looked pleased at the prospect of having one of Teresa's home-cooked dinners. Rog immediately thought of a trap.

Rog lagged behind the others as they walked to the Witchdoctor's home. Tanya, after walking with Carl, dropped back to where Rog followed.

"Look, I'm sorry I came on heavy with you back there. I was wrong." She hung her head and spoke towards the ground, as if an apology was one of the more difficult tasks she ever had to endure.

"That's okay." She continued to stare at the ground as they walked, and he felt a need to break the silence. "I'll talk with Carl later about you coming with us. I promise to be objective, and I don't dislike you. All right?"

She turned and made eye contact, holding his attention for several seconds. "All right. Thanks."

The dinner went fine with the guests staying well into the evening. Tanya gradually opened up again and was joking with Carl and Rog while Malcolm talked with Teresa. Rog saw glimpses of what his friend saw in Tanya, the quick, intelligent remarks to whatever was directed her way. Her humour often had a sarcastic ring to it, but it still made the others laugh. Her face and body, now that she was feeling comfortable and relaxed, showed more of her natural beauty. In fact, Rog observed, when she was like this, he could see why Carl had fallen for her. He could see that Carl hadn't given up on her and there was little point in trying to dissuade him.

"So, Tanya, are you still wanting to see the other end of the tunnel?"

Tanya quickly turned to face him, her eyes showing the excitement of being shown a great secret. "Sure. Have you two decided?"

Rog looked at Carl. "I have no objections, in fact it would be good to have another person with us to help us out. Carl?"

"Yeah, it would be good to have you along, Tanya."

Tanya beamed, while her mother frowned.

"I don't know if it would be safe for you to go, Tanya. You don't know what may be lurking out there."

"They've already been there. It's safe enough. I want to see this place that *Days of the Future* spoke about." She paused, clasping her hands together. "I need to know."

There was little Teresa could say. Her chief worry that Tanya was going to get too close to Carl, whom she believed was the leader who was going to bring forth the dark forces, couldn't be voiced. "Sometimes our wants and needs are confused, Tanya. Are you sure this is necessary?"

"It is."

Teresa sighed. The argument was lost. Her most serious objections couldn't be voiced with the others present, and she realized that Tanya was clever enough to arrange it that way. Tanya was the one who had suggested they cook a dinner in a way of a celebration, so she had the plan developed for a while. She knew her daughter was smart, and now she hoped she was smart enough to know what she was getting herself into.

After the others had left, she confronted her daughter about the danger of getting involved with Carl. "I'm not saying he is a bad person, in fact I admire what he has done since he found himself here. But he's going down a path that could well destroy what we have here and I don't want to lose you in the aftermath."

"Don't worry, I'll watch what I'm doing. But I can't live in a cocoon all the time waiting for a magic moment to try to live my life."

It was to both to their surprise and gratitude that at the last minute Malcolm decided to go along as well. The cart had a small open bed in the back that the others jammed into while Carl sat in the front with Malcolm, quickly moving the cart along down the tunnel. While Rog was prepared for the ride, he heard Tanya gasp and Malcolm ask for divine protection, though at least he did it in a joking fashion.

"Relax, he's drove this cart down here okay, we'll be okay." Rog tried to sound confident but there was a bit of tension in his voice. "Besides, if he hits the wall he'll provide a cushion for us when we pile on top of him."

"Great, I feel so much better now."

The cart was manoeuvred around another curve that caused everyone to lean a bit to maintain their balance. Carl heard Rog grunt from a bit of pain.

"Tanya, you can hold my arm as much as you want, but pull your claws out of my skin if you don't mind."

"That's because your arm is too thin to get a grip on otherwise."

Carl tried to ignore the comments behind him, concentrating on using the single control as he built up speed. Malcolm was quiet other than his first comment, but Rog and Tanya continued their bantering as he drove. He supposed that was a sign they were getting along better. They used to just ignore each other.

An hour into the trip Tanya tapped Carl on the shoulder. "Could I try driving for a while? It looks like fun."

He didn't have a chance to respond. Both Malcolm and Rog yelled out their feelings on her driving before he could even consider a reply.

"Lord no. We're tempting fate enough as it is."

Rog shook his head. "Tanya driving this thing? If I wanted to be maimed I would just jump off a cliff."

She punched Rog hard on the shoulder, crossed her arms and looked indignant at his insult.

"Ow. Why did you hit me and not Malcolm? He didn't want you to drive either."

"You were closer." She then kicked Rog for good measure.

Carl recalled his dad telling him and his friends to stop horsing around when he drove part of the baseball team home after a game. For the first time he could understand why it was so distracting to the driver. Still, it was better than having Tanya sulk, as she was prone to do in the past when she didn't get her way. At least she appeared to be actually enjoying the company of others for a change.

An hour later, the single control unit began to glow green, and a minute later the cart started to slow down, and then maintain the slower pace.

"What's happening there, Carl?" Malcolm leaned forward.

"Green light came on the control knob, and then it slowed down automatically. I think it must mean this thing is running out of juice. Low battery or something like that." He paused as he thought about it. "It might also mean 'requires service soon'. Like something is starting to break."

"I'm not entirely clear what you just said. Does that mean it's going to stop before we get there?"

"Don't know. If it does break down we'll be able to walk the rest of the way without a problem. We aren't that far away from the end of the tunnel."

"Good. I'm getting a mite cramped sitting here."

The cart did make it to the end of the tunnel and they slowly disembarked, stretching out their limbs as they looked around. Carl saw where a few of the other carts were parked. He noticed there were grey markings on the floor and when he examined them a bit closer saw that the grey markings were actually strips of dull metal.

The others watched as he slowly manoeuvred the cart over the markings. When he positioned just over the strips he suddenly heard a clicking noise and felt a small thump on the bottom of the cart. The green light now started to slowly pulse. He got out and looked underneath. Two thin metal strips had risen to meet with the bottom of the cart.

"Cool. It must be charging."

Malcolm looked at the others. "What is charging? Does it have anything to do with cool?"

Rog rolled his eyes. "He's thinking out loud. Think of it as speaking while in a Witchdoctor's trance."

Carl shook his head. "Come on. Let's finish the grand tour."

The four covered everything Carl and Rog had seen the first time. No one wanted to spend much time in the room where bodies floated in the large clear tanks, except for Tanya who sat in front of one of the tanks that contained the woman. She sat down, crossing her legs as she closed her eyes, silently mouthing words.

The others wandered around close by, not wanting to stay in the room and not wanting to leave her alone either. Malcolm finally offered to stay by the room's entrance so that Carl and Rog could continue their investigation.

All the doors appeared similar, sometimes they came across what appeared to be closets, other times an office. These had strange looking desks with simple chairs around it. The chairs didn't have arms but had padded seats and backs on four metal legs, appearing to have been designed for small adults. The desks were made out of a ceramic type of material and were supported by a single, fixed leg. The top was made of a thin ceramic material and tilted slightly forward like a drafting table. Other than the furniture, the room was empty, though Carl noticed there were a number of symbol embossed keys on the left corner of the desktop. Pressing them didn't bring about any response so he decided to invest his time elsewhere.

Rog opened the next door, revealing a room that held a number of chairs behind long flat tables. The chairs were again strictly functional and the table was about two feet wide and six feet long.

"Looks like a school cafeteria."

"A what?"

"Lunch room, you know, a place where a bunch of people sit down to eat their lunch."

"Oh. I guess it could be, if that's what a lunch room looks like."

Carl walked inside, reminding himself that he was still talking about things that most people in Sorbital had never heard of, as he scanned the front of the room. Like a school cafeteria there were shelves that could hold trays or dishes and behind those were counters that held empty containers set flush with the top. Carl inspected the containers that appeared to be made of a white stiff plastic-like material and concluded this was indeed a place where people could have eaten. Carl was still examining the room when Rog called from the doorway.

"Hey, you gotta come and see this." He waved him over and went into a room across the hall.

Carl followed his footsteps, entering a large room that had an extended ceiling. Two house-sized, round vessels were supported on their base by metal rods.

"Flying saucers! Rog, these are the spaceships that probably brought us here."

"Yeah? These things can fly through space?"

"Sure. I don't know how they work, but maybe they can be fixed."

The first spacecraft's interior was visible by a door that opened on the bottom that formed a ramp. Carl peered inside, seeing control panels around the perimeter along with chairs. He walked inside and saw that a centre hub had been removed to expose the inside cavity. The main feature seemed to be thick coils of different wires intertwined around each other to a diameter of over two feet. Close to the core were metal plates that contained what looked like circuit boards encased in a gold coloured epoxy.

"What is that thing?"

"I think it's what makes this thing fly."

"How does it do that?"

"I haven't the foggiest."

The other ship had its door down as well to form a ramp, but the saucer was also split open in the middle along its circumference. They tried to look inside but the shadows revealed little, save for support beams, some cables and some metal boxes that wires ran into.

Carl was excited to find the saucers, though they looked to be in a state of disrepair. Various tools and equipment could be found on benches along the wall as well as the now common flat monitors with the simple keypad. Carl tried to turn one on and to his surprise, it turned on to reveal a picture of various components and text along side of it. The text was composed of symbols he had never seen, but he had no doubt he was looking at a repair manual of some type.

"Rog, this must be the repair instruction to these things. If we can figure what these words mean, we might be able to fix them."

Rog looked over his shoulder. "Not in my lifetime. Come on, we better get back to Tanya and Malcolm."

Tanya found herself returning back to her own time and place. She was confused about the ghostly information whispered to her. She looked around and saw the three men quietly watching her. "I'm back."

"What did you find out?"

"It's odd. This place, this building is over a thousand years old, and is a replacement of another one that stood before it. This woman," she pointed to the tank, "has been here for several hundred years. The ones who live here, or sometimes live here, come from far away but have made this place, but not this building, their home."

"What do you mean by that?" This from Carl, who didn't know a Witchdoctor's dreams were not supposed be questioned or asked for an interpretation.

"They...they used to stay in this building but now only occasionally come here. They live on...on this world? But in a...a different area. They consider themselves to be renegades, searching for...searching for...meaning?"

"What is this place for?"

She looked at him, and then closed her eyes to remember the fleeting glimpse of her waking dream. "To learn about us...and to save some from the changes...the destruction. It is also to protect us...and to protect the others from us. I'm sorry, that's all I can bring up. Except...except that they are the ghouls that lived in the dessert."

She rushed out the last sentence, looking worried. "Can we get out of here now? Before they get back."

"Sure, take it easy." Malcolm crossed the floor and helped her up. "I reckon we have what we need."

"One minute. Give me one more minute. I want to check on something." Carl hurried out and went into the room where various monitors stood blank. He tried using the small keypad and succeeded in causing the monitor to spring into life. By that time, the others had followed him and grouped around the display. Again, the odd symbols danced across the screen, but he continued to push buttons and finally the image changed. It took a minute for him to recognize the picture, but he finally deciphered it into a map. The map was actually a photograph of part of the planet, though the image was static and it was difficult to guess how old it was. He moved the map across the screen, trying to pick out identifiable features.

"Let me try." Tanya pushed forward and held her fingers lightly over the small keypad. Closing her eyes and concentrating she slowly played her fingertips on the depressions. The image began to change, shrinking until Malcolm called out.

"It's Sorbital. See? That's its shape, and look, that's Silent Island. Only it's not an island after all."

The others agreed with him. Tanya looked at the map, with Sorbital having less than a quarter of the screen area. She moved the map across the screen again and then pointed to the base of a range of mountains. "There. That is where the desert ghouls live now."

Tanya returned the image back until Sorbital was in the centre of the screen and zoomed in. "Look, Tureck's house has not been built yet. This must be over a generation ago."

They talked constantly about their find as they headed back down the tunnel. The cart had come back to life during the time in its dock and carried them along with Carl driving. Tanya's second attempt to drive was met with a stern rebuttal once again.

Carl was now determined to find the ghouls. The aliens were the ones who brought him here and they could take him back. He would just have to convince them of that. Somehow.

He was also impressed by Tanya's ability to draw out information from thin air. Of course he had no way of knowing if what she said was the truth, but she was able to get the monitor to display what she wanted to see even though this was the first time she had seen one. *Maybe there is more to this Witchdoctor thing after all.*

Once again, Carl had to appear in front of the Elders, though although this time he was accompanied by Malcolm, Tanya and Rog.

Elder Bronwick once again led the discussion among the other Elders. They came to an agreement after a few minutes.

"We regret..." Elder Bronwick then suffered from a coughing spell before he could continue, "...we regret that we will require a few more days to come to a decision. We wish to thank your group, Newcomer Carl for their courage in exploring the ghouls' home. We will notify you when we have come to a decision."

Carl turned away slightly disappointed. He had hoped they would be as excited as he was about returning to the alien building when he suddenly felt a sharp pain on his shoulder. He turned around and saw Tanya holding a fist.

"What's this of us being part of *your* group, Newcomer Carl? I notice you didn't bother to correct them."

"Sorry, it wasn't my idea."

"Yeah, well don't get any ideas of bossing me around."

As if that could ever happen. "Relax, relax, I won't."

"Don't tell me to relax."

Two days later, they stood in front of the Elders as the edict was announced. Elder Bronwick stood in front and spoke before the large congregation.

"It is with careful consideration of all available facts that we have come to the conclusion that we cannot ignore what lies beyond the tunnel. Therefore, we will request that a group of dedicated people from Sorbit will explore the territory beyond the ghouls' home to learn more about this world. We implore that Newcomer Carl, as leader of this exploratory team, choose those that he believes will aid him in his task.

"We advise those that wish to follow Newcomer Carl on his great Quest approach us by the end of this week and ask for permission to join him. We will then consult with him for the best candidates."

There was considerable noise from the crowd afterwards and Carl was surprised by the scope in which he was empowered.

"Well, young fella, it looks like you are going to be leading an expedition. Congratulations, you have certainly earned this chance."

"Thanks, Malcolm. This was unexpected. I was just hoping to go by myself." He looked at the throng of people, mostly young men, who pressed in towards the Elders. "I'm not sure if I'm the right leader for this though."

"How so?"

"I...I've never been a leader before. Not even the captain of a pickup baseball game."

"Well, you are now. Just think before you do or say anything, pretend you are confident when you do it, and you'll be fine."

"Are you coming along on this Quest?"

"Well, I am a bit on the old side for that type adventure. Young men are the type you are looking for."

"Yeah, but you're in good shape—you hike around and hunt enough. I need someone with knowledge and experience, you know, someone who can give me advice."

"Well, I'll give it some thought. Let's get out of here and get a drink or two to celebrate. Rog, you better come with us. I think if you want to go on this fool hardy adventure, you have an in without checking with the Elders first."

They strolled off laughing, not noticing a pair of eyes watching them intently. Harbouring a bit of resentment that she wasn't included in the celebration, she forced her way into the crowd that lined up to see the Elders. The people she jammed past at first looked annoyed, but after seeing it was the Witchdoctor's daughter held back their comments. It wouldn't be smart to have a curse hanging over one's head while going on a Quest.

A week later Carl met with the Elders again. Malcolm went with him and Elder Bronwick greeted him at the door. The sitting room was how he remembered it, but now that he looked at the furniture, he recognized Malcolm's handiwork in the woodwork.

Bronwick heaped praise on him for what he accomplished in the short time he was here. He predicted that the Quest would be successful and that all of Sorbital would benefit from his work. "We have had many people request to join you, and believe that the best choices to join you are the following. You may discuss our decision with us, of course, but I think you will find we have made a wise assessment on who would be best."

He listed off several names, most of which Carl was familiar with, some he was not too sure about. "Most of these, as you would expect, are very capable with spears and a bow and arrow. There might be danger and you should have some protection that way. For camp cook, we have chosen Mattie and for spiritual needs and medical requirements, Florence has agreed to accompany you. Incidentally her daughter Katrina will also accompany her to help and provide other duties. That makes a total of thirty-four men and women to join you. Is this satisfactory?"

"Most of them are fine, but there are one or two others that I was thinking of."

"Such as?"

"Rog, I would like him to come, and Malcolm as well."

Bronwick glanced at the other four Elders in attendance. "Very well, they can be included as well."

"And if I may put my stone in the middle here, why was Mattie chosen over Hilliard? I heard both applied." Malcolm directed his question at Elder Bronwick.

"Oh, Mattie is younger and therefore would be able to keep up better."

"Hilliard may be older, and heavier, but she is in excellent shape and would be able to keep up easy enough. She's also strong enough to help with physical work if called upon."

"You believe she would be a better choice then?"

"Yeah, and she's also a hell of a better cook. Food may be in short supply but she can make most anything taste good."

"Okay, we can put her in instead."

"I'm not familiar with Florence. Is she also a Witchdoctor?"

Bronwick paused before answering. "To set it straight, the village has only one person who can carry the title of Witchdoctor, just as only one can carry the title of Hunter, or Woodworker." He nodded at Malcolm as he mentioned Woodworker. "That doesn't mean others do not perform those tasks, and when Witchdoctor Teresa, for example, passes on or decides she no longer is able to perform all the duties of Witchdoctor, we will appoint a new one. Florence has been practicing healing for many years now and is a likely candidate to become Witchdoctor eventually. When she is with your group outside of Sorbit, she assumes the title of Witchdoctor. I trust that explanation is satisfactory."

"Yes it is, but may I inquire who else applied for the position of Witchdoctor?"

Bronwick frowned. "Hmm, well there was Reinekke, but frankly her best years are behind her. Anita does not seem to possess the inner strength to do spiritual healing, at least not yet, but she has potential. Tanya, the Witchdoctor's daughter, also applied. We have hopes that she will someday learn to use her abilities in a more positive vein, but she is obviously too immature and headstrong to be of help to you now. We took into consideration that she has already travelled with you to the ghouls' home, but even when she applied, she failed to show proper respect for our criteria. She was, shall I say, resentful we were even looking at other candidates."

That sure sounds like her all right. "I understand what you have said, but I request that we have Tanya as our Witchdoctor. Please."

"But why, after all we have explained about her would you want her along?"

"I'm familiar with her temperament and I believe it won't be an issue. But I have confidence in her abilities, and would really feel better with her as our Witchdoctor."

Bronwick looked annoyed. "This puts me in a difficult position. At the end of our last meeting with Tanya, I rather bluntly told her she was not going to be considered. This puts us in a rather awkward position."

"I understand, but I still want her to come."

"Very well, I don't want you to feel as if you do not have fair input into our decisions. I will personally inform Tanya and Florence of the decision."

Carl did wonder why Tanya didn't talk to him first before applying. It would have made it easier and he could have her name as the selected Witchdoctor before the Elders started to work through the list. *That's Tanya for you, making life as turbulent as possible.*

The following day Tanya came to see him, thumping on the door to announce her presence.

"Hi, Tanya, how are you doing?"

"Fine, just fine." She didn't look fine, her eyes blazed with anger. "So you got me in your little Quest?" She glared at him, her forehead pinched in lines. "Well, thanks a lot, but it's not going to get you any closer to me, is that clear?" She was now practically shouting, and he winced from her attack.

"Yes but..."

"Good, 'cause I don't owe you anything." She turned and stomped off, leaving Carl bewildered at the animosity.

He closed the door, turned around and saw Malcolm laughing. "Seems like the fish you are trying to catch has a lot of teeth in it."

"Well, she sure took a bite out of me there. I can never figure out where I stand with her."

"Well, I doubt if she came all the way down here to scream at someone she didn't have strong feeling for. Now all you have to figure out is if she hates you or likes you."

Teresa wasn't pleased at all her daughter applied to go, and was dumbfounded when Elder Bronwick came to explain that the decision had been reversed on Tanya becoming the Witchdoctor for the Quest.

She was going to protest but noticed the glum, no-nonsense look on his face. Clearly, he wasn't happy about giving Tanya the appointment and arguing with him would be futile. And trying to change Tanya's mind, well it would be easier changing a rock into a flower. She consulted her copy of

Days of the Future again, shaking her head at the implications of the Quest.

Chapter Eight:
The Quest

It took another couple of weeks to prepare for the Quest. Several members of the group practiced by shooting arrows and using their spears. Others used the time to spend with their family and friends. Carl tried to help Malcolm finish as many projects as possible, including making some spare spears. Tanya kept to herself, refusing to attend a farewell party that was held for the group.

It finally came time to leave. The group, led by Carl with Malcolm and Rog next to him, walked down the long tunnel. A large assembly had been at the tunnel's entrance for the send off and Carl waved at them as they walked off. The party initially talked nervously among themselves, either talking in whispers or occasionally loud voices. After an hour, almost all of them had settled down and the usual conversation took hold.

Carl noticed Tanya stayed away from the main body walking either to the side or behind and she appeared to pointedly avoid looking at him. She was making it plain she was still annoyed with him and Carl inwardly wondered what he had to do to get her to act less hostile to him.

The hours dragged on and Carl decided to call a halt so that they could rest their legs. The hard floor was taking its toil on them and most of the group quickly sat down with relief. Two members of the group walked near the front and squatted, their eyes watchful and their spears at ready. Two more covered the back of the group. Carl knew there wasn't much risk in the tunnel itself but wanted a group of eight men to rotate guard duty whenever they stopped. He wanted to establish a routine for when they did move into dangerous territory and he was pleased they moved into position without being told. The journey down the tunnel went without incident. The following day, the rapid rise in the floor indicated they were approaching the end of the tunnel.

More excitement came when they finally reached the large grey metallic doors. He heard a few gasps as they moved first into the storage area for the carts and then into the main lobby.

"Okay, listen up people. This building is deserted, but if you touch anything, you may get hurt. We're going to rest here for tonight and head back outside in the morning. So feel free to look around, there's another level above you by the way, just don't touch anything. There're some tunnels and rooms that haven't been explored yet, and if you do decide to do some exploring, don't go alone. Also, inform Malcolm, Rog or myself where you're heading off to." Carl looked at the anxious faces staring at him. Obviously, some weren't too keen to do much exploring but several others nodded and soon went off.

He walked over to where Tanya was standing and tried without success to make eye contact with her.

"Tanya are you going to be mad at me for this whole journey?"

"What makes you think I'm mad at you? Just because you act like everyone owes you some big favour, why would I be mad at you?"

"For crying out loud, Tanya I don't think anyone owes me anything! I just tried to do what I thought was right, if you can comprehend that. Sorry if I hurt your ultra-sensitive feelings. Unfortunately you don't seem to care if others have feelings as well." He turned and went back to where Rog was sitting against a wall.

Tanya opened her mouth to speak and then stopped, pursing her lips as she watched him walk away.

"Wow, did I see that right? You got in the last word with the witch? Wonders never cease."

"Shut up, Rog. I don't feel so good about it."

"Maybe, but it's about time you stood up for yourself with her."

"Yeah, whatever. Look, Rog, you're my best friend and I'm gonna need you to help smooth things out at times, not make smart remarks when something goes wrong."

"Sorry. I didn't mean to get you upset. I just tried to add a little humour, that's all."

Carl lightly punched Rog on the shoulder. "I know. You're just being yourself. She just gets under my skin and I get a little stressed."

Rog knew it was a good time to be quiet and looked past Carl and noticed Tanya was still staring at them. Her eyes looked wet and her nose had a red tinge to it, giving the impression she was about to cry. She noticed Rog was watching her and quickly turned away and disappeared among the others.

Everyone slept close by on the main floor, not wanting to risk being by themselves in the dark as the possibility of the desert ghouls lurking somewhere in the building made everyone a bit nervous and apprehensive. Carl watched out for Tanya but didn't see where she spent the night. He assumed she was probably as far away from him as she could manage without being too far from the group. Or, as he reminded himself, she might be somewhere downstairs just to spite him. He decided to try not to think about her anymore and went to sleep at an open spot by a wall.

He woke up early the next morning, feeling tired but unable to sleep any longer. Hilliard was passing out fruit and bread from the provisions to those awake enough to eat. An hour later, he spotted Tanya sitting by herself eating fruit. Slowly he walked over to her and she quickly spotted him approaching, not taking her eyes off him as he came to a stop in front of her.

"How did you sleep last night, Tanya?"

"Okay."

"I didn't see where you ended up."

"You weren't supposed to."

"Alright then, where did you sleep?"

"Downstairs, by myself."

"Lord, are you nuts? Do you have a death wish or something? If I had known you were there I would've gone there and dragged you upstairs. You don't know if the ghouls may have returned here or were hiding." He ran his hand through his hair feeling upset and angry. He was feeling more exasperated than ever with her, and wondered if he should send her home rather than having a continual battle with her. He then noticed she was looking more pleased than when he had started his lecture.

She gave him a half smile. "Sorry to have made you worry. I checked, there aren't any ghouls here. Is it time to head out now?"

How she checked for ghouls, whether by mental abilities or by physically looking wasn't clear and he decided not to pursue the argument. He rubbed his chin trying to think of what to say next but nothing clever came to mind. "Yeah, it's time to go." He turned towards where the rest of group was gathering near the exit door.

The exit door was wide and was actually two doors that split open at the middle. The doors weren't in an obvious location but were at the end of another short but twisted tunnel. The sunlight was strong compared to the subdued yellow light of the building, causing everyone to blink as they made their way outside. Carl looked back at the doorway that looked like it was carved out from the solid rock face that stood behind them. The building looked like a large hill, with the doorway similar to the entrance of a cave. The hill appeared to be made largely of rock with only a few plants that covered the surface. Carl walked around the hill with Rog. The hill, or building, took several minutes to circumvent. The rear looked like an ordinary hill but with a rocky face. Behind the hill stretched the Ghoul Desert, with its yellow sand disappearing to the horizon. Other than the cave-like entrance at the front, the building appeared to be nothing more than a rock-covered hill.

Carl left the twin doors open, not sure if they would open on their return. There wasn't an obvious doorframe to open the doors on the outside and he didn't want to gamble on finding a way back in later.

The doors from the building led to a rocky path that led past large-leafed plants, bushes and grasses. Occasionally, they could walk two abreast but for the most part walked single file with Carl leading the way. Insects jumped or flew out of their way and the odd creature could be heard scampering away. Visibility ahead and to the sides of the path was poor, and Carl wondered how long the path was and where it was going to take them.

"Malcolm, could you ask one of the men to scout up ahead to see how far this path goes and where?"

"Sure, I'll get Reese to run ahead."

Reese, a young man that looked light enough to fly, took off down the path, disappearing a few seconds later.

He returned several minutes later, still running but not looking like he was tired at all.

"The path stops up ahead at this giant round stone. I don't know what it is but the path ends there. The plants thin out a bit as you go down so we can still make our way past that stone thing."

The stone thing turned out to be a stone wheel over twenty feet in diameter and two feet thick, standing on end into the ground. Carvings were made near the outside ring in what Carl thought was some type of lettering. The inside of the wheel had symbols etched into it as well, though they gave the impression they weren't letters but pictures that represented something. The extreme outside of the stone wheel had small holes in it along various points.

"What is that thing, Carl?" Rog squirmed his face trying to make something out of it.

Carl's first thought was that it was a stargate that could whisk him back to Earth, but it didn't seem realistic to think that a science fiction show could come to life here. "I don't know. Maybe something the ghouls pray to."

Tanya walked up to it, spreading her fingers as she touched it. Slowly she moved her head closer and closer to the stone wheel until her forehead touched it. She appeared to rest her head there for several minutes before she spoke. "The Ghoul, they worship it. It means the cycle of life to them and they use it to make important decisions. The stone is a single piece of rock that has been, not exactly blessed, but something like it."

They stood around and looked around the stone wheel for a few minutes and then Carl announced they might as well continue their journey. The path ended at the stone wheel but as the scout indicated the bush had thinned out to the point that they could travel through it. Carl followed Malcolm's advice and deployed two guards at the rear and near the front. He also asked Reese and another young man named Santana to scout ahead as a pair and report on any obstacles ahead.

Rog kept a steady bantering with Carl, Malcolm and anyone else who came within an earshot, generally making everyone either laugh or moan.

Carl was listening to him tell Malcolm how he could tell exactly which way it was to Sorbital just by closing his eyes and feeling the "waves".

"Well that may be, boy, but closing your eyes can get you in a heap of trouble if you're walking at the same time. I use the sun to figure my directions, with my eyes open."

"Yeah, what about night?"

"I sleep then, or use the stars."

Carl could hear Malcolm sounding just a little annoyed, which was exactly what Rog wanted. *Better him than me,* he thought as he poked at a bush with his spear causing something to leap away to another bush.

"Hi."

Carl turned, and was surprised to see Tanya next to him. "Hi yourself."

She was silent for several seconds and just when Carl was about to ask her what she wanted she blurted out what sounded like a planned speech. "Sorry I was acting a little strange the past few days. I was trying to prove something to myself and I didn't mean to hurt anyone's feelings, including yours. Especially yours. I know you're thinking you should send me back to Sorbital, but you can count on me. I'm going to do a good job as a Witchdoctor." She took a deep breath. "Okay?"

"Okay. I know you can do a great job as a Witchdoctor, Tanya. But try to remember to act with a little less anger."

"I know. Thanks. Talk to you later." She quickly dropped away before he could say anything else.

Carl had trouble guessing where she was coming from at times, almost as if she had two personalities. He had other problems to worry about, such as where exactly he was heading. He knew approximately where the ghouls lived but the path to get there was a long one. The best journey was to travel west, going over what Carl hoped to be low mountain ranges before heading north along a coastline. At least Malcolm and Rog agreed which way was west, and Carl led the way after the two pointed which way to head.

The scouts had not reported much change in the scenery ahead and the group stepped through the brush, trees and plants with the guards maintaining their position around them.

Carl found the temperature a bit on the warm side but the sun was hidden for the most part by trees. The shade made the travel less strenuous but he still decided to call a break to make sure everyone wasn't going to get too tired. Most of his followers were not used to long journeys.

Jose wasn't tired. He wasn't on duty until mid-afternoon, being one of the four guards that would be rotated with another group of four. He still felt the responsibility of making sure the camp was safe, so he decided to walk around the perimeter of the camp and look for any potential hazards. He waved at one woman he recognized who was making a small journey to a small grove of trees. She looked startled at his appearance, her eyes expressing alarm at being sighted. He wondered if he was intruding on a secret rendezvous meeting, perhaps to obtain some privacy from the others. Regardless, it was none of his business and he turned away.

Katrina watched him continue his walk and then satisfied he didn't suspect anything, resumed her own journey.

Jose struck the odd bush with his spear, using the heavier weighted end as a club. The fist size bulge was made from a long cord that had been soaked in tree sap and then wrapped around the spear end. The dried sap was hard but not heavy enough to upset the balance of the spear. Some of the other spears used the bone from the club tail of a kytle but he preferred the lighter weight of the sap. Occasionally he saw insects or small creatures scurry out of their hiding place. The last bush, a yellow leafed specimen provided a more interesting result. His knock on the branches produced a hissing sound and two green and yellow creatures jumped out. The reptiles were only two feet long from their long tails to the crest covered heads. Needle sharp teeth appeared in the open mouth as they stood on their hind legs, their front limbs dancing in the air that ended in three fingered claws.

"Mamma! You two gave me a scare. Just what are you anyway? Never seen the likes of you guys before. Maybe the boss would like to take a look at one of you." Jose balanced his spear in one hand and watched as one of them took a cautious step forward while the other moved to the side. Then, just inside the edge of his view he saw another reptile slowly advancing.

"Oh, trying to circle me are you? You won't fool me." With a flick of his wrist he launched his spear, impaling the one that had just taken another tentative step forward. It screeched a dying scream as it wiggled on the end of the shaft.

"Gotcha, you little devil!" Jose retrieved his spear but had little time for glory as a second reptile launched an attack at his leg. He stepped back and swung the other end of the spear at it, catching its body in a leap with a thud. The creature twitched on the ground as Jose swung his spear in an arc causing a half-dozen others to scatter. As he pulled the dead reptile off his spearhead, Jose surveyed the area around him, seeing there were at least a dozen more of the reptiles watching around the other bushes. The ones that had scattered were now advancing again, hissing as they bared their teeth.

"Sorry my friends, but it is time for Jose to go." He backed away as he swung his spear around again, bending down to pick up a loose stick that he threw at the ones behind him. As he predicted, they ran away before stopping to see if the threat was real. He turned and walked quickly towards the camp moving his spear in a slow arc in front of him. They continued to scatter and hiss but didn't prevent him from leaving. Occasionally he turned around and caught one on the club end of his spear as it came too close to his heels.

As Carl sat drinking water from a skin pouch he felt a peculiar tickling in his mind and he looked around, catching Tanya watching him while she sat among some trees some one hundred feet away on a small rise. She gave him a smile before looking away.

How can she act so angry and miserable one time and smile so sweetly another time at me? There has to be a reason behind it. Maybe it's related to her being a Witchdoctor and her powers. His thoughts on what made her swing from one mood to another were interrupted by the appearance of one of the guards.

Jose held the dead reptile by the neck. "Never seen anything like this before, boss. There're maybe two-dozen of them about a hundred yards from here. Nasty little things, tried to eat me."

Carl looked at the limp body. By itself, it wasn't too dangerous but a group of them would be something to be concerned about. *Reptiles that can stand on their hind legs. I don't even want to think about what if there are larger versions of the same things. Small dinosaurs, that's what these are. It sounds like they hunt in packs.*

"Good work, Jose. Take this thing around and show it to the others so they know what's out there."

He turned to his friend. "Rog, make sure that the people know it's not safe to venture too far from the main group, and they should always go in pairs if they have to do so."

"Uh, boss, there's one other thing. When I was walking around out there I saw Katrina, she looked like she was going somewhere to meet someone. She might be in some danger so maybe I should go back there and find her."

"Yeah, good point. I better go with you."

Together Jose and Carl retraced the steps where Katrina was last seen. There wasn't any sign of the small reptiles as they approached the small grove of trees that Jose last saw Katrina walk towards. Jose spotted her first and pointed his hand where she was sitting with her side towards them.

Carl noticed she sat cross-legged with her hands limp on her lap as she mouthed soundless words. He recalled seeing her doing something similar before, something she had denied at the time. It was no mistake, she was practicing the same thing Tanya did. He didn't know if what she was doing was permitted or not, but she was being secretive about it.

He had to say her name three times before she responded. She first looked surprised, then angry and then quickly gave a worried smile.

"Oh, you scared me. I was just, just daydreaming here. I had a headache and came to get some quiet."

"It looked like you were in some sort of trance, like Tanya does."

"Oh, no. That's silly. I don't know how to do that. I was just doing some mind clearing to get rid of my headache."

"Okay, but you better come back with us." Carl explained about the small reptiles they had discovered and she quickly agreed to return with them, chatting continuously as they travelled back. She also positioned herself close to Carl and occasionally grabbed at his arm for support on the walk back.

The camp was ready to continue their trek when they arrived. The green and yellow striped reptiles had made every one a bit concerned about where they were staying. The scouts returned as they set off, informing Carl of a river that ran parallel to their own trail about a mile to the north.

"Malcolm, wouldn't it make sense to try to follow the river bank rather than where we're going now? Maybe we could build a raft and float down."

"Hmm, well there're some things to consider. The vegetation near a river would be denser than out here. That might make the walking a little more difficult. Food would be more plentiful though, including the chance to obtain fish as well. On the downside, the number of predators might be higher as well but so far, we haven't seen much danger there. As far as building a raft, I reckon the river would be flowing the wrong way, towards the sea and away from the mountains." He shrugged his shoulders. "Six of one and a half-dozen of the other."

Carl considered what he was told. He pursed his lips as he surveyed the others waiting for him to make another decision. He noticed Tanya observing him as he wrestled with his choices. *Damn! I don't know what to do. I shouldn't be leading*

this group. They need someone older and with more experience.
"Okay, let's make for the river. If the going gets too tough, we can return to this route afterward."

Several others nodded in agreement and turned to resume the journey. Tanya frowned and shouldered her carrying pack before slipping to the outside of the group.

They made better time as the afternoon progressed. Everyone improved their own hiking techniques and the less able members of the group had some of their burden transferred to the stronger ones. Some of the weaker people wanted to carry their own share but Carl ordered them to relinquish what they could not carry easily, telling them there would be plenty of opportunity for them to aid the group in other ways later.

Carl looked onto the fast, wide river noting Malcolm was right about its direction. He couldn't guess how deep it was but judging by the clarity of the water he guessed that it would make good drinking water and harbour a fair share of fish. The last part of the journey had not produced any more signs of wildlife other than small mammals and reptiles similar to the one Jose had killed earlier. However, Carl could now see a small group of deer cautiously drinking from the water along the opposite bank. They looked skittish and suddenly they all bolted from the riverbank disappearing into the forest. A moment later several of the upright reptiles appeared, crashing through the trees where the deer had been and quickly turning to follow them. The reptiles were a larger version of the others they had seen, standing nearly five feet above the ground.

"Shit, did you see that, Malcolm?"

"That I did. Vicious looking things."

"Maybe coming to the river wasn't such a great plan."

"Maybe, but those things probably don't limit themselves to the river area anyway. Let's just make sure everyone is aware to keep their eyes and ears open."

Carl asked the guards to be on the lookout for more of the reptiles and for the scouts to look for a camping spot that could offer some protection from intruders.

Camp was established just off the riverbank on a grassy stretch. Fire was set along the perimeter on poles and in the centre of the camp as a bonfire. Some of the men went fishing while a group of four hunters explored the nearby forest for game. Katrina sat close to Carl and engaged in conversation with him and Rog. Malcolm told Carl to relax and walked away to make sure everyone was doing what he or she was supposed to be doing to make camp.

The hunters returned later empty-handed save for some birds that resembled pheasants. They did see other game, including the fleet-footed deer, a mountain lion that was stalking the deer and a large flightless bird standing nearly eight feet high. There were also some unusual cries from something that hid among the trees. The large bird was too far to chase and the hunters were not certain if trying to pursue it was worth the effort before the sun started to set.

The fishing went better with several large fish caught. There was a surprise when something in the water brushed up against one of the men. It knocked him over as it stole a fish another had captured on his spear. The fish and spear disappeared into the swiftly moving river.

All the same, Hilliard was pleased with both the fish and the birds and quickly started work on them to prepare dinner. Earlier she had obtained some berries, mushrooms and plant roots that looked like small yams. A reluctant young man, who she had called out to for help, joined her. Murray complained that he had already obtained firewood earlier but his complaints were ignored. Hilliard was surprised that Katrina walked over and offered to help, and soon the three of them had fish frying and the birds roasted on a stick above the fire.

Carl finished setting up his own tent and sat down on the ground in front of it. He was tired, the day of walking and the burden of having to make decisions for a whole group of people was taxing his energy. He was amazed at some of the things he was asked to decide on, like who should be in charge of the fire and that Jeremy was taking up too much space with his tent. He was hungry as well, and the smell of the cooking food was forcing him to consider getting up to get something to eat before he fell asleep on the spot.

To his surprise, Katrina brought him a plate piled with fish, bird, bread and vegetables. She had a smaller plate for herself and sat down in front of him to eat.

"You look tired. Pretty long day huh?"

"Yeah. Thanks for bringing me dinner."

"That's alright. Someone has to look out for the guy who is looking out for everyone else."

They continued to talk during the meal and after he had finished Katrina took his plate from him.

"Why don't you get some rest? There's not much to do now and I think Malcolm or Rog can handle any problems."

Carl looked over at his tent. The thought of sleep was inviting, but he wondered if he should stay up until he was sure everything was going to be okay. "That's okay, I'll do a quick check around."

Carl didn't find much to do around the camp. Two men, who had a large stock of firewood to use, were maintaining the bonfire in the centre. Tents of various descriptions surrounded the fire and outside of them, torches were set every ten feet apart. Four equally spaced guards stood watching carefully outside the perimeter. A few people stopped him to talk a bit but there weren't any problems. He found Tanya drinking a cup of tea inside her small tent and sat outside of the small entrance to talk to her.

"How come you're sitting inside the tent?"

"I was trying to get some solitude to try to read the Aura. Normally I would walk away from the camp but it's not safe out there right now."

"You mean those reptiles we saw that chased the deer?"

"Yeah, maybe. I think there're some other creatures out there as well. I've got a sense that there's a lot more out there than what we've seen." She closed her eyes for a moment, concentrating. "There's a lot of, how do I describe this? A lot of strong life energies around here, of different types."

"Okay, that certainly could be true. But we do have protection set up around the camp."

"Yeah, but...just be careful, okay?" It looked like she wanted to say more for a moment but then gave him a tentative smile.

"Sure, see you later." As he stood up, he reached over and touched her knee. His fingertips tingled where they touched her skin and he was curious why she left him feeling unsettled in one way or another whenever he saw her.

Dusk came and the violet sky turned black. As the glow of the sun disappeared completely, the sounds of the forest changed from the chirping of birds to that of insects and small creatures. The guards were changed and the new guards peered into the outside darkness for any sign of danger. In four hours, they would be relieved but until then, they would be utilizing their senses to their full capability.

Carl fell to an uneasy sleep, Tanya's warning following him into his dreams. He woke with a start to the sound of shouts. He wasn't certain how long he had been sleeping, perhaps an hour or two at the most. As he sat up, Rog pulled open the flap to his tent.

"Carl, better come quick! Problem at the perimeter, Jose and a few of the others are being attacked!" He ran off before Carl could reply.

Carl scrambled outside, pulling on his vest as he ran towards the loudest noise. He could hear people shouting but also the growl and screech of some creatures.

A dozen reptiles jostled with each other as they contested the perimeter just beyond the torches, waving their front limbs in frustration as they opened and closed their jaws to reveal yellow, pointed teeth. The reptiles appeared to be the same ones that were chasing the deer earlier, only in greater numbers, including some juveniles that stayed near the back. The fire in the torches held them back even more than the twenty men who brandished spears and pointed arrows at them. Every time the creatures screeched, the men waved spears and a few shot arrows at the closest one. That drew even more activity and noise from the reptiles. Malcolm was positioning the defence where the main group of reptiles stood, but also kept a guard at the other areas, correctly guessing that some of the reptiles may try to circle behind and at the sides.

Carl took in the commotion around him and made a quick decision, one that he later reflected he had no conscious reason for doing so. "Everyone, listen up. Stop moving around and be quiet. You're attracting their attention by reacting to their presence. Freeze your movements unless they cross the perimeter."

To his relief, everyone stopped running around and shouting. For the next few minutes, the reptiles continued their dance at the edge of the torches and then became quiet. Half an hour passed before the last of them turned back into the forest, leaving behind three dead reptiles from arrows and a very nervous group of people.

Carl was congratulated for his quick thinking and after making sure the guards knew what to do if another attack occurred, returned to his tent. He went over to Tanya and asked her if she was okay. She nodded, looking less worried than many of the men.

"I'm fine. Get some sleep, tomorrow might be a tough day too."

Carl walked slowly back to his tent and opened the flap to crawl inside. Katrina was waiting for him inside his tent, underneath his blanket.

"Katrina, what are you doing here?"

"I'm scared. I don't want to be by myself. Let me sleep here, please."

"You aren't any safer with me, if the reptiles..."

"I know, but I won't be able to sleep by myself. Please don't make me leave."

Carl was tired and didn't see the harm in letting her stay. "Alright. Just for tonight." He crawled under the blanket with her after taking off his vest. Her skin next to his felt warm as he closed his eyes. After a few minutes, he felt her snuggle close to him but he was well on the path to sleep. His last thought was that it did feel nice sleeping with someone after the terror of the reptile attack.

He woke up to her quietly getting out from under the blanket, her nakedness visible from the sunlight that strained through the cloth of the tent side. Through squinted eyes, he watched her as she carefully put on her clothes in the tent before slipping outside.

He considered getting up himself, but wanted to get a bit more sleep in first. Less than an hour later, he rolled out from under the blanket and stepped outside. He stretched and headed down to the riverbank to wash up, turning to the left to join the other men. The few women went to the right side, a slightly more secluded area. When he returned, he found Katrina waiting for him with breakfast.

"Good morning, you're just in time."

"Thanks." He took the plate and tea. "You don't have to do this, you know."

"I know. I wanted to." She finished with her own plate and stood to go where the food was being prepared. "See you later."

He wondered about her. He hadn't spent much time with her before other than they hung around in the same group. Now she was definitely trying to get close to him, and he wasn't sure what to do about her advances.

He finished eating and went to find Malcolm, finding he was close to where Malcolm had pitched his tent. They discussed how they should deploy guards when they resumed their hike. They also took a closer look at the dead reptiles, noting the skin was multicoloured making them difficult to be seen in the forest. Two of the reptiles had several bite marks on them, apparently from their comrades after they were killed though there didn't seem to be a serious effort to actually eat one of their own kind. Carl looked at the three-clawed front limbs and then the four claws on the feet, including one, over-sized claw, situated higher up the foot.

"What do think, Carl?"

"These reptiles look like a kind of dinosaur that lived long ago on Earth, they were called raptors and were rather deadly. I think they lived near the end of the dinosaur era, but from what I understand, were fairly smart as dinosaurs go."

"I reckon you know what you're talking about. They look mean even dead. Weren't dinosaurs big? These aren't any taller than my shoulder."

"I guess they come in all sizes, but maybe this is just a smaller type."

Carl returned to where his tent was, only to find Katrina had already packed up the tent and gear.

"You packed my tent?" Carl immediately regretted saying the obvious.

"Yeah, I thought you were busy doing stuff so I decided to help you out a bit."

"Thanks." Carl looked at the packed gear.

She slipped her hand inside his vest, resting it a moment on his chest. "My pleasure." She grinned at him and walked away.

As the last of camp was packed, Carl went to find Tanya, finding her sitting on her rolled up tent.

She gave him a smile as he approached and they exchanged greetings.

"Those reptiles—is that what you were referring to about other energies?"

"Life energies. But there's more than just those."

"Oh. Well, I'll just have to be careful."

"You do that." She paused for a moment. "It's really none of my business, but be careful with Katrina."

"What? But she, she just..."

Tanya laughed. "Relax, Carl. Despite your efforts, we are not a couple, friends for sure but not anything more. She, on the other hand, has kind of bypassed the friend stage and wants a relationship."

"I don't know what she wants."

"Don't be stupid, Carl. She wants you because you're the leader of our group. That's okay too, just try to understand where she's coming from, she wants something."

"I'd rather have you."

She cast her eyes down a moment and then looked up. "It's not possible. I'm a Witchdoctor and cannot have a man. So enjoy your time with her and see where it goes. You better go back and get this group underway." She gave his hand a squeeze.

Tanya watched him walk away, her smile gone as soon as he turned around, wondering if she did the right thing.

With Carl in front, the procession made their way, moving along the riverbank. The river must have been several feet higher in the past resulting in the present wide banks that made travel easy. The guards kept watching the nearby forest for any sign of danger with their spears held rigidly in front of them. The occasional noises heard among the trees heightened everyone's anxiety. Some of the guards also cast a wary eye on the water as the river splashed along its journey.

Carl himself peered into the bushes and trees only a few feet from the riverbank, watching out in particular for yellow and green five-foot raptors. What crashed through the bushes instead was a massive blob of brown fur directly in front of Carl. It turned to face him and reared up on its hind legs, growling and waving huge front paws.

Carl backed up quickly a couple of steps and raised his spear at the bear that stood a dozen feet high. Malcolm was standing next to him and swung one arm across his chest to push him back more. At the same time, several other men stepped forward with raised spears. Carl found himself surrounded by others, some holding spears and others aiming arrows. The bear roared again but this time it was answered by yells from the men. It shook its massive head and then dropped down on its four legs, turned and disappeared into the forest again.

Carl stood still, his heart still pounding and didn't feel her hand on his arm at first.

"I said are you alright?" Tanya raised her voice.

"Huh? Yeah, I'm fine."

"What was that thing?"

"A bear. Maybe a grizzly, but the biggest damn bear I've ever seen."

"A bare?"

"Yeah, a bear. A very large animal." He looked at her expression of confusion. "It's spelled b-e-a-r."

"Oh. Ohh! When I first met you, you talked about bears. No wonder you were worried."

"You have a good memory."

"You don't know how good. Are you sure you're okay?"

"Yeah, fine. Thanks."

They stopped for lunch by the river, using fish from the river again as the main course. Tanya continued her practice of sitting by herself, choosing to eat near the river while everyone else clustered near the fire at a small clearing in the forest.

She watched the river and heard someone approaching from behind. It wasn't Carl. She knew his walk and mental energies well enough to know it wasn't him. This person was familiar as well though. "Hello, Rog."

There was a short hesitation before he replied. "How's it going, witch?"

She grimaced and then smiled. Rog was the only one who could get away with calling her that. He seemed to follow his own rules of social convention. "It's going alright."

He sat down next to her watching the water as it tumbled along its path. "How come you're sitting by yourself?"

"I'm not now, am I?"

He shook his head. "You're difficult, even for a woman. You know what I mean."

"I don't get along with others too well. So, I sit by myself. Okay?"

"No, not okay. You've got to try to be a little more sociable."

"Why? I'm not hurting anyone."

"You are, in a way. By withdrawing away from the rest of us, you are depriving us of your company, wit and wisdom. Well, your company anyway."

She punched him on the shoulder. "Jerk."

"Ow! That's one part of you I don't miss."

"So who does miss me when I'm down here?"

"A few. There'd be more if you acted as if you're part of our group. You're not that horrible to know. Ouch! Stop doing that!" He rubbed his shoulder where she punched him again.

"Who put you up to this?"

"Tanya, it doesn't matter where I'm coming from on this, it's true regardless. Try to be a little more..."

"I know, sociable. Was it Carl? Or Malcolm?"

He laughed. "Maybe both. For what it's worth, I do like talking to you too. Okay?"

"Okay." She sighed. "I'll try to talk to others a bit more." She paused for a moment as he stood up. "You like talking to me?"

"Yeah, but without the punches. You got bony knuckles."

The path along the river became smaller as the brush moved right up to the river's edge. Carl led the way to higher ground and eventually to small rolling hills that was made out of a reddish, sandy soil. The trees gave way to grasses and bushes, which made their travelling easy.

One of the guards, Julien, first spotted the movement some one hundred yards away, streaks of yellow and green that stopped and sprinted among the bushes. The same movement was noticed on the other side of the group and Carl quickly called out the signal for the group to fall to the defence planned earlier. Slowly they moved closer to each other, becoming increasingly nervous as they made their spears and arrows ready.

The raptors approached from two sides at the circle of twenty men. The men on the perimeter held spears while inside the circle were six women, Carl, Malcolm, Rog and seven other men. Carl and Malcolm shouted out directions, trying to make sure everyone maintained their positions on the outer circle. Rog and the rest of the men and most of the women held bow and arrows.

Individual reptiles charged the perimeter, coming within a few feet before veering off. The tactic was probably effective in breaking up most collections of their prey, trying to get one or more to bolt from the protection of the group. However, this new quarry resisted their thrusts and the reptiles began to get restless and approached closer.

The men were terrified at the snapping, drooling growling beasts. They held their spears chest high, extended about three feet from their own bodies.

"Carl, they're getting closer. Reckon we should start with the arrows?"

Carl considered. They had thought about using the arrows as they came into range, but Malcolm pointed out the raptors may become even more violent if the arrows only injured them. "We better try. Let's make those arrows count."

Several arrows were launched and most were on target. Most of the injured raptors screamed in rage and retreated away, confused on what happened. One took an arrow above its forelimb. Rather than turn away, it screeched and then leapt at the men. Its leg raked the arm of the defender as he raised his spear in defence, the spearhead plunging into the chest of the raptor as the man screamed in pain. Both tumbled down and while the injured man was pulled inside the circle, his partners used their spears to stab at the writhing reptile. As they finished it off another raptor attacked, locking its jaws on the neck on one of the men as he opened his mouth in a wordless scream, falling backwards and trying to push it off with his hands.

Carl watched in horror as he lifted his own spear to help. Rog aimed an arrow at the raptor when he caught a glimpse of someone charging into the fight.

Tanya didn't stop to think of any part of her assault. She found herself picking up the dropped spear and turning it around in her hands and swinging the club end at the reptile's head again and again even as an arrow pierced its cheek. Eventually the raptor died with its teeth still in the neck of its dead victim.

Another raptor jumped at one of the defenders, a spear killing it as it ripped open the chest of the defender with its clawed foot. He was pulled inside the circle looking in dismay at the blood, torn skin and the white bones of his ribs.

The intensity of the raptors' attack lessened as several more reptiles died from arrows and spears and suddenly, they vanished into the bushes.

Several guards protected the area as attention was given to the injured. Tanya directed Malcolm to rub an oily substance on one guard's injured arm as she tended the torn, open chest of the dying defender. The blood loss was too severe and his shallow breathing became increasingly ragged as he stared with wide-open eyes at her.

Carl watched her hold his head in her hands as she whispered a prayer for him. Despite what had happened to him, he did not appear to be in pain and as she spoke, he slowly closed his eyes and stopped breathing. She continued her whispers and then stood up, staring at his still form. She turned towards Malcolm and the injured guard and Malcolm saw tears roll down her cheeks.

A minute later, she was working on the arm of the other injured defender, holding her hands around it. Carl knew better than to disturb her as she worked with her eyes closed, her body swaying to her quiet chants. Two men had died and several had injuries, though only the one with his arm ripped apart by those black claws looked serious. Carl directed four men to start digging graves for the two fallen defenders, wishing he knew what to do next.

Chapter Nine:
Predators and Prey

Tanya worked frantically to help the injured, her movements becoming automatic as she laboured. Philip's damaged arm took most of her energy and she desperately wanted to rest just a bit, but there was still too much to do, including a prayer service for the two dead men.

Malcolm brought her a hot cup of tea and bread as a snack and she gratefully took it, consuming both quickly before returning to her work. She noticed Rog was setting up her tent, and then realized they had decided to make camp rather than try to travel anymore before sunset. Tanya checked on Philip once more, and then headed towards the two graves.

She gave the standard poem of the spirit returning home at each site, and as was custom, invited friends and relatives to speak about the deceased's past life. She was pleased that Carl also spoke about each man, though he looked as if he was almost catatonic himself. After the last speaker spoke, Tanya closed her eyes and listened to the Aura, whispering silent words to the air. The service finished when she gave a blessing to those who would carry their memory. Wearily she headed back to the campsite knowing her work wasn't over but happy she managed to go through the service without preparation before hand. She was aware of Malcolm leading her by the arm to her tent and shortly after climbing under her blanket she fell asleep.

The morning came and she stumbled out of her tent, yawning. Tanya realized she couldn't remember a thing after going inside her tent, apparently not even bothering to undress. She went to the river and washed the cool water over her face until she felt awake. A cup of tea and some breakfast presented an irresistible image to her, and she headed to the centre of the camp. She spotted Carl ahead of her, walking with his head down.

"Carl."

He turned and gave a weak smile. "Tanya, how're you doing?"

"Tired."

"Maybe you need some more rest." He put his arm around her but she resisted the urge to collapse into him, instead she held herself straight and turned to give him a smile back. He looked worse than she felt.

"Carl, you look awful." She felt his arm tighten.

"Damn it, Tanya, I caused the death of those two men! I should look awful. I feel awful. And I don't know what to do about it."

"Do you want to do the right thing? For them and everyone?"

"Of course. But I haven't the faintest notion what."

"You didn't cause their death, those reptiles did. Your planning probably saved a lot of lives."

"But if..."

"But nothing. You did what you could. But now you're screwing up."

"Huh? What do you mean?"

"Look, everyone is feeling down, wondering what is going to happen next. And their leader has the longest face of all. If you're going to act like this, what kind of an example is that for those who need reassurance everything is going to be okay?"

"Not a very good example. But I still don't..."

"Carl, you're in charge. Act like it."

He sighed. "Okay, I will."

The rest of the day Tanya checked on minor injuries and, before the camp broke after lunch, she replenished some of her medicinal supplies from the forest.

Carl was watching her from the camp and she waved to him as she returned. He walked to meet her, looking concerned.

"Tanya, you shouldn't go out there by yourself."

"It's okay, I can tell when there's danger close by."

He frowned. "I still don't think it's safe. Please bring someone with you just in case."

"I don't think it's necessary."

"Damn you're stubborn. Going out there by yourself is a bad example to others, so take someone with you next time."

"Is that an order?" She began to raise her voice. "Just because you're in charge…"

Before she could react, he leaned her backwards with one arm behind her shoulder and another around her waist and kissed her. Tanya waved her arms around before putting them tentatively around his neck for a moment and then to push him away at his shoulders.

"What're you doing?"

"Acting like I'm in charge." He grinned at her.

For a moment, she held her hand poised to slap his face, but his grin overcame her resolve. Instead she laughed. "You're impossible."

She wanted to run away but instead she walked as fast as she could. *What a sneaky way to get a kiss, using my suggestion to act like he's in charge. The whole camp probably enjoyed that little show, damn him. Good kisser though.*

Tanya worked on Philip's arm some more. She rubbed an oily liquid on his arm after giving a healing touch with her hands.

"Am I going to lose my arm?"

"I don't know. I hope not."

"I heard some people say that it doesn't look good, that you may have to cut it off or it may infect my whole body."

"Listen to me." She put both hands at the sides of his head as she knelt in front of him. "You have to believe you can stop the infection. Tell your body to heal. Do this and I'll save your arm."

"Okay, okay I will."

"Good." She relaxed and smiled. "Get some rest."

"Sure."

Tanya stood up.

"Hey, Tanya. Are you and Carl going together?"

"No, we're just friends."

"Oh. Can we be friends like that?"

She laughed as she walked away, not certain if she was annoyed at Carl for that kiss. Her attention was drawn to the fire that was being extinguished in the centre. Carl was pointing and directing two others as they spread out the ashes, sounding like he was very much the leader in control again. Standing nearby him was Katrina. She noticed Tanya watching and glared at her.

Tanya walked away, shaking her head, wondering if Katrina really thought she could tell her to keep away from Carl. *Katrina, you fool. If I wanted Carl, you wouldn't have a chance. Don't make me regret pushing him away.*

The camp was established again with similar defences in place, fire along the perimeter and a bonfire in the centre. They had made good time on a shortened day and Carl was glad suggestions to return to Sorbital had not materialized. He walked around the camp, talking to anybody still up and around and then headed to his own tent. Katrina had set up her own tent next to his. She had a habit of being close to him whenever he looked around. Carl was enjoying her company, though she seemed a little too pushy for his liking. Tanya had refused his advances so far, other than his stolen kiss, and if she didn't want him, he had limited choices in a camp of only a few women. The advances of Katrina were compounding the problem. Tanya had indicated to him not to wait for her, but he felt he could change her mind.

Yawning he climbed into his own tent and a few minutes later he drifted off to sleep, only to be waken by the warmth of another body when Katrina joined him in his bed.

"Katrina, I thought we agreed you were going to sleep in your own tent."

"But I'm scared. Please don't make me leave."

Carl sighed. This was something he should have seen coming, with her asking if she could put her tent next to his for safety. "Alright. Last time though. Let's just go to sleep."

But, she had other plans than sleep that night.

As they trooped along the next day, Tanya decided to try to walk closer to the others as Rog suggested. She actually found she enjoyed the odd bits of conversation, though most looked a little hesitant to talk to her at first. Tanya found Hilliard humming softly to herself and approached her.

"Hi, Tanya. You look like you're in a good mood."

"I guess I am."

"Anything to do with Carl?"

Tanya laughed. "No. Did everyone see him kiss me?"

"Probably. You two look good together."

"Please. Carl's seeing someone else. Katrina." Tanya didn't like saying her name but it looked silly to avoid saying it.

She winked. "Maybe not for long."

"Hilliard, you know that as a Witchdoctor I'm not allowed to have a man."

"Maybe, my dear. But sometimes the heart wins anyway."

Tanya shook her head, amused at the older woman's suggestion. *As if I would ever be lucky enough to follow my heart. If only...* She dismissed the rest of her thought. "I was wondering if you happened to see any jetile plants when you were searching for mushrooms."

"Jetile plants?"

"Yeah, they're a small plant with small white bell flowers that live in the shade. I need them to make a poison that we can dip arrowheads in. I think it'll help against the raptors."

"Oh, do they have light green stalks and large leaves?" When Tanya nodded, she continued. "Yes, I saw them earlier today. They were under those oak trees. I didn't know they were poisonous."

169

"Just the roots. You have to boil a lot of them to get a bit of poison, but it's very deadly and quick acting."

"Well, you learn something everyday. When we stop again I'll help you look."

Tanya said thanks and continued to walk with the others. She reflected how much easier it was to talk to others lately—how her own mood had improved. Gone were the long periods of self-doubt and unbidden anger that followed her everywhere before.

But not now. It disappeared as I went further away from Sorbital. Is it something about this Quest? Or, was it something in Sorbital that did that to me?

Now that she had thought about it, she really did wonder why she felt so different. But answers weren't forthcoming and after a few minutes her attention was diverted to other things.

While there was enough fish to make lunch, Hilliard indicated to Carl that she would like to have some birds to cook instead. Carl also felt it was important not to give the impression that they were scared to do the things they should be doing. As a result seven men left to hunt, but not without some apprehension as they left the security of the camp.

Terrace watched behind for a moment and then scanned to the left. Nothing moved behind the trees but he still felt nervous. His hands were getting sore from gripping the shaft of his spear too tightly. Terrace glanced at his counterpart, Belone, who was walking parallel but was responsible for anything behind and to the right. Together the two were to make sure nothing was hunting the four hunters that were being led by Malcolm. Terrace was glad Malcolm was in charge of the hunting party. While he respected Carl's ability to make smart decisions as their leader, there wasn't anyone better than Malcolm when it came to understanding terrain and how to track game.

Terrace watched Malcolm suddenly give the four hunters a quick wave of his hand and they all froze their positions. He couldn't see what was up ahead that caused the stoppage and quickly looked behind. When he looked forward, Malcolm was pointing and whispering that there was something in the trees overhead. A few seconds later several arrows flew upwards, half of them bringing down blue and grey feathered birds. The rest of the birds made loud chirping noises as they scattered into the sky.

The party continued on, securing the birds on a short rope by their legs. Terrace thought that after killing the birds they would go back but Malcolm indicated there was more game up ahead. He was following a trail of something that to Terrace looked like ordinary ground. However, a short time later they came across a herd of deer that were warily eating in a small grassy area. Two of the hunters circled around to the back of the deer, using an exaggerated route to avoid detection. The plan was simple. They were to drive the deer towards the remaining hunters and hopefully one of them would be able to take one down.

Terrace looked around behind him one more time before the deer were to be chased when he saw the quick movement behind the trees. What it was he couldn't tell—it could be raptor or almost anything else. He waited, straining to see through the bushes and leaves when he saw the movement again. It wasn't a raptor. This creature was on all four legs and had a yellow coat. He breathed a sigh of relief, but was still concerned what was watching them so closely.

His attention returned to the front as he heard a noise from one of the hunters waiting in ambush. Several deer exploded into the trees around them followed by the two yelling hunters sent to flush them out. Malcolm and the remaining hunters took down one of the deer. Malcolm plunging his spear into the buck after it took an arrow into its shoulder and veered towards him. The rest of the deer went by them but one more fell to the cat that was prowling behind the hunters. Terrace watched the short-tailed cat sink its teeth into the neck of the deer and quickly make the kill. The power in its jaws and shoulders caused him some concern if it were to attack their group. The cat was over five feet long and might have weighed close to two hundred pounds. Malcolm watched with concern as the predator ate its kill, ripping chucks of flesh off the carcass. A second cat then joined in on the feed.

The hunting party began the return to the camp, taking a wide circle around the cats. Terrace continued his periodic checks to his left and behind. One moment he saw Belone make similar checks, and the next time he looked, Belone was gone. Terrace immediately shouted out an alarm and Malcolm and then the others quickly converged towards where he was last seen. One of the large cats could be seen carrying the body of Belone by the neck at a speed almost equal to what they could run. Behind it were another large cat and two juveniles.

Terrace started to move after the cats, but Malcolm stayed him with his hand.

"No, boy. If we were to follow them, there could be serious trouble. We don't know how many there are, and something tells me they know the area a lot better than us. We could take one or two of them but I'll wager there's at least a half-dozen of them. Let's return to camp, tell Carl what we saw and say a prayer for poor Belone."

The return to camp was a solemn one. The camp held a prayer service in the evening for Belone, and then went about its business, though the mood was reserved.

A bit of good news was that Philip's arm seemed to be in recovery as he announced that he could both feel and move his fingers.

Carl talked with Rog and Malcolm as they made their way. The large cats were another disturbing predator and Carl was hoping they could kill one so he could see exactly what they were.

Malcolm considered the problem. "Well, we may not have much choice. Seems to me they'll likely find us and then we'll see if we can handle them."

"What difference does it make what they look like exactly?" questioned Rog.

"I'm not sure yet, but a lot of these animals I've seen lived on Earth at one time but became extinct. Like those raptors, and then there was those trilobites and the small sabre-tooth cat back in Sorbital. I'm wondering why. There has to be a reason."

"So you think these animals were planted here?"

"Yeah, a long time ago. By whoever put us here too."

The level of greenery increased as they travelled, with an abundance of trees, ferns and bushes that made hiking difficult. Twice, raptors were spotted but the reptiles didn't take an interest in the humans this time. Rog claimed that they had learned their lesson from the last encounter, but Carl was of the mind he and the rest didn't understand what provoked them to attack.

Carl led the way until they suddenly broke out onto a plain, the grasses replacing the trees. A herd of deer broke and ran at their approach though they were still some distance away. Camp was set up far enough away from the forest to make sure it didn't present an easy hiding spot for any predators.

Carl checked the camp and made sure everyone was busy. The tents were more spread out from each out than at the last camp without the boundaries of trees to hinder them. Carl noticed Katrina had set both their tents side by side. He realized after last night he had given up trying to keep her from getting too close to him.

Oh well, there sure are worse fates than being stuck with Katrina in the middle of nowhere.

Rog approached Carl about checking out the plain to see how far it extended and to take a few men with him to explore the area. Katrina was at his side as usual, suggesting that they agree to return one hour before sunset or they could send a search party for them. Rog disagreed, saying if they couldn't be back by that time it would be dangerous to send out a rescue team.

"We'll be fine. If it gets dark too fast we'll sleep out there and return in the morning."

"Carl, tell him that's stupid. We have..."

Rog got excited at her rebuttal. "Look, what do you know about what is dangerous or not dangerous? Who made you the grand advisor to Carl? Keep your opinions to yourself."

"Carl!"

"Settle down, both of you. Rog, if you run into problems handle it the best you can. I'll have a large bonfire made so that you'll be able to see the glow in the sky some distance away in case you get confused in the dark. Try to be back before nightfall though."

Rog nodded at him and strode off without looking at Katrina.

Carl sighed. "Katrina, you just can't voice your thoughts like that. Talk to me first, and if it's reasonable I'll bring it forward."

"I was just trying to help."

"I know. But you have to do it the right way, okay?"

"Alright." She continued to pout for a few minutes more but followed him as he made his way to the centre of the camp.

Tanya and Hilliard were laughing at some private joke together but then tried to staunch their giggles as Carl and Katrina approached.

"Hi, what's so funny?"

"Nothing. Just something between Tanya and myself. How are you, Carl?"

"Fine." He noticed that they ignored Katrina and it made him curious if it was something about her that provoked their laughter. "Are you two still planning a trip to the forest edge?"

"Of course." Tanya gave him a very friendly smile, tossing back her almost shoulder-length hair. She had let her hair grow out again from her earlier short haircut.

Carl felt Katrina's hand on his arm after Tanya's flirt and he didn't like to see the trouble that was brewing between them. "Then make sure you two take a couple of guards with you."

Tanya didn't argue with him like she did last time, instead she teased him. "Oh, Carl, are you worried about us getting into trouble?" She sang out the question in a soft voice.

"Please, just do as I ask."

"Okay, you're in charge." She laughed and headed out with Hilliard.

"I don't like her acting like that. Provoking you like that, especially when I'm standing right here."

"Yeah, well, she was just having some fun with me."

"*Humph.* Whatever."

Malcolm was examining the ground with care, turning over loose clumps of dirt now and then. He frowned, walked a few more paces and explored the ground again, putting a reed of tall grass between his teeth as he thought. After another twenty minutes of walking around, he returned to the camp and sought out Carl.

"We may be in a situation here."

"How so, Malcolm?"

He looked between Carl and Katrina. "Katrina, would you mind if I talked to Carl alone for a few minutes?"

She looked back at Carl and when he nodded, she turned on her heel, looking slightly annoyed.

"Looks like bit of a problem there, Carl." He jerked his thumb at the departing Katrina.

"No kidding. What's the other problem I have?"

Malcolm chuckled. "Always a problem somewhere, right? I was looking at the ground around here and I noticed some patterns on the surface. To make a long story short, this plain has been run over by large herds of something—large footed creatures in particular. I noticed hoof prints of some smaller animals as well, possibly deer. With the larger prints, I have no idea what made them other than they are round and flatfooted. They also left some rather large droppings. I suspect they came by here sometime in the last couple of weeks and it's tough to say when they might return."

"Not good news. Would it be safe to say they're plant eaters?"

"Yeah, nothing to eat here but grass. For the time being it's just information for you, no point in getting the others alarmed for something that may not come about."

Dusk came but Rog and his company had not returned. Carl tried not to worry about it and wandered by the campfire to get some dinner. Katrina saw him coming as she helped with the cooking and immediately made a plate for him. He thanked her but wished she hadn't done so. He really didn't want to solidify their relationship. The way Tanya had flirted with him earlier had made him think there was still a chance to change her mind.

Nightfall came and Rog still hadn't returned. Carl went to the perimeter and peered out into the darkness but didn't see any motion. Malcolm walked over and stood by him.

"I reckon he's okay. Smart boy, he won't try to find his way back in the darkness. Too easy to get lost or hurt that way."

"Yeah, you're probably right." He paused before speaking again. "Tell me, Malcolm, what the hell do I do about Katrina? What should I do about Tanya? I'm getting mixed signals from her and I don't know what to do."

"You're asking me? What do I know about women? Still, I see your difficulty there. Do you want to spend the rest of your life with Katrina?"

"No, I don't think so."

"Well she might want to with you. How about Tanya? Still got the hots for her?"

"Yeah, but she believes Witchdoctors can't have a man."

"And meanwhile Katrina is hanging around you like bees to honey. Before you can do anything with Tanya, you have to cool off with Katrina. My boy, with what I do know about women, you gotta have only one at a time."

"One at a time what?"

Both men turned around at the sound of Tanya's voice.

Malcolm laughed. "I'm going to turn in. See you in the morning. Good night Witchdoctor."

"So what were you two talking about?"

I wonder how much she heard. Especially with that hearing of hers, she might have heard the whole thing. "Just stuff, guy talk."

She was grinning at him. "Guy stuff huh? Can't share with me?"

Carl laughed. "If I thought I would get the right answer out of you I might. But no, I won't let you in our talk."

She pretended to pout for moment. "Oh alright. I came by to tell you I made up a poison. If you use it with those arrows they'll probably be effective to kill those predators."

"Great. We'll try it out on our next attack, if one comes." She continued to stand near him as he looked out into the darkness.

"You're worried about Rog. Don't be, he's okay. They're sleeping right now."

"You're sure?"

She gave him a quick glance. "Of course. Am I ever wrong?"

"Well..."

She punched him hard on the shoulder. "Well what?"

"Nothing." He reached for her hand and they stood listening to the insects chirp for a minute. He turned towards her but she suddenly broke her hand free.

"I better go. See you in the morning."

He watched her disappear. *Damn, just as I thought about kissing her. I've got to find a way to hide my thoughts.*

He went to his own tent, not surprised Katrina was waiting for him. She questioned where he was, what he was doing.

"Katrina, what I do is my business. I don't have to justify my time with you."

"Sorry, I was just curious." She tried to kiss him but he didn't respond with any enthusiasm. "It looks like you need some sleep. Would you like a back massage?"

"No, no thank you. I just need to sleep."

He didn't sleep well, waking up in the middle of the night. He felt Katrina quietly get up and steal out of the tent. He continued to lie for a few minutes and then opened his eyes, seeing her clothes still in the tent. *Where could she have gone? She's naked, not likely to have left to answer a call of nature.*

Curious, he put on his shorts and went outside. He didn't see her and walked the few steps to her tent. He caught a glimpse of her sitting in her tent through the slightly parted flaps. Kneeling close to her tent he heard her speak in whispers, words that he couldn't quite comprehend, almost like a chant.

This isn't good. I've got to ask someone about this tomorrow. He went back to his own tent, not falling asleep until after Katrina returned.

In the morning, he felt tired but went about his business of getting the camp ready. Katrina had been up earlier and was helping making breakfast. She, as usual stopped what she was doing and prepared his plate. He noticed she looked rather pretty this morning, her blonde hair catching the morning sun.

He thanked her for breakfast and then thought about her. *All in all she is rather nice. Could do worse than spend time with her.*

He spied Tanya sitting by herself and walked over to her. "Hi, Tanya. Sleep well?"

"No, not really." She didn't look at him. "If you don't mind I'd rather be by myself."

Taken back he nodded and walked away. *What the hell was that? Last night...* His thoughts froze, remembering Katrina getting up and doing something by herself. He found Malcolm, seeking his advice.

"The arts? Well, I ain't no expert, let me tell you that. What you describe sounds very bad indeed. Katrina may be invading the minds of others to give suggestions. It's not supposed to be allowed from what I understand, unless it's very special circumstances that the Elders are consulted on."

"Could she be making someone feel angry or something?"

"Yeah, it's possible." He paused as he scanned the horizon. "Or make someone fall in love." He raised his eyebrows. "How do you feel about Katrina?"

"I like her better today than yesterday. Damn, could she really be doing that?"

"I dunno. Ask her. Maybe there's another explanation. Hey, I see some people approaching. Must be Rog and company."

Rog and the rest waved as they approached the camp. "Sorry we're a bit late. Key here sprained his ankle in a hole. We decided not to push it to make it back last night."

A few minutes later, the men were finishing up the remains of the breakfast. Tanya checked Key's ankle while Carl questioned Rog about the trip as the others prepared to break camp.

"Okay, Rog, what did you find?"

"Well we decided to spend the night in this weird tree, I'll show one to you later, and I ended up climbing to the top. Due west I saw a blue haze, maybe an ocean and a smudge of some kind of structure. A town or something, hard to tell. We thought we best return in case it was inhabited by unfriendly people. It looks like it sits on the shore of the ocean."

"Might be worthwhile to take a look. Let's head in that direction."

Carl sought out Malcolm and informed him of their plans. He agreed it was something they had to check out.

"By the way, I was giving some thought to your problem. Teresa was appointed Witchdoctor some time ago, but there was some controversy. Teresa didn't have near the power her mother did and there was considerable talk that Florence should be made Witchdoctor. She seemed to possess a lot of natural ability as a practitioner, but in the end Teresa won out because of her blood lines and well, she had made a lot more friends than Florence. Florence can be a bit of a bitch at times."

"Florence is Katrina's mom."

"Right. Now keep in mind, once a Witchdoctor is chosen, that title is never taken away. At least it's never happened."

"So Florence, even if she uses her power on Teresa, it wouldn't do her any good."

"Yeah, but what if she worked on Tanya? Tanya has more ability than the rest put together but despite that she is unlikely to become the next Witchdoctor because she's pissed off too many people."

"You mean Florence, and now Katrina have been working on Tanya?"

"Possibility, my boy, possibility. From what I understand, these powers may be limited by distance, or at least become weaker. Tanya could well be out of range from Florence."

"Maybe that's why her dispossession has been improving, until today."

"Remember, this is just a theory. But if it's true, I sure wouldn't want to be Katrina if Tanya finds out."

"She would hex her?"

"More likely punch her teeth in."

Carl approached Katrina during the stoppage for lunch. She looked happy when he suggested they go for a short walk.

"So what do want to talk about, Carl? About us?"

"In a way. I found out you have been practicing spells on Tanya and myself. I'm not sure what to do about it."

Her eyes widened and she crossed her arms in front of her. "Who told you that? It's not true. I swear."

He grabbed her shoulder and stopped, making her face him. "It is true. I know it is. What the hell am I going to do with you?"

She hesitated as she looked at him. Her lips trembled for a moment before she spoke. "Please, Carl, don't tell anyone. I...I...didn't mean to hurt anyone. I just...just wanted to...to be needed." She dropped her head.

"Please, that's one pathetic excuse. Maybe I should just send you back to Sorbital."

She looked back up at him, her eyes glistening. "No, please. I promise I won't do it anymore."

He stared at her. "Maybe you can stay. If you tell Tanya what you did."

"No, she'll kill me."

"She's gonna find out one way or another. Want me to tell her?"

"No, no. I will." She burst into tears and Carl found himself holding her.

The journey continued. About an hour later, there was a commotion of shouts and Carl turned to see Tanya yelling at Katrina, and then grab her hair and raise her arm. Katrina raised her forearms in front of her head as Tanya began to rain punches down on her. Several of the men tried to intervene, grabbing at Tanya to pull them apart. Katrina fell to the ground, covering her face. Two men were restraining Tanya, both looked amused by the turn of events. She continued to struggle against them, but then began to kick at the dirt towards Katrina. Carl rushed over and told someone to take Katrina away and he turned to Tanya.

"Okay, Tanya, it's over now."

"Says who? I'm gonna kill that fucking little tramp."

"I said it's over. No one is going to hurt anyone, let alone kill someone. Understood?"

She glared at him. "Who do you think you are that can..."

"Someone who's in charge here."

"Okay, In-Charge-Here, what the hell are you going to do about my whole life that's screwed up because of that bitch and her fucking mother? Huh, what can you do about that?"

"Past is done, Tanya. As for the rest of your life, I'm prepared to be there if you'll only let me."

She continued to glare at him. "I'm getting really tired of that line of yours." But the steam of her temper began to dissipate and she stared at him intently for several seconds before speaking again. "You never give up on that, do you?"

"Never will."

She sighed. "Alright, just let me be. I promise to leave that fat-ass bitch alone."

"Good." He reached out and squeezed her hand and for a fleeting moment, she squeezed back. She turned and walked away, holding back her own tears.

"I reckon that girl could out-swear a sailor." The camp started to move on again with Malcolm, Rog and Carl leading the way.

"I haven't seen her that angry before."

"Then you're lucky, young fella. I have known her since she was born. The stories I could tell you when she went to school. She has settled down some, until now."

"When I went to school I saw her beat up boys bigger than herself, and use words that I hadn't a clue what they meant at that time. She was a handful for the teachers."

Carl laughed. "And who would have thought she would turn out to be this quiet, meek girl we have now."

Rog laughed. "I told you before, she's a demon in disguise."

Chapter Ten:
The Savannah

The savannah stretched out before and behind them. The temperature continued to rise and the lack of the forest allowed the sun to bear its full strength on them. Carl swatted at an errant insect determined to land on his nose.

A small herd of animals resembling elephants trooped by and trumpeted a warning to stay away. The elephant-like beasts stood slightly taller than their Earth counterparts but their tusks were inverted, pointing downward towards the ground. They weren't the only herds they came across. Groups of small horse-like creatures mixed with long-necked antelope to provide mutual protection from predators. The predators not only included a group of raptors, but also a pride of large cats and a creature that looked like a cross between a dog and a hyena. The raptors were spotted early into the journey but didn't seem interested in them. The large cats watched as they passed by, appearing to be resting but their gaze followed their movements. Carl looked closely at them and noticed rather large canines. Coupled with their large shoulders, he felt they looked more like a type of sabre-tooth cat rather than lions. The large flightless birds weren't apparent here—they seemed to prefer the edges of the savannah where they could ambush their prey.

The odd trees that Rog had spoken about earlier were strange indeed. What looked like a clump of several trees turned out to be one tree with several trunks that fed to a common centre. The outside of the tree was covered in small leaves while the inside was a maze of leafless branches that intertwined with each other. Branches inside had died, turning white in the process and ended in a sharp point. It made navigating difficult to get into the middle where the tree developed a sweet fruit that looked like dark pineapple. Several birds and small animals made their home inside this area, an entirely different ecology than the one outside. With care, humans could penetrate the barriers that were difficult for the larger predators or the large prey that wandered about.

Carl was impressed by the size of the tree, which covered almost two hundred feet in diameter and agreed with Rog that it was a safe place to stay at night.

"A lot of noise, my friend. Every small creature must hide here and they sure don't like us sharing their space."

"They probably thought 'there goes the neighbourhood'."

"What?"

"Uh, just an Earth expression."

Rog tapped him on the skull. "Hello in there. We here, not there."

Carl chuckled. "You're right. If I climbed to the top would I see what you were talking about?"

"Only if your eyes are better than your love life, which, if you don't mind me saying so, is really a mess."

Carl sighed. "It's a mess, but it's my mess." He climbed to the top, not difficult with the numerous branches but they overlapped each enough that he had to duck and crawl as he made his way up. Once on top, he saw the hazy blue of the ocean and as Rog indicated the odd looking structure near its edge. A green belt surrounded a brown group of buildings.

Rog called up. "See them?"

"Yeah."

"Think it might be the ghouls' city?"

"Don't know. If they could build that tunnel and building back at Sorbital, you would think they could do better than that."

The journey continued, heading towards the odd structure after Carl talked to Rog and Malcolm. The afternoon stayed hot but fortunately, clouds appeared to take away the heat of the sun.

Carl saw the blur of yellow and black spotted fur rush at him and at the same time was shoved to the ground. Malcolm stood by him, holding his spear at ready. Within seconds several more cats attacked, initiating shouts and screams from the group. An arrow just missed Malcolm's head when he turned to face a cat that was set to jump at Carl. His spear plunged into the cat's chest when it leaped. It fell dead, only a yard away from Carl, cracking the spear shaft in two when it landed. Malcolm wasn't the only one using his spear. Another sabre-tooth roared in pain when a spear found its mark and then was silenced from arrows that pierced its hide. Within a minute, the battle was over with four cats dead and several disappearing into the tall grass. The poison Tanya had made worked well with the arrows and killed the cats quickly. When the cats saw their own fall dead, they retreated as fast as they attacked. Unfortunately, two more men died and others were injured. Carl had the dead and injured taken quickly to one of the multi-trunk trees that they now called the thorn trees.

Tanya worked on the injuries. Fortunately none of the injuries appeared to be life threatening. Some of the cats had left a few deep gashes in the victims and she quickly dressed the cuts to prevent infection. She looked over to her side and was surprised to see Katrina working on a gash on someone's arm. She wished Katrina would look at her so she could scowl at her but the woman was intent on her work.

The thorn trees made an excellent place to camp, providing protection with fresh fruit to give a change from the usual diet. Carl walked around the tree trunks checking on everyone and saying a few words to those who were close to those who died. It bothered him that the deaths were easier to take than the first ones and he felt guilty over his lack of remorse. He did have other things on his mind, especially the heavy tension between Katrina and Tanya. Though Katrina and Carl were no longer going with each other, he still felt sorry for her. Perhaps that was irrational, after all the problem was her own doing, but he thought she still was a decent person, a bit selfish, but maybe that was more from her mother's influence than anything else.

There I go trying to justify her actions again. Like how I think Tanya will come around. Rog is right about me and women—no sense at all.

Tanya was sitting by herself when Malcolm approached her. She wanted time to reflect after the funeral service but he was perhaps the only one she didn't mind interrupting.

"Nice service, Tanya. You helped a lot of people with your prayer."

"Thanks. I was just doing what I was suppose to do."

"Maybe, but you did it well." He sat next to her on the grass under one of the tree trunks. "Something else I'd like to talk to you about, if you don't mind my intrusion."

"No, not at all. Go ahead." She watched him carefully select a blade of grass and start to chew on it.

"It's hard when someone dies, sometimes hard to let go."

"True. But the cycle goes on, as they say."

"It's also hard to let go of hate, too. The stuff that can harm a person."

Tanya looked down. "You mean me and Katrina."

"Yeah. You're doing yourself no good girl, holding up this wall of hate."

She pulled out a group of grass with her hand. "But what she did to me...I get angry just thinking about it."

He put his hand on hers. "When you were first born, Teresa was so proud of you, showing you off to the whole village. I was one of the first to see you. She even let me hold you, a rare honour. You were a beautiful baby."

Tanya grinned, feeling a little self-conscious. She was also very aware of his big hand holding hers. She was puzzled by a tingle that went through her starting at her hand.

"But, I've got to tell you, even then you had a nasty temper—throwing tantrums, screaming and waving your fists and feet in the air. Things didn't change much as you got older either. About the same time you learned to walk, you learned to kick things when you got mad."

She laughed a bit as he chuckled. "So you're saying I always had a temper?"

"You got it. Now I'm not saying Florence didn't try to push you more so in that direction, and that would be a horrible thing to do to a child. But I'm not sure Katrina did much of that, she'd be too young and untrained."

"She did it a few days ago."

"Yeah, that's true. No excuses for her there. But consider this, she was told by her mother this was the right thing to do and so she followed her directions. Second, she didn't make you into something you're not. You, my girl, are just a passionate person and a little too intense at times."

"So am I just supposed to forget what happened?"

"No, just get by it. You're hurting yourself more than her by this brewing about what she did. This problem is causing Carl a lot of grief as well. He's supposed to come out with a suitable punishment for her."

"Carl's not much for handing out judgements like that."

"True, he doesn't want anyone hurt. You do know that when we get back to Sorbit the Elders will try Florence?"

"Yeah. What will they do to her?"

"Probably send her to exile and not allow her to return to Sorbit for years. That might still happen to Katrina."

"Okay, I'll try to work something out." She sighed. "I just feel she's getting away with it too easily."

"Thanks for being understanding. From what I've seen, Katrina is not getting off lightly. She looks miserable." He stood up.

The tingle faded in her fingertips, and suddenly she needed to ask him something. "Malcolm, when those big cats attacked, I saw you push Carl out of the way."

"Yeah, have to protect our leader, right? I saw that cat charging and I just reacted."

"Right. But I saw you move *before* the cat appeared, otherwise you never would have time to move over and push him."

Malcolm was curious, squinting his eyes. "I don't get it. What are you getting at?"

"You said you saw the cat charging but the cat wasn't there when you moved. You wouldn't have time and then your back was turned and you couldn't see it when it was there."

"You saying I didn't see that cat?"

186

"You saw the cat, but before he was there. You have the gift, don't you? You can see things that aren't there yet."

Malcolm sat again. "Yeah, it comes and goes by itself. Sometimes when I'm awake, sometimes when I dream. I have no control over it. Don't tell anyone, a man ain't suppose to have the gift and I don't need to be thought of as any more peculiar than I'm already."

"Sure, it'll be our secret."

Tanya went to the centre of the camp where dinner was prepared and took a larger portion than usual. The activity during the past few days had increased her appetite and she knew the next few days could be taxing as well. After the meal, she saw Katrina, almost hiding behind a tree trunk and walked to where she sat.

Katrina stared wide-eyed at her approach.

"Relax, I'm not going to hit you. Maybe I'm still a bit upset about what happened, but...well, I have better things to spend time thinking about."

Katrina scrambled to her feet. "Uh, thanks. Tanya, I'm so, so sorry for what I did. It was so wrong, and I promise I'll never, ever do anything like that again."

"Okay. Let's just drop it." Tanya watched as Katrina started to cry again. *Well at least she feels miserable about it. Malcolm is right, it's more her mother's fault than Katrina's.*

Then Katrina took a hesitant step towards her, and then another. Finally, she hugged Tanya muttering thank you several times.

Great, I let her off the hook and now she's blubbering all over me. Tanya gave a small hug back and they parted company.

Tanya went to where Carl was sitting at the edge of the protective thorn tree, looking out at something. She noticed he had some meat scraps next to him. She felt remarkably pleased with herself now that she thought about how she dealt with Katrina. She sat next to him and related what happened without much prodding on his part.

"...then she ended up crying on my shoulder."

"You know what they say, no good deed goes unpunished."

She laughed. "I never heard that before. You and your crazy Earth sayings." She looked out to long shadows past the tree. "What are you looking at?"

"Some animals out there. I think this tree is a normal refuge for them but we're here and they're scared to come any closer."

"Oh. So why are you watching them? I don't get the sense they're dangerous."

"I don't think so either. I'm trying something. Keep your voice down." He tossed a piece of meat towards the brush and after a short time, three animals came to retrieve the food. After they remained where the food was tossed, he threw another piece, this one closer still.

She whispered, "You're getting them to come closer each time."

He nodded and tossed another piece a few feet away. It took several minutes but eventually one took the piece but then retreated.

Tanya looked at him as he patiently tossed another piece and waited. She enjoyed sitting next to him, their bodies in contact as evening continued to advance into night. She thought about Katrina and Carl and realized part of her anger was jealousy. Now that Carl had stopped sleeping with her, she was able to let the issue of Katrina's mental invasion drop. She leaned into him and thought of the grey powder that would give her one night with him, but a night he wouldn't remember.

Morning came, and the ground had quickly absorbed the light rain that had fallen during the night. Carl led the way across the yellow grass heading towards the odd looking structure. Tanya caught up with him, asking him about the animals he fed last night, that he continued to feed after she went to bed.

"Got them about a foot away. I finally ran out of scraps, but I thought they might even feed out of my hand."

"You're crazy. Anyway, one of them is following us. To your left."

He looked and saw the gold and brown coat of the animal about twenty feet away. The animal appeared to be one of the two smaller ones he was feeding last night. Carl thought the animals looked to be a cross between a dog and a bear in appearance and about the size of a medium-sized dog. He suspected the largest one was the mother with the two smaller ones possibly pups that soon would have to make it on their own. It seemed one of the pups had decided to do just that.

"Interesting."

"I suppose so. The place we're heading to, no one's living there anymore."

"You can tell that from here?"

"I checked with the Aura last night before I went to sleep."

"Oh. Well that's good to know."

"Carl, how come you never cook at the camp?"

"What? That's what Hilliard is for."

"Then why don't you heal the injured?"

"That's silly. That's what you do."

"Right. Who's the best at direction, Rog or Malcolm?"

"Uh, well Rog has this built-in compass and Malcolm can spot things in trails. Both pretty good. Why?"

"Both better than you?"

"Sure."

"Then why are you out in front of everyone? That's Malcolm or Rog's job."

"I'm supposed to be the leader!"

"And you are. You're putting yourself at risk, risk that's avoidable. Everyone would feel better if you let someone else in front. No one is questioning you as a leader but everyone thinks you shouldn't be so far in front."

She watched him as he thought what she said. She expected some sort of argument or that he would think about it. He surprised her.

"I guess you're right. I never thought about it before. At lunchtime, I'll switch with Rog and Malcolm. They can take turns."

She continued to walk with him, longing for him to reach out and hold her hand. But she had made it clear in the past that she was off limits to him and she resisted the urge to encourage him.

At lunchtime, Carl announced that Malcolm would alternate with Rog as lead. Everyone nodded, some it seemed with relief. Some came up to him and told him after the sabre-tooth cat attack, they were concerned about his safety and were glad he would be less exposed.

After lunch, Tanya watched Carl as he carried some food scraps to where Chester, as Carl had named it, waited in the tall grasses.

This time the animal didn't run away and allowed him to slowly approach it. Carl stopped within a yard of Chester. Carl carefully placed a piece of food on the ground and kept another piece in his hand. Dozens of eyes saw the animal tentatively take the food in front of Carl and then from his hand.

Katrina walked cautiously to Tanya, standing just behind her. "What is he doing? Isn't that dangerous?"

She glanced at her former adversary. "I doubt it. He said it reminds him of his best friend back on Earth."

"His best friend?"

"He can be strange."

Chapter Eleven:
Triceratops

The odd looking settlement took form as they approached it. A ring of thorn trees stood along the perimeter of a group of mud and stone buildings. The twenty-foot thorn trees, and it was difficult to differentiate between individual ones, provided an effective defence. The multiple trunks of the individual trees overlapped each other made a dangerous barrier for any large creature to cross. Behind the trees stood a wall, eight feet high made of clay bricks, stone and mud. The only entrance was through a set of large wooden doors located in the middle of the thorn trees, standing ten feet high and a dozen feet wide. In front of the doors stood a pair of stone towers, one shorter than the other due to its top crumbling down. The doors were falling down under their own weight, helped along by the intrusion of the thorn trees. The rotting wood had split wide enough that Malcolm and the others could slip through. The inside of the compound surprised them.

The walls were thick, almost two feet, but they hadn't been able to stop an attack from penetrating.

Many of the buildings had fallen down. The mud and stone had collapsed from the elements in some cases, but others appeared to have been knocked down by something long ago with their walls scattered about in chunks. Among the debris were broken clay pots, wood pieces and bones. Beyond the buildings, the rear of the settlement was open to the ocean with large rocks positioned along the shore to discourage easy access.

Malcolm looked around. It was difficult to take more than a few steps before coming across a skeleton. He looked at the white bones and quickly concluded they belonged to more than one type of creature.

"What do you think Malcolm? What happened here?" Rog bent down to examine a skull. "Is this skull human?"

"A battle, I would hazard a guess." He pointed at a nearby skeleton. "Broken spear in the ribs of that creature. As far as that skull is concerned, I guess it might be human but different from us." Malcolm wandered into one of the small buildings that was still standing. Although the roof had disappeared, the walls stood with an opening for a door and a small window. Inside he found more human skeletons, including that of an infant without its head. He winced at the obvious violence. Malcolm heard Rog calling him and he went to where the younger man was pointing at yet another skeleton, this one dominated by a large head that had three horns attached to it.

"What the hell is this thing, Malcolm?"

Malcolm looked at the size of the four-legged creature that was half the size of one of the elephant creatures. "Haven't a clue to be truthful."

A voice came from behind him. "It's a triceratops. They lived on Earth at one time and died out, like the raptors."

Malcolm didn't turn around, standing in awe at the huge array of bones. "Doesn't look like they died here, Carl. God almighty that's a fierce looking animal."

"Uh, actually a plant eater. There's a few more by those thorn trees, a couple are actually among the tree trunks. Those skulls of the people, they look human but I think they were of a species that died out. Maybe Neanderthal, maybe something in between."

"You mean these aren't human?"

"Human but a little different than us. I'm going to check with Tanya, maybe she can get a read on this."

Malcolm watched him walk away with his new companion. Chester, he recalled, as Carl had decided to call her.

Tanya walked among the ruins and the bones and then stood looking at the ocean. A twelve-foot boat lay disintegrated on the shore, the timbers a dark grey on the ground. Large rocks could be seen on both the beach and the shallow water. The scene looked peaceful to her and she realized that because of the lack of bones, it probably wasn't the area where the battle took place. With a sigh she turned back to the main site, glad Katrina had stopped following her around. Forgiving was one thing, being buddies with her was quite another.

Rog came running up to her. "Hey witch, Carl's looking for you."

She pointed her finger at him. "One of these days I'm going to put a curse on you for calling me that."

"Wouldn't that just prove that you're really a witch then?"

She laughed. "Jerk. Maybe I'll just beat you up then."

He fainted a defensive position. "Hey, I heard Carl's got a new lady friend. You waited too long to make your move."

For a moment she felt irrationally jealous, and then she suddenly understood his jibe. Tanya hoped her face didn't show it. "Oh, yeah, his pet. What did he call her? Chester." She shook her head. "That animal never had it so good, free food and a fire to sleep by every night."

"You could've had all that, if you been nicer."

"Sleep by the fire like an animal?" She started to chase him but he sprinted out of her reach. "One of these days I'm going to teach you a lesson."

They found Carl looking at some of the bones lying around. He picked up the skull of a raptor, turning it over in his hands.

"Hey, Carl, look who I found hanging around the beach while the rest of us were working."

Carl wiped his hands as he smiled at Rog's joke. Tanya tried to look exasperated at the slight but was amused. Since leaving Sorbit she had established friendships of sorts with Malcolm, Rog, and Hilliard and an odd relationship with Katrina, who was now trying to be her friend. Then there was Carl—Carl who was tempting her to abandon her commitment to be a Witchdoctor.

"Tanya, I was wondering if you could use your talents to determine what happened here? Do your Aura thing."

"Aura thing? It's a little more than just that." She looked around. "Sure, I'll give it a try."

Tanya searched for a quiet spot and found several near the ocean, but didn't like the feel of the area. She walked along the beach and found a secluded spot on a rise that overlooked the ocean. This was going to be difficult for her. Trying to read the far past was not easy and she had taken one of the bones with her to aid her search. She tried to get as comfortable as possible, taking off her sandals and loosening her skirt and top. Her best contact with the Aura occurred when she exposed herself as much as possible to the outside, and while she didn't dare undress with the potential of someone seeing her, she tried to give herself the illusion of being naked. She started her chant, quickly finding the rhythm that allowed her mind to reach the trance state where she felt herself disappear from her physical self. The Aura came strong and fast this time, much stronger than it had before and for the barest of moments, she almost withdrew from its space, feeling almost overwhelmed by its strength. She pictured herself falling upward and allowed the Aura to take control.

It never had close to this power before and it made her a bit nervous. She heard her own voice telling herself to relax though her own lips didn't move.

Suddenly, she found herself in the middle of the settlement, the image soft as if she was looking through a fog. She knew instinctively where each person was, and when she watched Carl talk to Malcolm, his voice became clear as if she was next to him. What was interesting she found she had an image of everything around her, as if she had suddenly developed 360-degree peripheral vision. When she used to call on the Aura in the past, the best she could see were smoky, shadow images on a grey slate.

She tried to contain her excitement at her new powers for fear she would slip out of the trance state. She felt the bone in her hand, concentrating on its shape and then its being. The images of Carl and others began to fade, to be replaced by the ghostly images of events long ago.

She found it confusing to sort out the various images at first, but then she concentrated on a thread of energy that twisted its way out of the settlement. She felt herself moving in both time and place, to the start of the battle.

She ran next to a thunderous herd of triceratops, the thousand hoofs churning up small trees, grasses and soil in a cloud of dust. The smell of fear and excitement stimulated her, causing her to cry out. She looked at the long spear she was using to poke at one of the beasts, to keep him charging at full speed regardless of what lay ahead. In her mind she could feel the need for revenge, for the death of their young and strong alike. A raptor ran past her, brandishing a spear as well and its scream mixed with the bleating of the triceratops. She knew that over three hundred like her were chasing the creatures towards the settlement. Once again, the stone towers were an effective deterrent to the triceratops. The towers did not offer enough space between to squeeze through and caused them to veer away from the doors. But this time the triceratops were sent towards the thorn trees and a rumbling storm of yellow and brown crashed into the green perimeter. The first few triceratops died, impaled by the pointed branches and then trampled by those behind them. Soon a path was made through the trees to the brick and stonewalls before they collapsed under the weight of the three-horned dinosaurs. They did more damage inside the compound, trampling people and buildings alike as they panicked.

Tanya's ghostly raptor leaped among the stalled triceratops, as they were no longer being driven into the thorn trees. She and her comrades poured into the opening screaming the death-kill at the humans, the smell of blood and fear sending the raptors into a near frenzy.

Tanya saw her raptor plunge a spear into a woman's back. Around her several raptors fell to arrows, another took a spear in his throat. The raptors, almost two feet shorter than the six-foot humans, continued to flood in.

A raptor used her spear and then a claw on her foot to maim and then rip open a human. The humans were in disarray from the triceratops trying to escape and the assault from the raptors.

More raptors died from the cornered humans but they continued to be attacked from the combined clans of the raptors. Some humans died as they tried to open the heavy front doors but they weren't quick enough to allow escape.

A few lucky ones managed to escape in a boat, leaving the raptors howling in anger. The raptors could not swim and did not like to venture even into shallow water.

Suddenly, Tanya saw a face of a human up close. His eyes were full of fear and rage and then the image became dull as the raptor that carried her spirit fell to the ground dying. A moment later she found herself back in the middle of the settlement but in her own time. She drew back on herself and emerged from the Aura, trembling, sweating and exhausted.

Tanya rested an hour before she walked back to the centre of the settlement. She walked around until she came to the spot she last remembered seeing through the raptor's eyes, spotting a white bone poking above the ground. A few minutes later, she dug into the sandy soil and came across the remainder of the skeleton. A broken rib showed where the blow entered to kill it. For a moment, she paused to briefly touch the skull and then replaced the bone she had taken from the area earlier. She stood up and found Carl, standing near Malcolm.

Tanya related her vision to them, without telling them that she felt she was there at the actual battle.

"So these raptors killed these people out of revenge?" Carl had listened carefully and now tried to figure out what made the raptors work together so effectively.

"I guess so, at least they thought the people were killing them. Some got away by boats, but not very many."

"It looks like we're dealing with intelligent raptors. What about the people, did they look like us?"

"Somewhat. Bigger, heavier anyway. Ugly faces, though compared to the raptors they were at least human. Those raptors were small, only about this high." She held her hand about four feet off the ground.

"But their skulls are large for their size, maybe they have bigger brains. I hope we don't come across them."

Malcolm had been listening but until now hadn't joined in the discussion. "Any image of where they might live now?"

"No, I didn't try. I could go back to the Aura and see if I can find out."

Carl shook his head. "No, you look pretty beat. You said clans had joined together so we can assume they would be in more than one place anyhow. We're going to hold up here for a couple of days. I've got a couple of people cleaning out an area so we can camp here. We'll secure the door and maybe try to relax for a change. You..." he pointed at Tanya, "...should get some rest."

"Is that an order?" She heard herself speak in a tired voice and wasn't sure if her reply sounded challenging or as a tease. It didn't really matter, she knew she had to sleep.

"Yeah, do you want me to tuck you in?"

She decided not to dignify his question with a reply, rolling her eyes upward and then walking away. She heard Malcolm laugh and say something to Carl but by then she was no longer paying attention.

Tanya woke up in one of the few remaining buildings. She had wrapped a blanket around herself and curled up in a corner. She expected to have vivid dreams but instead opened her eyes to dancing shadows on a wall. Her only memories were of curling up to the wall to rest. The shadows were from the fire that lighted up the open doorway. She yawned and went out to where people were mulling around the fire. She wondered how much different the scene was a hundred years ago when the odd looking humans lived here.

Tanya, like most of the people in camp, slept in. Carl had decided this was a good place to let people relax for a change and most took advantage by resting. Tanya took care of some minor medical needs but not much was required. The busiest person was Hilliard who still had to cook and now made breakfast almost on an ongoing basis as different groups of people rose.

Tanya ended up having breakfast with Rog, Carl and Katrina. Katrina was helping Hilliard make breakfast but the older woman indicated they had caught up again with the cooking and suggested that she join her friends. Katrina knew she hadn't reached the status of friend with the others. Many were ignoring her after they found out she was using her abilities in the arts to influence others. Tanya had forgiven her, which at least stopped the suggestions of banishing her from the Quest. That prospect of being banished had worried her. She knew she wouldn't be able to reach Sorbit alive by herself. Katrina was grateful that Carl instead assigned her to extra duties including helping Hilliard, gathering firewood and maintaining the campfire. Katrina joined the others to eat breakfast, feeling a little uncomfortable doing so. As usual, it was Rog who was talking the most, trying to probe a reaction out of them.

"So what we should do is organize a hunt for those triceratops. Just one of them would provide us enough food for the whole journey."

Carl almost reacted to the absurdity of trying to kill one of them, let alone trying to transport the carcass the size of a truck. Instead, he closed his jaw as soon as he thought about answering, realizing Rog was only trying to bait them into arguing.

Tanya responded however. "What makes you think their flesh is edible? Could be like eating tree bark."

"Maybe, but you could help Hilliard and learn how to cook it. She really can make anything taste good."

"Me? What's wrong with you?"

"Hey, I'm a hunter. You're the expert on collecting plants and things." Rog then jumped on another argument before Tanya could react. "Besides, a dinosaur might be what you need to put some meat on your bones."

"Meat on my bones? I'm not skinny, but you're..."

Rog didn't let her finish. "You and Katrina are so thin, both of you could hide behind that tree." He pointed at a sapling, not more than an inch thick at its trunk.

Now Katrina was caught in his tease. "There's nothing wrong with my weight! Rog, you're just asking for trouble."

Laughing, he stood up. "Whatever you say. Let's just hope the wind doesn't blow too strong tonight." He walked away, happy with the result of his barb.

Carl tried to hide his grin and a quick glance at Tanya and Katrina told him they were not amused by Rog's humour.

"Damn, I swear one of these days I'm gonna pay him back for all his little jibes." Tanya sat with her arms crossed.

"I feel like an idiot for falling for his trap. I should have ignored him too. He pulled in both of us."

The woman pouted for a minute longer and Carl was glad they didn't ask his opinion on their weight—there just wasn't a right answer for that.

Katrina touched Tanya on her forearm to get her attention. "Hey, Tanya, do you want to go swimming? I need to wash off all this dust and dirt."

Tanya thought about it. On one hand, she didn't want to encourage a friendship with Katrina, but a swim did sound good. Carl had a rule of no one going anywhere alone, and Tanya couldn't think of another swimming partner readily.

"Sure, why not? Let's find a secluded spot though." Tanya preferred not to swim in a large group, especially if men were around.

The shallow water near the shore was warmed by the strong sun. The two women placed their clothes on a large rock and then ran into the ocean, splashing and laughing.

Higher up the slope leading to the beach, the noise attracted the attention of a hunter. He crept among the trees, pausing to watch before signalling a companion to join him. They hid among the trees as they stared wide-eyed at the two women. The first man smiled at a thought that came to him as he reached for his knife.

Tanya decided this was the best she had felt on the whole trip so far, despite having to share it with Katrina. After spending over an hour in the water, they decided to return to the shore. Katrina waded onto the beach first and looked around.

"Hey, wasn't this the spot we went in?"

"I think so. Yeah, there're those rocks."

"But our clothes are missing!"

Tanya immediately reacted by covering herself up with her arms. Katrina wasn't as modest and continued to look up and down the beach.

"I don't think the wind could've blown them away. Someone must have taken them."

Tanya was getting upset. "What do we do now? How do we get back to camp like this?"

"Oh, well, if you're shy I'll go and get a change of clothes. It won't be the first time a bunch of people saw me naked." The two women stood by the rock where their clothes were and looked around again.

"There! I think I see them on that tree." Tanya hurried to the spot only a dozen feet away past the beach with Katrina following.

Their clothes were there, each set on a small tree. Each tree had its limbs cut off until only four limbs remained on the thin trunk.

Tanya looked at the result. "Rog. That idiot put our clothes on a tree that's suppose to resemble a skinny person." She yelled out at the surrounding trees. "Rog, I'm going to kill you, slowly and painfully."

Katrina laughed as she pulled the clothes off. "Actually that was pretty funny. Though I can just picture him rolling on the ground laughing at us."

"Yeah, and the worst part is he's going to retell this gag at the next large grouping around the fire." Tanya was not as amused as Katrina, and wasn't comfortable with a man seeing her without her clothes on. She was going to find Rog and tell him off.

The two women returned to camp and Tanya immediately started to look for Rog, but he was still out of the camp. She went to where Hilliard was cooking and took a large chuck of brown bread to eat. Hilliard went over to her, looking concerned.

"What's wrong, dear?"

Tanya didn't immediately answer, taking another bite.

"Tanya, you don't normally eat between meals and that big piece of bread tells me you're upset. What is it?"

"Well, I went swimming with Katrina, and after we finished we found our clothes were missing. Rog, and I don't know who else, dressed them on a couple of trees that were suppose to resemble two skinny women. It's bad enough I had to be buddies with Katrina but the fact Rog and company went spying on me makes me mad."

"Oh. Are you sure it was Rog? And if so maybe he wasn't spying on you two but just happened to come across you two swimming."

"It had to be Rog. Maybe he just came across us, but he shouldn't have kept staring at us and then steal our clothes."

"Tanya, if you were walking where he was and saw him swimming would you have stopped to watch a bit? I know I would have."

Tanya gave a tight smile at the thought of Hilliard peering through the trees at Rog. "I guess so."

"So what you are really upset about is the joke he pulled on you."

Tanya nodded. "But, well, a guy had never seen me naked before, and I guess I felt...I don't know."

Hilliard patted her leg. "I know what you mean. You should be glad men want to see you naked. They would run at the sight of me." She laughed, forcing a smile from Tanya.

"Thanks, Hilliard, for your advice." She stood up. "Nice bread."

Rog avoided the centre of the camp, figuring Tanya would need time to cool off. He was quite pleased with his inspiration to put the clothes on the altered trees, though Carl appeared to be reluctant to help at first to prune the saplings. He skirted the outside of an almost collapsed hut where one brick wall had fallen and was dragging the others with it. Tanya stood there with her arms crossed as he passed the corner, giving him a start.

"Oh, hi, Tanya."

"Don't you 'hi' me, why were you spying on me? Is that what you do in your free time, sneaking up on people when they're swimming?"

"Whoa, girl. I wasn't spying on you or anyone else. I was hunting when we saw you two in the water."

"Yeah? Who's 'we'? What's the big idea of stealing our clothes?" She uncrossed her arms and held her fists up.

She looked upset, but with her fists clenched, he had to stifle a laugh. "We didn't steal your clothes, just moved them. The trees were just your size too." Now he grinned, showing off his white teeth as he stepped back to sit on part of the wall that stood about two feet high.

"You didn't answer who the other person was."

"Come on. It's a secret. Maybe he don't want you to know who he was."

"I'll find out who you were hunting with. Was it Carl?" She wasn't sure if she wanted the other person to be Carl. *I don't like the thought that it was him peering through the bushes at me. Though I'd rather it was him than some other guy. A long time ago I saw him naked so maybe that's fair turn around.*

"Girl, you just ask too many questions." He laughed. "It's nothing personal, just a joke that could have happened to anyone."

"Maybe I'll plan some revenge."

"You can try, you can try. Rog here is the master of funny stuff. You don't want no quarrel with me." Rog laughed again.

She stared at him, wondering if she really wanted to escalate his joke. "You are really making me pissed off at you, you know."

"I know, but don't blame me for your own problems."

"My problems!"

"Yeah, you're frustrated and now get mad at a little gag."

Tanya sighed, getting exasperated at Rog's ability to divert the problem on her. "So why am I frustrated, man-with-all-the-answers?"

"Simple, you're scared to get serious with Carl."

She stepped forward and grabbed his shirt with one of her hands. "I'm not scared of anything! Even an idiot like you knows a Witchdoctor can't have a serious relationship."

"Says who? Where did that rule come from?"

"It's been a rule forever, ever since Witchdoctor Mariah. Maybe even longer."

"Yeah, let me tell you a few things about rules as ol' Rog sees it. First, I never seen you pay particular attention to rules before. In school you was always getting into trouble over them. Second, there has to be a reason for a rule and there ain't none there for that one. But I know the real reason you follow that rule and none other."

"What?" She released her hand from his shirt. She was reading his emotions as he spoke and felt his sincerity. Whatever he was about to say he believed it and not just to win another argument. "Well, why?"

"It's because..." his voice dropped a little, becoming softer, "...because you're scared of a relationship, especially with Carl. You is hiding behind a rule that was made up long ago for reasons unknown."

Tanya felt her mouth open to deny it but her voice stayed silent. She felt Rog grab one of her hands in each of his own.

"You and Carl, you're meant to be. I didn't always think so, but it's obvious to anyone who sees you two together."

Tanya felt her stomach lurch. "But, but my mom said...said men cause negative..." She heard her voice trail off, feeling almost foolish for saying it.

"Maybe that's true. But it's your life, and the cycle continues whether you're a married Witchdoctor or not. You gotta ask yourself what's important to you. I think you can be the Witchdoctor either way. What do you want to do?"

She stood there, not knowing what to say. She had sought out Rog to tell him off and now he left her on the brink of changing her life. "I don't know. Maybe you're right. I just can't think straight right now." She felt the beginning of a tear. "Damn, what's going on with my life?"

Rog smiled. "Everyone asks that now and then."

She turned to leave and then turned around once more to face him. "Uh, thanks, Rog."

"Sure, anytime. Witch."

"You didn't tell me, was it Carl?"

He nodded. "Yeah, I think he wanted to jump in the water with you."

She walked away, feeling better it was Carl.

Chapter Twelve:
Tanya Decides

The savannah was longer than it was wide and as they followed it, the entire group kept close to each other out of precaution. A few predators menaced them but they didn't suffer any more casualties. Food was not scarce, both game and fruit were available in large supply. Carl was content to allow either Rog or Malcolm to lead and he spent more time checking with various members of his Quest to make sure everything was going well.

Tanya was, as usual, a mystery to him. She appeared to be on her friendly side to him, but he never knew how long that would last. From experience, he found if he pushed their relationship she would immediately withdraw. He was also puzzled that she didn't appeared to be annoyed with him when she told him that she knew he had watched her swim. He had expected a rather cold reaction from her, but she didn't act like it bothered her very much. She even initiated a bit of hand holding with him and, while he enjoyed the contact with her, he was still at a loss what to do about it.

When they stopped at a group of thorn trees, Carl had one of the smaller men climb to the top. The tree was not hard to climb but the branches on a thorn tree were thin and brittle. They could snap without warning and the remaining part of the branch could cause injury to the climber. From the top of the thorn tree, the climber announced he could see distant hills or cliffs. They looked grey in the distance, lacking any detail and it was hard to guess how far they were away. Still the news was greeted with some excitement. The place where the ghouls live may have been sighted and within reach.

Carl tried not to show his impatience as they headed across the savannah once more. Rog was in the lead and was using his spear to sweep through the tall grasses to chase away some of the insects, rodents, snakes and reptiles. Malcolm and Rog found that the pests were more likely attack or bite the lead person when startled and by the time the rest of the group came by they had either gone into hiding or run away. The sweeping of the spear at least woke them up and they were less likely to try to bite the leader.

An hour's journey from their latest stop at the thorn trees, Tanya came up to Carl, her eyes wide.

"What's the matter, Tanya?"

"I'm not sure, but I feel something. I sense anger or fear. But whatever is causing it is also large, massive."

"What should we do? Take cover?"

"I don't know. Probably. I'm just warning you, I'm not sure what it is."

Carl went to Rog and asked him to head towards the next large group of thorn trees. The thorn trees usually lived singular lives, their seeds hidden inside their fruit, would only germinate with some distance from the parent tree. The ground under a full-grown tree was too dry and blocked the sun for most plants to survive, including their own seedlings. Occasionally, two or more thorn trees grew at the same time in close proximity with each other and formed a grove of the multi-trunk trees. Rog looked for a group of the small leaf trees, and spotted a group of them in the distance.

The group swung to the east towards the trees, though some grumbled a bit about the detour and stoppage. The trees were less than a half-mile away and they made steady progress towards it. Predators such as raptors and sabre-tooth cats didn't impede their progress or threaten them, deciding there was easier prey than a large group of humans.

Rog heard the low rumble of thunder and looked at the sky for the dark clouds that would bring about another short but furious shower. Instead, the sky was clear, save for low clouds on the horizon. Then he heard shouting from behind and he turned to hear their warning better.

Tanya couldn't wait any longer. The oppressive feeling was too strong. She first asked Carl to tell everyone to start running, and while he looked dubious about her request, he did tell everyone to hurry up. Tanya added to his directive by yelling for them to run, knowing it looked like she was trying to usurp his authority. It would be more than embarrassing if she was wrong, but it never occurred to her she might be mistaken. Tanya started to run herself, grabbing Carl by his hand and pulling him along. At first, she could feel his resistance as he jogged behind her before increasing his lope to run beside her.

Tanya looked ahead to the green grove of thorn trees, wishing it wasn't so far away. The thorn trees started to change in her vision, the individual leaves became clear and sharp. She began to feel as if she was in a dream, she continued to be aware of her breathing and the pounding of her feet on the ground but it was as if her body belonged to someone else and she was merely observing. Tanya thought about the others behind Carl and her, wondering if they were running as well. Suddenly she was seeing what was behind her, watching the others chasing after them in a ragged cluster. It was similar to the vision of the settlement when she went into a trance state, but this time she went into the Aura without the relaxation exercise. Everything was clear, details jumping out at her if she thought about them. It was odd and she wondered what she looked like while she ran hand in hand with Carl. Then she saw herself, running next to Carl but with her eyes closed. Her face looked relaxed, without the fear that was on so many of the others' faces. It looked odd but now she remembered what Rog had said, anyone who saw them together knew they were meant to be. It did look that way, and not just because they were holding hands. They ran close to each other, step for step, their bodies dancing to the same rhythm.

Pleased, she looked back, behind the pack that followed them. The small horses and deer were running as well and gaining ground on them. She also saw raptors and the large sabre-tooth cats running, but they were running away from something and not interested in any prey. The hunters were not inclined to run along the savannah for long and headed towards the forest that lined the edges. The deer, the fastest of the creatures behind them, were on a collision course with the humans and Tanya was worried about someone getting seriously hurt.

Hilliard was lagging far behind the others when Katrina turned back to help, telling the older woman to drop the supply bag she was carrying. Hilliard paused, not wanting to give up supplies, but Katrina yanked on the bag and it fell to the ground. Moments later Hilliard increased her speed, thankful that Katrina did what she had done. For a large person, Hilliard moved remarkably fast and soon caught up with the others.

Malcolm knew he was in trouble. He had started near the front and was now among the last. His legs ached and his lungs couldn't gulp enough air. He started to slow down, his run not much better than a jog, trying to conserve some energy and reduce the pain in his knees. Then, as he dropped well behind the others, he heard a whisper, telling him to let go, that she would help him run. He couldn't understand why he heard that insistent whisper, other than he was dying and hallucinating. But he wasn't in any condition to resist and gave in, letting himself float free. Now, he felt as if his legs were an alien part of him as they started to churn faster and faster but without the pain. His lungs breathed in air as if they were open to the sky while the voice, Tanya's voice, told him not to be afraid. He saw himself pass some of the others as he floated above the ground. He didn't understand what was happening, but he didn't care as long as he could make it to safety.

Tanya felt as if she had split herself in three. She had seen how Malcolm began to slow down and knew the danger to him. It took a concentrated effort, but she managed to find his consciousness in the chaos of energies and tried to block his feelings of pain and stress. It worked, to her relief and surprise, and he started to propel himself quickly along the ground. She hoped it was not putting too great a strain on his heart but the alternative was worse.

A second part of her watched helplessly as some of the deer crossed into the path of the humans, sending several people tumbling to the earth in a cloud of dust. Two managed to jump back up quickly and started running again, yelling a warning at the others up ahead. Another man dropped his broken spear and holding his left elbow in his right hand started to run again. Tanya watched Katrina lay on the yellow grasses, crying out as she held her ankle. She tried to get up but fell over in agony and then was clipped by another deer. The second deer left her motionless on the ground.

Tanya was also aware of Carl yelling at her, pulling at her arm. It occurred to her that she had stumbled while trying to help Malcolm and Carl was trying to get her to wake up. *Or at least he probably thinks I'm sleeping since my eyes are closed. I should be able to drop my concentration on Malcolm soon. He's almost made it to the thorn trees. But what can I do about Katrina? She's going to get killed lying there.*

Malcolm finally reached the safety of the thorn trees and she released the block she put on his mind. Almost immediately, he staggered against one of the trunks of the thorn trees and fell down in a heap.

Tanya cast one more look behind them and saw the reason for the stampeding deer and horses. Triceratops were rushing down the savannah, chewing up almost anything in their path. The huge creatures weren't moving fast, but they spread out over a vast area and left little room for escape. In hindsight, Tanya thought it may have been better to head for the forest like the raptors did but for some reason she thought the raptors were part of the danger as well, making the thorn trees a better place to defend.

Fatigue was setting in fast for Tanya, and not just because of the running. The mental exertions had taken their toll and she wanted to sleep and wished her headache would go away. She decided it was time to return to her more normal state and opened her eyes, looking right into Carl's face. Another moment of disorientation occurred and she realized he was carrying her in his arms. Her legs were still flexing as if she was running and her arms swinging. She knew it must have been rather difficult for Carl to carry her while running and with her limbs flailing about. Apparently, the invasion of Malcolm's mind caused her to lose her own control of her body.

"You can put me down now. I'm...I'm back."

"Almost there, faster to keep going." He puffed as he spoke.

"Please, this is silly. I'm too heavy for you to carry."

"You're a bit lighter than Hilliard."

She hit his back with her free arm as he ran into the grove of trees. "A bit lighter?"

He put her down slowly, almost reluctantly, and then sat down.

She looked out and saw the herd of triceratops approaching, hoping they would avoid the thorn trees. She thought about the unconscious Katrina lying prone on the grass and wished she could help her. It was then she saw the tall thin man running towards Katrina.

Rog knew it was perhaps one of the dumber things he had done in his life, and it looked like it could be his last. Still, he felt he was one of the leaders of the Quest and it was his responsibility to try to save Katrina. He could make out the huge three-horn crests of the dinosaur and knew he probably wouldn't make it even if he weren't going to carry her.

She was moaning as he bent to pick her up and he yelled at her to hang on. He tossed her over his shoulder and started to run back. He felt her grab on tight to the waistband of his shorts and he concentrated on returning to the shelter of the trees, ignoring his shortness of breath.

He could feel the vibration of the ground as the two-ton animals pounded towards him, their bleats high-pitched compared to the thunder of their hoofs.

"They're gaining on us Rog! Drop me, save yourself." He didn't answer and she knew he wasn't going to stop. She wanted say thanks to him and that it was nice knowing him. That would have sounded overly dramatic though and he needed to concentrate on his running. Her ankle meanwhile was sending out a new pulse of pain with each step he took, and she felt her neck had to be broken it hurt so much.

Rog caught a glimpse of the triceratops running past him to his left. It was veering to the side to avoid the thorn trees and he hoped the others would do the same and spare them. Another ran alongside him for a moment and then turned in front of him, causing him to try to brake and turn at the same time. He missed the monster by inches and then resumed his sprint to the shelter as more of the triceratops passed by and swung to the left of the grove of trees. Another minute passed and then arms were hauling Katrina from him and he fell to the ground exhausted as he heard the triceratops roar past the thorn trees.

Tanya watched with the others the heroics of Rog as he raced with Katrina on his back. She wished she could do something, anything. But, like everyone else, she found herself holding her breath as he tried to stay out of reach of the yellow and brown monsters.

Katrina's ankle was badly swollen and it was hard to tell if it was broken or sprained. Tanya's healing powers were compromised by her mental fatigue, though she was able to provide some relief to her. Katrina's neck showed the sign of a severe bruise where a deer had kicked her and Tanya used a simple cream to ease the stiffness.

"Sorry, Katrina. I don't have much reserve power right now. I kinda used it up during our run on something else. I'll try again later, okay?"

"Sure, that's fine." She gave a smile that showed through the pain. "How's Rog?"

"Oh you know Rog. According to him, he ran fifty miles with you on his back screaming while he fought off triceratops. We're going to hear about this for years to come."

She grinned. "Sorry. I told him he could drop me."

"Drink this and try to rest." Tanya handed a cup of a yellow liquid to her.

After Tanya left, Rog came and saw Katrina as she sat against a tree trunk. "How're you feeling?"

"Alive, thanks to you. You were very brave to do that."

He shrugged. "I needed the exercise. Nasty looking ankle."

"Yeah, gonna slow me down some. Rog, I owe you my life. If there's anything I can do for you, just ask. I mean it, okay?"

"Sure. Buy me a beer sometime."

Tanya was watching the sunset after camp had been established in the safety of the thorn trees when Malcolm joined her.

"Carl said you were over here."

"Yeah, I like to watch the sunset."

"You want to tell me what happened back there?"

She sighed. "I don't know how to explain it. I saw you were in trouble, but not how you see things. I have a second kind of vision, only not through my eyes. I just sort of reached out with, with my thoughts, I guess..."

"I heard your voice telling me to let go."

"Yeah, I tried to block your pain so you could run again."

"It worked. I felt like I was floating. But it almost killed me when you let go of me later. I thought my lungs were going to collapse. And my knees, they still hurt."

"Sorry."

"Don't be. I'm alive." He picked up a stick and played with it. "Can you read minds? Do what you did to others?"

"I never tried before. I don't read minds, only emotions. I can find individuals sometimes mentally. You're the easiest. I can find a couple of others. Katrina, and Carl now. I used to be able to find my mom but the distance is too great. I haven't really tried lately. I suppose I should."

"I never heard of anyone, past or present, being able to do what you do. You're getting very powerful in the art."

"Yeah. It scares me. The Aura seems to be around me all the time now. Like I can switch it on without much of a trance at all."

"You'll learn how to control and use it in time I suspect. Don't worry, you'll do fine."

She bit her lip, thinking. "Rog said I could have a relationship with Carl and still be a Witchdoctor. Is that true or do I have to choose one or the other like my mom told me?"

"Hell, I don't know the answer to that one. But for what it's worth you been getting closer to Carl, and yet your powers have been growing all the same. Maybe there's an answer for you somewhere in that."

"Yeah, maybe." She brightened up. "Thanks, Malcolm."

"Glad to be of help. By the way, I think it's best if we keep what happened between us a secret for a while. No point in getting the others worried you're able to take over their minds. Some people jump to conclusions a little fast."

"I think Carl already knows. I kind of hinted what happened."

"That's okay. He won't say anything that could hurt you. The young fella has been smitten by you something fierce."

"I don't know why. I haven't always been very nice to him." She laughed.

"I guess he sees that as part of your charm. Come on, it's time for chow and Carl's likely given our portion to Chester."

The next morning Carl announced that the group was going to split into two. Katrina was not in condition to travel and Malcolm looked tired and was suffering from a sore throat. A few others were having trouble with the constant walking, and would slow the group as a whole.

Carl left Malcolm in charge of the group that was to stay behind. When, and if, they decided they could journey again, he was to take them back to the abandoned settlement. Carl felt they could reach the area where the ghouls now live in two or three days and perhaps could return to the settlement in a week's time. Providing, of course, everything went well.

A few hours later, Carl walked hand in hand with Tanya with Rog in the lead. The group now numbered eighteen, and made it easier for Carl to keep track of what everyone was doing. Safety didn't appear to be an issue as the sabre-tooth cats and raptors left them alone. Carl wasn't sure about other predators that might be present but concluded they weren't a threat or would have been noticed by now. Chester was quite at home moving around the group, though he kept close to Carl most of the time. It had a dog's face with bear-like ears with the body much like a canine with a short tail. The legs were heavier and the paws broad, each with five toes causing it to move in a rather ungainly fashion. Still Chester appeared to have found a notch in Carl's heart and the rest of the group gradually accepted her presence.

Tanya called out to Rog as he swung his spear at a hesitant reptile that stood on its hind legs and hissed at the intruders. "Hey, Rog."

"What?"

"That was quite a kiss Katrina gave you when we left."

Without turning, Rog waved his free hand in a downward fashion. "It was nothing. Just thanking me for saving her."

"Yeah? Then what were you thanking her for when you kissed her back?"

Carl laughed with Tanya. Even from the back, Rog looked uncomfortable.

The ground changed from a mixture of flattened grass in packed earth to the freestanding grasses of softer ground. Carl noticed the change and saw Rog point far to their right where a herd of perhaps two hundred triceratops grazed. A couple of the huge beasts noticed them and lowered their heads, placed their front legs forward and then bayed a low hooting sound at them as they raised their massive crests. They repeated the gesture and several more of the dinosaurs turned towards them. Rog wasted little time in leading the group away from the agitated animals and, after a few minutes, they returned to their grazing. The triceratops fascinated Carl, who noted that a pattern of yellow and brown covered the beasts but the crest also sported two large black dots and jagged white lines that gave the impression of an enormous face. He supposed that the crest provided both a real and a simulated danger to predators. The size of the dinosaurs was impressive with their backs eight feet above the ground though Carl recalled seeing skeletons of them in museums and felt these were smaller than their Earth ancestors.

The savannah gradually gave way to a wetter climate and green plants and trees replaced the thorn trees and yellow grasses. A cheer went up when they came across a talnut tree and soon the tree was common among the palms, fruit trees, ferns and other plants that preferred warm and wet climates.

Carl felt it was good to be out of the direct sun, though the footing became a bit trickier. Rog was picking out paths quite well and they continued to make good time as he led them to a small pond that was being fed by a small stream. They paused to refill their water containers and eat. Tanya had taken over the cooking chores with Daniel after Hilliard was left behind, and provided a simple lunch.

An hour after their stoppage, the terrain climbed higher and together with the heavier growth of plants the travelling slowed down. Still, Carl believed the home of the ghouls was within a day or two of travel.

$\wp$

Malcolm had two of the six designated guards on duty at all times, rotating them on a six-hour schedule. They grumbled that there wasn't any danger around the thorn tree grove but Malcolm refused to give in. The afternoon came and a few creatures ventured towards the thorn trees, including several sabre-tooth cats, but they all turned away when they became aware of the human presence. The cats growled and acted annoyed but weren't in a mood to fight for the shade and wandered off to find another place to hide from the sun.

Katrina who was sitting on a low tree limb noticed them first. Eight raptors advanced to the grove where the humans rested, not noticing or caring that it was already occupied.

Malcolm noticed the oddity immediately. The raptors, six adults and two youngsters, were coloured different than the earlier ones, sporting bright yellow and red stripes along their bodies. They were also shorter, less than five feet high but their skulls were at least as big and their forearms longer in proportion to their body. All of this made them quite distinguishable from the larger raptors, but the biggest surprise was that they carried spears in their clawed hands.

Malcolm quietly had everyone prepare for a possible attack. Although the raptors weren't being aggressive, Malcolm felt they just hadn't noticed the humans yet. With the leaves that bordered the thorn trees, it was hard to see creatures that hid inside. Large predators like the sabre-tooth cats found the numerous branches awkward and preferred the outside perimeter to find shade. The raptors likely weren't worried about anything large inside the grove of thorn trees and approached in a relaxed manner. Malcolm reasoned if that was the case, they didn't need to surprise the raptors in close combat. The raptors were within thirty feet when Malcolm stepped out, knowing several arrows and spears were aimed at them. He hoped they didn't want to fight—the dinosaurs were excellent fighters without the spears.

Malcolm held one arm high, his palm outward in a stopping motion. He kept his spear vertical so the raptors didn't think he was attacking and hoped they would back off without fighting. The lead raptor stopped dead in his tracks when he saw Malcolm and barked out a hissing command to the others. The raptor stood, swaying from side to side on its legs, as it sniffed the air. Malcolm held his position, not moving and watched intently for any aggressive move on the raptor's part, ready to run back into the trees. One of the smaller raptors stepped around the leader and took a hesitant step forward, baring its teeth. It was a short-lived gesture when another raptor used one of its front limbs to sweep back the youngster and hissed at it.

The lead raptor was looking at the rest of the thorn trees and seemed to come to a conclusion. It snapped out another command and the raptors turned away.

Malcolm breathed a sigh of relief. The thought of an intelligent, weapon-carrying raptor scared him. He hoped Carl and company didn't come across any.

Chapter Thirteen:
The Desert Ghoul

Cha-lui-x emerged from the canopy of twisted tree limbs that covered the front of his dwelling. The large dwelling indicated his high position within the Cha Clan, and was made from the talnut tree. The inside was partitioned by a wall at the back two-thirds of the oval-shaped home that served as sleeping quarters for him, his mate, Cha-dos-r, and their four offspring. The offspring did not have names, choosing them when they moved out on their own as their older sisters and brothers did. Like all offspring, they were simply called Cha-x or Cha-r depending whether they were male or female.

The clan was a successful one and was growing at an acceptable rate, which made them a threat to some of the other clans as they pushed their boundaries. Just a few months ago, the Cha Clan attacked the Rhos Clan after the Rhos Clan killed two of their hunters. The battle cost the lives of many raptors on both sides before the Rhos Clan withdrew from the disputed territory.

The leader of the Cha Clan, Cha-trtr-r, was considering launching another attack on the decimated Rhos Clan and either killing or absorbing the clan unto her own. The key to such a strategy was to maim the leader of the opposing clan during the battle and then challenge him or her to a fight for the leadership. Cha-trtr-r was thirty years old and now in the declining years of her prime. In another five years she would likely hand over her command to her strongest offspring, keeping the power within her own family.

Char-trtr-r leapt down from the second-level of her home. The second-level could be accessed from the inside or outside using a four-foot and then an eight-foot platform made out of three-foot diameter tree trunks that looked like the start of a giant staircase. The raptors made a series of three easy leaps to reach the second-level but one leap was normally used to return to ground level.

In the courtyard, several hunters waited for her. Already her three lieutenants were clearing an area for her to enter and making sure the hunters were isolated from the throng of onlookers. The lieutenants, two males and a female, had several duties. They had to handle small disputes among the clan members, advise Cha-trtr-r on matters when she requested it and protect her from other families looking to usurp her power. In other clans, one family member may attack the leader without warning, usually dying in the process. While the leader was still trying to recover from the wounds, a second member would make the challenge for ruler of the clan. A challenge for leadership could only be made at least one half-year after the last one, so challenges were usually planned out carefully to optimize their chances.

One of the new hunters spoke for the rest, an old male who Cha-trtr-r respected for teaching new hunters how to capture or kill prey. This time he had gone out to kill rather than bring back live food and came back with a horrible message. She listened to his tale of finding several of the flat-muzzled beasts.

She was sceptical. First, he admitted he had seen only one—the others were hidden among the tree leaves. Second, their appearance was a bit different than the records indicated. They were smaller with less fur than their old enemies. They also wore skins, which gave them an odd form. The oddest part of the story was that the flat-muzzles did not attack them, not taking advantage of an easy ambush as they hid in the trees.

Cha-trtr-r was troubled with the news. The triceratops hunt did not go well, with the herd charging out of the trap set for them, resulting in fewer kills, plus a longer journey to bring back the meat. If that was cause for Cha-trtr-r to feel annoyed, she now had this tale of the possible reappearance of their old foes that her ancestors fought over a hundred years ago. These were the ones that forced several clans to join to eliminate them. The enemy was treacherous then, killing clan members on sight, attacking whole clans and then returning to hide inside their fortress. The flat-muzzles would also kill game indiscriminately and leave the carcass to rot. This attracted the huge theropod scavengers to the raptors territory, making life more precarious. It took many more years after the flat-muzzled beasts were killed before they were able to drive off the giant megaraptor theropods.

Cha-trtr-r thought carefully about the information. She considered that it was quite possible another of those flat-muzzled creatures had returned. The fact that they hadn't attacked was interesting but pointless to debate. There could be several reasons for that, including that there was only one adult and several youths in the tree grove.

She needed more information and she looked to her lieutenants for help.

Cha-lui-x led the party of fourteen raptors. The number was significant, any less and Cha-trtr-r felt they might have trouble defending themselves against the vicious flat-muzzles. A group of a dozen raptors would be seen by the other clans as a large hunting party but any more could be interpreted as a possible raiding party of the neighbouring clans. The Cha Clan was one of the larger clans and was watched suspiciously by the other clans, with good reason. They had absorbed two other clans in past two years.

Cha-lui-x headed towards the grove of thorn trees where the sighting of the flat-muzzles took place. It wasn't clear exactly which grove of trees were the ones, but Cha-lui-x suspected they would be moving around in any event. As long as he had the general area, he could begin a thorough search. What would happen when they found the flat-muzzles was a different matter. The old drawings on the clay tablets depicted a creature that was as cruel as it was clever. To fight such an enemy would take strength and cunning. The other clans had not been informed yet. There was little point in spreading speculation and still less in letting the others know the Cha Clan was occupied by a new danger.

Carl reached the apex of one row of hills only to be confronted with another. He cursed under his breath. The ripple of hills made the journey longer and tiring. He stopped to take a long drink of water, thankful that at least water wasn't in short supply with the numerous streams and ponds. More wildlife was present and though they weren't large, they still had to be respected. Chester was actually earning her keep for a change by yelping out in distress when a hidden predator was nearby.

Tanya was quiet as usual, though Carl thought there was more on her mind than normal. Several times he caught her staring at him, occasionally favouring him with a smile. Still she didn't get distracted from the business at hand, preparing meals and pointing out to Rog and himself where she felt the ghouls now live.

Camp was made towards evening in a relatively clear area. Fires were lit but Carl didn't feel the threat of predators close by. Raptors apparently didn't like the uneven landscape anymore than he did and it had been some time since they had seen any. After dinner, Tanya came to see him by his tent, carrying something in her hand.

"Hi, what do you have there?" He gestured with his hand to sit beside him on the ground.

She frowned. "I have a story, a confession to tell." Tanya slowly sat in front of him.

"How so?"

She looked troubled. "Do you remember how I told you Witchdoctors don't have relationships? Don't marry, don't know their own fathers?"

He nodded.

"My mom is going to kill me for telling you this, but I can't do this to you." She swallowed and then plunged on. "You see, each Witchdoctor has to pick out a suitable partner, one to father her daughter. On a night that she feels is right, she slips this powder into his drink, and, well, in the morning he remembers nothing. Like the night never happened." She held up the powder in the vial and then threw it into the bush. She looked at the ground as she spoke. "I was going to use it on you, but I can't. It felt so wrong, so deceitful."

He watched her look at him, her eyes wet. "Tanya..."

She held up her hand and started to get up. "I'm sorry, please forgive me. I never wanted to hurt you. I..."

He grabbed her hand and pulled her towards him. "It's alright. I'll have you any way I can."

She fell onto his lap, holding him tight.

For a long minute, he thought they would stay in each other's arms all night, then she whispered in his ear. "I still want to, if you'll have me."

He answered with a kiss and pulled her into his tent.

"Just one thing, Carl."

"What?"

"You may be eager, but I'm a virgin, so..."

"So I'll take it slow and easy. We have all night." And, he hoped, maybe our whole lives.

The next day was like most other days of travel except that the leader and the Witchdoctor wouldn't let go of each other, causing everyone else to move slower. They ignored the comments around them and put up with Rog's snide remarks. Nothing removed their smiles and grins until Rog announced there was an odd looking hill a few miles away.

Tanya looked at the white rock that covered the surface of the hill. The colour was not interesting but the black holes that looked like a cave entrance was.

She pointed a shaking finger at the hill. "The...the desert ghouls. They live there now."

She wasn't alone in her trepidation. Carl noticed everyone was silent as they peered at the ghouls' home.

"I'll go by myself. The rest of you wait here."

Tanya grabbed his arm. "Not so fast. Let me go check the Aura first to see if it's safe. Then, and only then if it's safe, we'll go together. You're not leaving me by myself now."

Rog put his hand on Carl's shoulder. "I'm coming too. Someone might have to carry you out of there, and I'm used to saving your ugly hide."

Carl gave in. There was a general concurrence among the group that they all would head down. That was later revised to half going down with the rest waiting at the camp.

Carl watched Tanya slip into the trance, her eyes fluttering under her eyelids. Occasionally she would move a limb or move her head as she moved about in the Aura. Carl expected she would be in the trance for an hour but she returned fifteen minutes later to their world.

She looked at Carl with wide eyes, her voice higher pitched even as spoke in a whisper. "They know we're here. There're so many of them, they live inside the four cave openings we saw on the face of the hill."

They made their way to one of the cave openings. It was larger than what he first thought, measuring almost fifteen feet high in a rough semi-circle. Carl stepped inside noting an artificial wall stood about ten feet inside facing them. The wall, which was made of a solid ceramic type of material, went to the ceiling and stretched about five feet past the cave opening on either side. Carl looked left and then right, wondering which side to go to when a ghoul appeared to the right. The creature placed his right hand on its left shoulder and spoke a single word in a raspy, clipped voice. "Follow."

He stared at them, waiting for them to either obey or not. Carl turned and started towards the creature, guessing that if Tanya or anyone felt different about following it they would speak up. Tanya squeezed his hand tighter as they approached the ghoul. The creature was dressed in a white sleeveless shirt and pants and its pale skin made it appear rather ghostly as it turned to lead the way. Carl had trouble making out details in the low light. The walls of the tunnel glowed from a yellow plant that clung to the sides, almost obscuring the rock surface completely. The tunnel didn't go straight, twisting and turning. Several times the ghoul stopped at forks in the tunnel so they wouldn't go down the wrong path. The tunnel would not only split left and right but sometimes up or down. The air felt damp and too warm and Carl soon found himself sweating. So far, no one spoke a word and Carl heard only his own quick breaths as they tagged along behind the silent ghoul.

Without any advanced warning, the tunnel suddenly opened up into a large cavern, about the size of a small football stadium. More glowing plants clung to the walls and to the stalactites hanging down from the ceiling. As Carl's eyes adjusted to the yellow light he noticed the benches that lined part of the wall. The seats appeared to be made out of some type of wood-like material and the ghouls occupied a few of the seats. In the centre of the room stood two ghouls, one appeared to be on the older side as it hunched over slightly and its skin appeared a little more grey than white. The ghoul that led them turned and stood off to the side.

It was the younger of the two ghouls that spoke in the clipped but raspy voice of the first. "Why they come?"

Carl turned to Tanya and whispered. "Try to get a read on their feelings." In a louder voice, he spoke to the ghoul. "To understand you. To go home, back to Earth."

The ghoul didn't reply for several seconds. "Earth?"

"The planet where I came from."

It considered the information for several seconds before speaking again. "Difficult to do. Possible. Not soon."

Carl decided a different tack might give more information. "Who are you? Do you come from this planet?"

The ghoul seemed to be expecting the question and had an answer ready. "We come from another star. Closer to the centre of the colony of stars. Seen many lives on planets rise, fall, disappear. We try to help, protect and know. Earth, yours? Showed good signs but hazardous system. Too many small planets. Saved walking lizards, smart, by bringing here. Then new creature like you and bring here. Terrible fight. Lizards win. Try again but in isolation."

It stopped as if the explanation was complete, but then suddenly started again. "You learn very fast. We worry too fast. Try to understand motive, reasons. Too different from us, maybe better. Someday be dominant. Want to help you learn. Not all at once."

Tanya whispered. "From what I sense it's being honest. The other one is conversing with it as the other talked."

"What? How? I didn't see its lips move."

"By smell. These creatures give off scents to communicate. And by reading each other's mind."

"Oh. Pheromones." He addressed the ghouls again. "How come that building is empty now? The one by the desert."

"We live in units. When unit gets too big, split. We unit get tired of new way, return to old ways. We to look after protected area, but later decide to stop intrusion. No need. You last to arrive, mistake. Not know what else to do, sent here. Cause of problem."

Rog poked him in the ribs. "Hear that? Said you were a problem."

Carl looked around again. The ghouls all looked passive but as Tanya had indicated, they communicated in different ways. He didn't doubt they would be in trouble if they tried to do anything aggressive. "So we are here for good because you wanted to learn about us? What made us tick?"

The ghoul was silent for several seconds as it considered how to respond. "True. No harm wanted. Just learn and maybe save."

"How many of you live here?"

More time went by as the creature stared at him. "Million plus several. Not just here. More on other side of water." It paused before speaking again. "Go now. Will speak again. Answer more."

"When? Where?"

"Desert building. Signal then."

The ghouls turned and walked away and the first ghoul approached. "Follow."

Carl was glad of the guide. He wasn't certain if he could find the way back. On their return, they did see some of the ghouls walking quietly down the tunnels and an occasional creature dart among the glowing plants. They reached the tunnel entrance and had to squint their eyes at the daylight.

"Wait." Their guide went back inside and behind the wall. He returned with what appeared to be a rolled up sheet of paper. Carl accepted the roll from the ghoul, stepping to the front of the wall where the light was better and unfurled the roll. It felt like plastic covered paper, around eight inches wide and twenty-five inches long, and looked like a world map. Several landmasses were scattered about in various sizes and perhaps half of the globe was ocean. The ghoul pointed at a peninsula with one of his fingers. Carl noticed the hand had six digits, four fingers and two opposable thumbs.

The peninsula was Sorbital and Carl recognized the small islands around it. As the ghoul rested his finger on the map, it changed, expanding the area several times in size. The peninsula now covered an area four inches square. The ghoul continued to place his finger on the expanded area and the area increased its size again. Carl made out the desert area of the top of the peninsula easily. Satisfied in showing Carl how to enlarge an area of the map the ghoul wiped the enlarged area with the palm of his hand and it returned to normal. The ghoul stood up and returned to the interior of the cave. Carl shouted out thanks and it turned around, placing its hand on its shoulder once more before disappearing.

Rog tried out the map himself and any area he touched, expanded in detail. If he held his finger down, the area would continue to expand and show detail as small as a meter. It was impressive and Carl wondered how it was accomplished as he rolled up the map again.

Tanya was quiet as they returned to the others. After they established camp again, she sat with him at his tent and related what happened to her as he was speaking with the ghoul. Apparently, the second ghoul was able to speak to her through the Aura, telling her much the same thing as Carl was told but in more detail.

Tanya closed her eyes as she recalled the information given to her. "The ghouls, or Keepers as they called themselves, are as they indicated, a very old race. They told me their age is not relevant because they continued to evolve after they became sentient and after they learned to conquer space travel. Their original ancestors were small hand-size creatures that lived in colonies underground, coming out at dusk to feed."

"So that explains why they live in caves now. They like dark, small places."

"True. They had male and female sexes, but didn't bond with each other. The females would lay a cluster of eggs and passing males would fertilize the jelly-like clusters that were left in small alcoves within the tunnel. The colony as a whole would raise the healthy young, killing the weak. Since each cluster contained several hundred eggs, the Keepers had to prune the population or the young would overrun them. It was one of the reasons the Keepers did not feel individuals were important, the colony took precedence."

"So they thought of us as a colony like ants?"

"In a way. They were amused by your annoyance that you were taken to Sorbital against your will. The Keepers felt the Earth colony as a whole was left alone and taking a few individuals was okay."

"So why did they take people and other creatures from Earth?"

"It took the Keepers two million years from the time they became sentient to the time they became able to travel among the stars. They found other intelligent species and most took approximately the same time, anywhere from just over a million years to five million years. The raptors were already several million years old evolving before being transplanted to Sorbital.

"The humans to them were a different story. Apparently, we mysteriously showed up as just below the sentient level a few hundred thousand years ago. It was noted in their records and hope was given a new sentient species would arise in another million years. Instead, a return visit to Earth showed humans had leaped to a sentient stage only a hundred thousand years later. Several species, including the Keepers, took a strong interest in the rapid development and watched more closely. They expected the advancement to slow down but to their surprise, the humans continued its rapid progression. The Keepers expect us to reach interstellar flight in another thousand years and this has caused some concern among the other intelligent species."

"What does that mean?"

"Just that they want to learn more about us. The Keepers are trying to understand humans, and are puzzled by so many aspects of our behaviour. They see that we live in colonies, but are able to survive quite well as individuals. They see that the two sexes form strong bonds to each other, often stronger than to a colony. What puzzles them is the two sexes are so unalike in temperament and physical appearance it was hard for them to understand why we are so strongly attracted to each other."

"I ask myself the same question about you."

Tanya gave him a smile. "Don't make me lose my train of thought. The Keepers also were impressed by human ability to withstand diverse climates from dry to wet and from cold to hot. The Keepers can only live in a relatively narrow range of humidity and temperature as in the case of most intelligent species.

"The other quality creatures from Earth have is sound. The music and singing of humans is considered an oddity and the Keepers don't understand its importance. The Keepers are aware we have lost a large portion of our sense of smell and they speculate one has taken over from the other. The last thing the Keepers told me was my mind was the next step in the evolutionary ladder. The ability to communicate using the Aura is something most species try to breed into their race."

"So you're the next great leap in evolution?"

"No, just that there will be more and more people able to use the Aura."

"It told you all that while I was doing one syllable words with its buddy?"

"Yeah, the Aura is much better to communicate with. Like, I get images and ideas instead of just words."

"Obviously it's better. Why haven't they talked to you before?"

She shrugged. "Probably wanted to stay hidden. I get the impression we scare them a bit, they aren't certain what we'll do next. They were relieved when we didn't attack them. They did have weapons to fight back but I don't think they know how to fight very well. Their first instinct would be to run or hide."

"So are they going to be our friends now?" Carl laughed as he asked.

"No, but they respect us. Which may be better." She wrapped her arms around him, resting her head against his shoulder, and they sat quietly until it was time to go inside the tent.

The travel back to the savannah was faster than the other way, as they understood the terrain better. Still it took a full day to reach the grassy plain where they had camped. Within another half-day, they would reach the grove of thorn trees where they left Malcolm and his company.

Chapter Fourteen:
Ambush

Cha-lui-x watched as Cha-guee-x used his spear to spread apart the remains of the fire. The ashes were long cold but there was a chance that something else might be revealed about the earlier campground. One thing Cha-lui-x noted was the flat-muzzles had at least cleaned the campground. This was not what he had expected from the old reports about the beasts. It could mean these were a slightly different species, which meant they have learned to be more responsible, or perhaps they covered up their remains to try to hide from any pursuers. The raptors sniffed the area, picking up the peculiar smell of mammals. Not much more information was available other than the direction they went, which was confirmed by the bent grasses. The raptors followed the trail uneasily.

ℰℭ

Rog rolled his eyes at the sounds behind him. Tanya and Carl were acting like they were the only ones who could hear their kisses, giggles and the simplistic words they uttered to each other.

"Enough you two already! I liked it better when she was acting like a witch and you as a know-it-all."

"Times change, my friend." Carl didn't sound concerned about Rog's outburst, despite some shouts of support from the others that travelled with them. "But don't worry, I still know everything."

"Then you gotta know what you're doing is really annoying."

"Sorry, Rog. Don't stay mad at us." Tanya ran up to where he was walking and hooked her arm into his. "I'll try to behave. How much longer until we come across where we left Malcolm and the rest?"

"Not soon enough." He grimaced and then looked into the distance. "I dunno. Maybe another half-day. They may have gone on to that old settlement, which would add another day."

"Oh. Well in that case maybe we should stop for something to eat. Are you hungry? I have some of that deer meat left over."

"Sure. We'll stop by that big rock over there." Rog knew she was trying to make up to him by offering him one of his favourite foods, and he began to relax his frown. He was aware she could read his emotions enough to know he had been getting more and more annoyed by their behaviour and Tanya was trying to make amends. He was also aware she was working on his disposition by bumping her hips against his as they walked. It was an obvious and deliberate attempt to use her sex to get him to change his frame of mind and he reluctantly admitted she was making it work.

"Okay, I'm not mad at you anymore. You can walk with your boyfriend again."

"That's alright. I'll walk with you 'til we stop if you don't mind. I figure I better learn how to get along with you since you're Carl's best friend."

"He won't be if he hangs around with a witch all the time."

"Watch it or I'll make you fall in love with a raptor."

"It's always about your side of the family isn't it?"

Carl watched from behind as Tanya punched Rog in the shoulder and laughed. Things were good right now and he didn't want it to stop. But the return to Sorbit and Teresa might change all that. Would Tanya and he be allowed to live together?

Malcolm wished they could move a little faster. But Katrina was hobbling the best she could with a walking stick. That also meant someone else had to carry her load of supplies, slowing them down as well. Malcolm himself wasn't certain how well his knees could hold up to a faster pace. His wish that they could travel faster remained just that. He felt that there was something following them and the sense was getting stronger which indicated the gap was getting smaller.

Katrina moved from the middle of the pack closer to Malcolm. Malcolm heard her uneven stride as she drew closer and slowed down to make it easier for her.

"Malcolm, I feel another presence behind us and I don't think it's Carl and the rest."

Malcolm didn't tell her he felt the presence as well, letting Tanya know he had the gift was enough of a disclosure. "Might be raptors or cats thinking we're prey. We better get someone to watch our backside."

"When we stop, I could try to use the Aura to find out what it is, but I'm not certain what the others would think if they saw me trying to use it."

Malcolm considered her suggestion. The others would certainly be apprehensive if they noticed her using the art again. Of course, if he were to make the request in front of them, it would probably be okay. "Well, let's keep that in mind. It's a good idea, but let's wait and see if anything else develops first."

"Sure. I'll ask Benny if he'll keep an eye out behind us."

"Thanks, girl. We'll take a break in an hour if your leg holds out that long."

Malcolm considered the different possibilities of what was trailing the group. For both Katrina and him to have sensed they were being pursued probably meant there had to be a fair number of animals. Neither of them, he felt, was sensitive to discern only one or two pursuers. That meant a pack animal of some kind, maybe a large family of the sabre-tooth cats but more likely raptors. Neither was an inviting possibility, especially if the spear carrying raptors were the ones. Malcolm knew they needed to stop soon and hoped to see a shelter or grove of thorn trees soon.

Cha-lui-x sent several of his pack after the deer. As usual, the raptors attacked from two sides, breaking apart the deer into smaller groups. A selection of four deer was made and they were steered into the waiting spears of more raptors ahead. The kill was done quickly and soon the prey was divided among the raptors. Cha-lui-x, as was custom, ate first and choose the best portion. A large portion of one deer was left and cooked to eat later. Fresh meat was best but when it was cooked, the spoilage slowed. Some raptors actually preferred slightly cooked flesh to fresh but Cha-lui-x would not admit to such pampering. A hunter of high rank had an image to protect.

The raptors were closing in on the flat-muzzles but not as fast as Cha-lui-x would have liked. They temporally lost the scent at a watering hole and had to circle around to find the trail again. The trail went by some sabre-tooth cats that had just made a kill of their own causing the raptors to circle around. It was fortunate the trail was still fresh, meaning they were gaining. Cha-lui-x resisted the temptation to increase their pace to a half run. He didn't want to tire out his hunters if a battle was to be fought. How a possible battle was to be fought depended on the number of the flat-muzzles. He needed time to plan a strategy, and was not planning to get himself killed on a fact-finding mission. Many of the raptors looked down on mammals, considering them inferior to reptiles and certainly dinosaurs. Certainly, the allosaur and the forty-foot crocodile were the dominant predators compared to the sabre-tooth cat. The only reason, some claimed, the cats were still alive was because the raptors had chased away the other two predators from the nearby habitats. The deer, as prey, lacked the size and protection of the triceratops, proving again the superiority of the reptiles. Cha-lui-x and Cha-trtr-r had had several conversations about such arguments in the past. They both boasted to the tribe how superior raptors and the Cha Clan were over other life, but in private admitted to other thoughts.

Cha-lui-x knew the mammals were smart. The sabre-tooth cats were very cunning, at least as smart as the raptor's less fortunate cousins, another type of dromaeosaur. The deer may not be as strong as the triceratops but their numbers were growing at the expense of the larger plant eaters.

He had listened to Cha-trtr-r tell how many small mammals were fighting the small reptiles for a small bit of ground to live on, and were winning. Slowly, so slowly that it was not noticeable at all in only a year, the mammals were gaining position.

It was a depressing thought for Cha-lui-x and worse of all was the possible return of the flat-muzzles, the beasts that almost destroyed the raptors over a hundred years ago.

Carl took the lead after dinner, letting Rog relax for a change. Being the lead meant keeping ones eyes and ears open—concentrating on what lay ahead. For that reason he also had Tanya stay back. She had become a serious distraction to him whenever she was close by.

A few hours later they came across the grove of thorn trees Malcolm had stayed at. It was deserted and Carl supposed the trees were not the best for an extended stay and Malcolm had decided to make for the abandoned settlement. Which meant, he reasoned, that Katrina had healed sufficiently well to be able to walk. They stopped only long enough to drink water and then headed onward in Malcolm's footsteps. The path was easy to follow, and it was Rog who first mentioned it was a little too easy.

"These grasses should not be lying down like this. Some, maybe. I would guess there was more than just Malcolm's group walking down here. We didn't leave a trail like this when we arrived."

Carl bent down and looked at the yellow grasses that were stomped down. "A lot of feet did this. Maybe a herd of deer or triceratops did this."

"Hmm, maybe. But since when do deer follow people?" He pointed at Chester. "Your friend there sure is excited about what she is smelling."

Carl watched as Chester went around smelling the ground, looking nervous. "Good point. Let's look for some tracks other than human."

Tanya spotted the telltale prints first. "Raptors. Not big ones fortunately, but raptors all the same."

Carl stood up. "Tanya, see if you can use the Aura to find out what's happening. Rog, I need to talk to you."

He unrolled the map and enlarged the area they were in. "See, there's the old settlement where Malcolm has gone. When we went from there to this grove of thorn trees, we went in a round about way. Like to this watering hole."

"Sure, we circled that way and then there." He moved his finger along the previous route.

"Right. I'm thinking we use a more direct route to get back to the settlement. I think we will be able to catch up to them before they arrive there, especially if Malcolm and Katrina are not walking too fast. They may need our help and if we move quickly maybe we can arrive in time."

"Gotcha. We can increase our pace without much of a problem. If someone finds the load too heavy, they can dump it. Nothing too valuable here."

They waited almost half an hour before Tanya could tell them anything. She had trouble reaching Malcolm's group, the distance weakened her sensitivity and she only felt Malcolm and to a lesser extent Katrina. Both, she believed, were nervous about being pursued by something dangerous and smart. She did sense the others were okay but there was a disturbance that likely came from the raptors that were trailing them.

Carl outlined to the rest what Rog and he had planned and soon they were off, slowly diverting from the original trail. Rog took the lead, promising his built-in compass would not lead them astray.

The problem was what to do next. Cha-lui-x waited patiently far enough away from the grove of thorn trees to remain hidden from the flat-muzzles. One lone raptor was given the job of watching them from a closer vantage point behind a large rock outcropping in case the flat-muzzles started to leave. That was unlikely to occur soon as he could smell the cooking of food. Keeping downwind from their quarry was second nature to the raptors and so far, they believed they were completely unnoticed. Cha-lui-x had a look at the flat-muzzles long enough to believe they were the same, or nearly the same, beasts his ancestors had tried to eradicate long ago. How or why they suddenly showed up again was important too. Even if they could kill these flat-muzzles hiding in the thorn trees, that wouldn't help know if there were more, where they came from and why they were in the Cha Clan's territory.

A decision had to be made one way or the other, events were going to happen and it was better to be the instigator of them than just reacting. Cha-lui-x sent a runner back to the Cha Clan to report to Cha-trtr-r that the story of the flat-muzzles reappearing was true, though they may be of a different type. Next, he sent four more hunters behind the grove of thorn trees to make sure if the quarry were to try to flee, they would be circled. He waited now for the four hunters to make their way in a large semicircle to their new position. Likely their scent would be picked up by the flat-muzzles as the raptors would be downwind, but Cha-lui-x felt detection couldn't be avoided forever in any event and certainly wouldn't matter soon anyway.

Twenty minutes later, Cha-lui-x and the rest of the raptors walked boldly towards the flat-muzzles hiding in the thorn trees. When he got close enough to see their faces, he stopped, holding his spear in his two paws towards them. Ideally they would try to escape and Cha-lui-x would be able to kill or capture one or two of them to take back to the Cha Clan for inspection. The rest of the flat-muzzles would be followed to see where their nest was and then the raptors could learn how many others there were. That was the ideal situation. But, he thought, it was unlikely they would flee, more likely they would attack and Cha-lui-x did not want to fight yet. If they were aggressive, he would retreat and pass their fighting methods on to Cha-trtr-r for assessment on what to do next. He hadn't been this nervous since his first triceratops kill as a youth, and he could smell the fear among some of his hunters. No doubt they believed these creatures were the demons sent to destroy their land, unlike the white ghosts who gave life to the raptors. Cha-lui-x resisted such superstition. He had never seen the white ghosts and didn't believe these beasts were demons either. Still, it was wise to consider such possibilities.

A few minutes passed and a flat-muzzle emerged, holding his spear in his hands like Cha-lui-x did. The flat-muzzle stopped a few feet from the thorn trees. It was not the response the raptor had expected. He thought they would attack, stay hiding among the trees or flee. Instead, this creature was standing out in the open with a weapon. It might be a challenge, or simply imitating Cha-lui-x's stance. The creature's smell indicated it was nervous, though not overly fearful. Cha-lui-x considered that the creature, by standing with its weapon at the ready, was going to simply wait for him to make the next move. This was not going well. The flat-muzzles were making this a complicated situation. Perhaps it would be best to retreat and wait for a response from Cha-trtr-r, though it would be a long time to hear her suggestion from a return runner. Regardless, Cha-lui-x felt an attack would be foolish. The flat-muzzles numbered about the same as the raptors, were protected by the thorn trees and had unknown weapons at their disposal. The problem with a retreat was that it made the Cha Clan appear weak and their sudden appearance to the flat-muzzles would have accomplished little.

He studied the flat-muzzle's face, noting the blue eyes were not looking at him any longer, but at something behind him. It was odd because his hunters had remained in their position along side of him. Then he heard a strange call behind him and he whirled around. Disaster!

Cha-lui-x stared at the new group of flat-muzzles, who had come from behind them into the small wind and thereby not giving a scent of their approach. His own hunters were now in a difficult situation, pinched between the ones in the thorn trees and the larger group behind them. The four members of his group behind the thorn trees were not much help now. He cursed for allowing himself to fall for their trickery. They must have detected the Cha hunters some time ago and laid this trap. He wondered when the leader of the flat-muzzles would yell out the battle cry, signifying the end of his reconnoitre team. They certainly wouldn't go without a fight, but the odds were long anyone could escape back to the clan home. The delay in the attack caused him to wonder if they were perhaps being given a chance to prepare for death, something that was common among the raptors when one clan had overwhelming odds in their favour. He didn't expect the flat-muzzles to have such beliefs, so perhaps this was supposed to be a chance to lay down their weapons and surrender. It was not an option he would normally consider for himself, but one had to think what was best for the rest of his hunters as well. He stared at the new group once more and saw two members were advancing, but not with menace as they held their spear points down. The taller one appeared to be the leader as it walked a half pace in front of the shorter one, stopping about eight feet away. They were communicating verbally, not using scent to express themselves, and Cha-lui-x admired their ability to hide their thoughts completely by using sound alone. Cha-lui-x considered carefully what was taking place. Apparently, they were being given a chance not to be killed in battle, and he was not going to lose that opportunity by bravado actions. He lowered his spear and barked out a command for the others to do so as well. The flat-muzzles had all lowered their spears save for a few that rested small, thin spears between a string and a curved stick. Cha-lui-x recognized the weapon, it could throw the tiny spear very fast from a distance but had proved to be difficult to use. Of course, these beasts had long arms that they could bend behind their back making such a weapon practical. After lowering the spear, Cha-lui-x waited impatiently for the next move.

"Okay, Tanya, now what?"

"Uh, well, he's still worried and a bit anxious. Hard to read his emotions being, well, a walking lizard. But I sensed a lot of relief when you lowered your spear."

"Their spears look a bit crude, like the spear shaft is just a long stick with a point on the end."

"With their claws I don't know why they would bother with a spear."

"Killing a triceratops is too hard without a spear is my guess. These raptors are smaller than the other kind, bigger head though. Their arms are longer as well and their claws can hold stuff, maybe they're getting civilized."

"Maybe. We better do something, this is getting on everyone's nerves."

"Right. I know what to do." Carl placed his spear on the ground slowly and then took out his knife from his belt. With slow steps he advanced, holding the knife by the blade and extending it towards the raptor. The raptor stared at the handle for several seconds before reaching out slowly to grasp the handle. The raptor turned his head to bark out a short command and another raptor advanced with a weapon.

Carl watched as the curved sword was slowly handed towards him. The broad sword was two feet long and made out of worked bone. Carl guessed that it might have been a rib from a triceratops, an impressive looking weapon.

It was time to part company, the encounter had proven to be awkward but successful. Carl turned around and gave a short whistle, causing everyone to walk slowly around the raptors towards the thorn trees.

The raptors looked at the open savannah and immediately started to walk towards it, then increased their speed after they went past the last human.

Malcolm was relieved when he first saw Carl and the others. He wasn't sure what the raptors wanted but certainly wasn't looking forward to any confrontation. The raptors didn't appear to be too aggressive but it was hard to read another species, though any thought of battle disappeared when the raptors became outnumbered.

As surprised as Malcolm was when Carl showed up, he was just as surprised when Carl and Tanya had walked up to the raptors and gave their leader a knife. If it had caught Malcolm off guard, it did the same to the raptors who tried to respond in kind by giving a sword. Malcolm thought Carl had lost his mind, but his tactic seemed to work when the raptors walked away peacefully.

"Any particular reason you gave them your knife?"

"Couple of reasons. One, an exchange of gifts might show them we don't want to fight them. The other is I saw how crude their spears were. They obviously don't have a sophisticated civilization. The knife's metal blade may indicate to them we may have weapons too advanced for them to attack us."

"Well, I reckoned it worked. Come on, time to find out what you learned about the ghouls."

Carl held up the rolled up map. "Boy, do I have a story to tell."

૪૭

Cha-trtr-r examined the knife in her home. The shiny blade was strong, sharp and not like anything she had seen before. The encounter with the flat-muzzles hadn't gone as she expected, leaving her perplexed. At least they didn't appeared to be an immediate threat, but that might still change. The knife worried her a bit. The flat-muzzles obviously had an ability to make weapons that the clan could not counter. She would have difficult decisions to make.

If she were to ignore the flat-muzzles, there was still the danger they could attack the Cha Clan. Their apparent non-aggressive attitude might be a ruse. Another possibility was that another clan might make an alliance with the flat-muzzles. The added strength and advanced weapons of the flat-muzzles would make that clan a formidable opponent.

However to approach the beasts again could anger them and that was something she wanted to avoid. She turned the knife in her claws, examining the blade and the carved wooden handle. Whoever made this weapon had a secret way with materials, something the white ghosts might use. The wooden handle was of interest too. A design was made on a well-shaped grip. The handle was not designed for her claws but she still appreciated the feel of the weapon and the ease it could be used against an opponent. If they could make this type of weapon, and give it away as a gift, she wondered what else the flat-muzzles had developed. The risk was too great that another clan may vie for their weapons and help. The Hea Clan in particular would present an almost unbeatable rival if they formed an alliance with the flat-muzzles. Cha-trtr-x considered what to do next.

Chapter Fifteen:
Sorbit Bound

Carl felt light on his feet as they headed on the homeward journey to Sorbit. He had done what he had set out to do, contacting the ghouls and perhaps setting the stage for a return to Earth in the future. Certainly, the ghouls had the knowledge and the technology to do so and they hadn't ruled out considering his request. Tanya was an even bigger reason for his happiness, she continued to be with him as he walked and had not gone back to her former hostile mood. His friend Rog had taken to being quite close to Katrina and Carl teased him he was going out with a witch as well. On a more serious side to his Quest, he had shown that there was a world outside of Sorbital that they could live in and discover.

"So how long are you going to have that silly grin on your face?"

"I don't know, as long as you stay by me I guess."

"That could be a long time." She paused and grabbed his hand. "I was going to tell you tonight but I just can't wait. Carl, I'm pregnant."

He tripped and fell. He looked up at her laughing face and grinned himself. "Pregnant? We're going to have a baby!"

Chester walked over to where he was lying down and began to lick his face, whether out of concern he fell or to help celebrate the pregnancy.

"Yes, we. A daughter."

"A girl? Are you sure?" He got up and hugged her.

"Witchdoctors can only have daughters."

"That's great news! Whowee!"

Carl and Tanya took in the congratulations from the rest of the group. Rog gave Carl some good-natured ribbing and wondered out loud if the baby was going to be as miserable as her mother was.

"Serve you right if she is."

"She'll be just like me, sweet and smart." Tanya smiled smugly.

"Yeah? The first thing she'll do is make a fist."

"Only to hit you for your idiotic remarks."

Cha-lui-x wasn't happy following the flat-muzzles. He had only three others with him and one of those was a runner to deliver a message to Cha-trtr-x when needed. He tried to keep downwind from the beasts but they were clever in ways he had little knowledge of. Last time he had found himself surrounded from the front and rear and he was leery of that happening again. There was also the danger of predators such as the sabre-tooth cats, and they would be difficult to handle with only a few hunters. Then, too, there was the possibility of running into another clan. Some clans were friendly, though another might take him and his companions prisoner and try to force out the Cha Clan plans. Despite his reservations about being caught or killed, he did relish the challenge of sneaking up behind the flat-muzzles. A few million years of being a predator that depended on stealth did not disappear easily.

"We're being followed again." Tanya sighed. She was about to use the trivoli when, as she began to relax, she picked up the murmurs of another intelligence close by.

"By whom?" Carl looked out beyond the campsite of the thorn trees where they had stopped for lunch.

"The same raptors, I think. They're keeping their distance and there's not very many of them. Not much of a danger, I suppose."

"Yeah, well I don't like it all the same."

"What can you do about it?"

"I don't know yet, but I'll think of something."

The raptors approached the thorn trees where the flat-muzzles had stopped to eat. The burning green leaves left a strong smell this time. Cha-lui-x knew they ate plants as well as meat, but didn't expect they would cook the green leaves as well. There wasn't much interest here though and they started along the trail of their quarry once more. A few minutes after they left the campsite, half of a dozen humans dropped from the tree branches. Rog congratulated himself on suggesting using the burning leaves to hide their scent as they moved behind the raptors.

The noise was obviously meant to attract their attention and Cha-lui-x snapped his head around at the noise. Several flat-muzzles stood there, spears held vertically, not as threat but as an indication of the confidence of their holders.

As soon as Carl heard Rog yell "Hey!" he doubled back with a few hunters of his own. He arrived a minute later to see the raptors looking at Rog and his company. He called out to his friend and watched as the raptors looked back at him and then back at Rog. Once again, the raptors had found themselves between two groups of humans, though this time they weren't completely surrounded.

Cha-lui-x cursed. It wasn't possible for the same thing to happen twice, but it had. Where did the flat-muzzles come from? How were they discovered? So far, the flat-muzzles had not harmed them but he wondered if their patience was going to hold up. They could run, of course, but that was how prey acted and not how a true hunter should act. He did have an obligation to protect those under him however, and he hoped his next act was not to be his last.

He threw his spear into the ground and walked half the distance between one of the groups of the flat-muzzles. Going down to both knees, he raised his head to expose his neck. If the flat-muzzles were to take his life, hopefully, they would understand they were to allow the others to live. A flat-muzzle approached carrying his spear. Cha-lui-x's tail twitched as he wondered if this was to be the end of his life.

Rog watched for any signs of aggression but the raptor remained with his forearms limp and his head raised. It certainly appeared to be a sign of surrender but who knew what the raptor actually was thinking. Perhaps Tanya was able to understand some of its emotion but he didn't think she could give him much warning before it attacked. One thing he tried to focus on was remaining calm, it wouldn't do any good for it to smell fear on him as he came closer.

When Carl signalled him to approach the dinosaur, Rog felt his stomach tighten. He wasn't about to yell back that he was scared, though he did consider the option for a brief moment. He wished the creature had walked towards Carl and not himself when it decided this unusual gesture. The next problem when he was close enough was what to do with the raptor. He didn't expect Carl would have him kill it with his spear.

Cha-lui-x watched as the flat-muzzle slowly stepped towards him. He could smell the fear and apprehension emanating from it. He didn't consider that unusual, no doubt the beast could pick up the same scent from itself. When it was within a few feet, it stopped and he heard the other mammal call out instructions to it. Cha-lui-x resisted the urge to close his eyes as he saw the spear, with its peculiar shiny end, arc towards him. The spear point touched him on his shoulder for a moment and then withdrew. He watched as the flat-muzzle then walked away. In a few minutes, all the flat-muzzles were walking away, leaving Cha-lui-x relieved and embarrassed. One flat-muzzle stopped and looked at him, and using one of its long, flexible arms, reached up and paddled the air. It was an odd gesture, but after a moment, Cha-lui-x was able to interpret the movement. He got to his feet, giving a quick verbal order to the runner. Cha-lui-x followed the flat-muzzle after sending a scent order for the last two raptors to continue to trail but at a reasonable distance. If the flat-muzzles were to kill him, at least the other two could escape and inform the Cha Clan.

The flat-muzzles walked without apparent order or reference to status. One did go in front but the others all acted like they were on the same level, save for one who did appear to be the leader. That caused Cha-lui-x to ponder as the leader was not the one in front, certainly a contradiction as far as raptors were concerned. Cha-lui-x was not able to decipher the scent instructions sent by the flat-muzzles other than obvious ones such as fear. Some of the beasts were giving an indication of fear but the leader was exhibiting signs of happiness. It was all rather confusing and Cha-lui-x wondered if he could ever make sense of the conflicting information. The leader and his female companion were obviously mates and they did a lot of physical contact, such that if they were raptors he would expect them to start having sex in another minute. Cha-lui-x wondered why he had been invited to join the flat-muzzles as they marched towards the east. Obviously he was expected to learn or understand something, but what that was he hadn't discovered yet. Cha-lui-x was also curious about Chester, wondering why the mammal acted like it was part of the flat-muzzles group. He knew its meat wasn't that good to eat so its purpose wasn't apparent.

Carl looked at the raptor. It had behaved itself as they walked. One of the archers kept an arrow trained on him in case he suddenly attacked but it appeared to be only curious as it looked around, sniffing the air constantly.

Carl finally spotted what he was looking for and lightly touched the raptor on the shoulder, then pointed at a flat, barren area that was a dried-up pond. The raptor followed Tanya and him while the rest waited nearby.

The dry ground made a good drawing surface as he made small figures of stickmen. Tanya told Carl the raptor seemed to understand what he was drawing, though she professed the reptilian brain was hard to interpret.

Cha-lui-x headed back with his two companions, they were curious to what happened but he simply informed them his information was for Cha-trtr-r only. The flat-muzzle showed him that they had come from the land-arm that went out to the sea to visit the white ghosts and were now returning home. The land-arm was the one area the raptors could not enter, with a hill made by the white ghosts standing on the only land entrance while the sea protected the rest. Water was an effective barrier to the raptors who didn't swim nor wanted to learn. The flat-muzzles also indicated they had conversed with the white ghosts, something the raptors had rarely been able to do. The white ghosts had made it plain in the past that they preferred a solitary existence.

The flat-muzzles also wanted to know where his clan lived and Cha-lui-x drew an area slightly more distant than that the actual site. There was a danger in being too forthcoming with information. One thing Cha-lui-x decided was that he had best forget about trailing the flat-muzzles. Twice he had been caught and until he learned how they detected him, he was not going to risk a third time. Cha-trtr-r may not approve but it wasn't her neck that would be sliced open. She would have to be satisfied with his information.

Tanya had revealed that the raptor was not entirely forthcoming in his answer on where they lived. That was expected, as the raptors obviously didn't trust them yet. Carl used the map to look for areas where they might live and spent considerable time enlarging one area of the map and then checking another possible site. When they finally stopped to make camp for the evening, Tanya held the raptor's sword and used the Aura to locate their home. Once Carl knew where to look, he spotted the change in the landscape on the expanded map. The village was large, at least as big as Sorbit, but the size of the population was impossible to guess at.

Tanya had tried to use the trivoli to divine a little more what lay in the future, but the small trivoli objects only gave vague indications of turmoil ahead. Once again, Tanya was tempted to see who her father might be but to use the Aura and the trivoli for personal use or gain was against the creed of being a Witchdoctor. She continued to speculate on two or three men she thought might be her father. Perhaps her mother would relent and give up his name to her now. She was going to announce to Teresa that she and Carl were going to marry, and that if called upon she would fulfil the role of Witchdoctor. There was a chance her mother would be so angry with her that she wouldn't have anything to do with her, but no doubt, a granddaughter would heal any bad feelings.

Tanya stole a glance at Carl as he ate. Smiling she reflected how much he had changed so much since he first arrived on Sorbital and how he had become a leader on this Quest. He was now bigger, stronger and much more confident in what he did. She knew she had changed herself, and while he had a part in that too, it was this Quest that allowed her to become what she wanted to be. Her powers with the Aura had suddenly exploded and with the removal of the negative influence of Florence and Katrina, she felt she deserved the title of Witchdoctor.

The group increased their pace on the homeward trail and Carl reminded them there was danger at hand. The new world was a strange mix of reptiles, mammals and dinosaurs that all competed aggressively. The ghouls, in their hope to help understand and preserve sentient life from Earth, had created a complex world that was looking for a balance among the life forms.

The door was still open when they arrived back at the ghoul-built hill. If it had closed by itself, Carl would have tried to break in through one of the windows or wait for someone to open the doors from the inside. Carl had to coax Chester to enter, though once inside she was happy to follow along the tunnel.

Carl now understood why the tunnel twisted the way it did and the soft glowing lights from the walls. The tunnel was meant to imitate the cave the ghouls lived in.

As they completed the long tunnel, Tanya heard a shout at the end, "They're here!" and then the rumble of feet as the greeters poured in to meet them. Tanya had sent an advance message to her mother by using the Aura and wasn't surprised Teresa had notified the rest of the village. She had been tempted to tell her more but held back her information on Carl and the pregnancy, preferring to tell her mother face-to-face.

Tanya walked with her mother back to her home. Everyone had broken into small groups as they journeyed back to Sorbit.

Several of the villagers took an interest in Chester who seemed quite happy at examining the people and the new smells.

Carl broke away almost immediately to talk to the families of those who died on the Quest. Tanya winced from the sudden change in emotion of joy to grief from the families. The Witchdoctors would have a lot of healing to do later.

Tanya listened to the latest gossip about Sorbit and then took a deep breath and blurted out the news that she couldn't hold any longer.

"I'm pregnant."

"What?"

"It's Carl's and he knows."

Teresa stared at her daughter and then gave her a hug. "Congratulations, dear, I know you'll be a great mother." She then put her hands on her hips. "But what did I tell you about using the sleep potion on him? This is going to cause a big problem in keeping him away."

"No, it won't. I'm going to marry him."

"You...you can't do that!"

"Yes I can. And I will. I love him and I want him to help raise her."

"But your Witchdoctor training?"

"I can be a wife, a mother and a Witchdoctor. There's nothing to prevent me from doing that."

Teresa just stared at her for a long moment, not speaking or moving. Thoughts and emotions raced between the two minds and Tanya suddenly felt her mother's resolve.

"You're too stubborn to argue with. If that's what you want to do, then you have my blessing." She hugged her daughter again. "But remember I warned you."

When they arrived at Teresa's home, Tanya divulged what happened between her and Katrina. Tanya believed Katrina was going to behave now but Florence was a different matter. The Elders would have to decide her fate.

Tanya also explained how she was able to use the Aura to live in the past of another creature, how she had been able to save Malcolm and her close connection with him.

"When he touches me I feel something like tingling. At first I thought it was because he had the gift." She looked at her mother as they sat at the table drinking tea. "But that's not the reason, is it?"

Teresa slowly shook her head, a tear finding it's way down her cheek. "God knows how I wanted to tell you, it's just that I was told by my mother not to ever tell you. But unlike you I always listened to my mother." She swallowed hard. "Yes, it's true. Malcolm is your father."

The party was a big one, celebrating the return of those on the Quest, Tanya's pregnancy and her announcement that Carl and her were to marry. Malcolm was drunk by the time Tanya pushed her mother towards him, telling him Teresa had something to say to him. From being inebriated with his eyes half-closed to looking cold sober took only one sentence.

Carl's home took a month to build with the help of the whole village. He was offered a prime area in the centre of the village where the Elders resided but choose instead a hill not far from where Teresa lived. Tanya created a garden in the backyard where she could focus on the Aura while Carl spent a lot of time writing about science, math and the various creatures they came across during the Quest. While the Elders still governed the village, Carl became the leader and was constantly called upon to help with disputes and to solve problems.

The months passed quickly and at exactly sunrise on the longest day of the year Tanya gave birth. For those who had read *Days of the Future* it wasn't a surprise.

The hundreds of deaths seen were at the abandoned settlement. The dark witch was either Katrina or Florence because of what they did, or Tanya who did have black hair. Florence had disappeared the day Carl and the rest had returned from the Quest. She was reported being seen in different parts of Sorbital and rumour was that she was going to live on Rhume Island.

The long line of Witchdoctors giving birth only to daughters was broken when Tanya delivered a son.

∞

She played with her son on the grass near her garden while Carl and Chester looked on. "So what would you do if the ghouls offered to take you back home to Earth?"

Carl looked at Tanya, at Edward and finally at the huge talnut tree growing beyond the garden. "I guess I'd tell them I'm already home."

She looked back at him and smiled. "Talnut, Carl. Talnut."

About the Author

To learn more about JH Wear, please visit www.jhwear.com. Send an email to jhwear@jhwear.com.

A no-nonsense starship captain and a billionaire financier,
Fairfax and Cavendish are the ultimate odd couple.
Until an insidious government conspiracy leaves
them with nothing—except each other.

Starchild
© 2007 Katriena Knights

When billionaire financier Harrison Fairfax boards the EarthFed starship *Starchild*, Captain Trieka Cavendish knows he'll bring trouble. Earthlubbers always do. But she has no idea "trouble" will come in the form of a vast government conspiracy that will turn her whole world upside down.

Harrison Fairfax has spent the past seven years trying to find out what happened to his wife, an investigative journalist. But his wife's disappearance is only the tip of the iceberg. What lies beneath is bigger—and much, much worse. It's a conspiracy reaching to the highest echelons of EarthFed.

Government strongmen, who are on to Fairfax's meddling, drive him and Cavendish into the wilds of the colony planet Denahault, where they discover even more secrets—and a passion that may be the only thing that can save them.

Available now in ebook and print from Samhain Publishing.

Enjoy the following excerpt from Starchild...

The roar of the engines rose louder. A strange enervation passed down Fairfax's limbs. Suddenly he was afraid to stay strapped in the chair. He pulled again at the restraining straps, his fingers weak and uncertain. The engines seemed to scream inside his head. Blood pounded behind his eyes like fingers trying to push his eyeballs forward, out of their sockets. The walls of the small cabin shimmered.

He closed his eyes, panic rising in his chest. The howl of the engines drowned out everything but the sound of his own heartbeat.

"Harrison..."

Fairfax gasped in shock, his eyes snapping open. The voice had been impossibly soft, a murmur he shouldn't have been able to hear over the engines. But the sound of it closed a fist around his heart.

"Kathi."

The room was empty. The shimmering had intensified. Looking at the moving walls made him sick. The voice came again, a breath of memory, carrying with it a soft odor of roses.

"Harrison..."

Colors came together from the air and suddenly she stood in front of him. Straight black hair framed an oval face. Her eyes were dark, and she smiled. A hard lump rose in Fairfax's throat.

"Kathi..."

"It's all right," she said. She faded, becoming translucent. He tried to reach out, but the webbing held him.

"No."

"Don't stop searching," she said. "You have to end this. She can help you."

The lump rose into Fairfax's sinuses, filling his head with thick tears. She had become a wisp of color against the cabin's gray walls. She lifted her hand to her lips and kissed her fingers, then turned her palm toward him.

"I love you." Her lips moved, but he could no longer hear her voice.

"No!" he howled, and tears came behind it. He sagged against the webbing, weeping.

ℛ

They settled nicely into hyperspace, the ship weaving a stable course through folded space. Trieka returned to her cabin to enter her daily log. She was just finishing when her comm panel buzzed.

"Cavendish."

"Captain, it's Commander Anderson."

"What's up, Jeff?"

"Not a lot. I just thought you might like to know that Fairfax called medical right after we stabilized in hyperspace."

Trieka frowned. "Is he all right?"

"I don't know. I assume it's not serious. He was treated in his cabin."

"All right. Thanks."

Trieka broke the connection and considered, tapping her keyboard with a short, blunt fingernail. He was probably fine. If there had been an emergency, she would have been notified by medical. That didn't stop her from worrying, though. Apparently Fairfax had awakened her maternal instincts. Funny—she hadn't thought she had any.

He didn't answer her buzz immediately. She was about to buzz again when she heard the soft click of the door lock disengaging. She pushed the button and the door slid open. With some trepidation, Trieka stepped in.

Fairfax lay on the too-short bed, on his back. He had one arm bent behind his head, the other rested on his stomach. His legs were crossed at the ankles. As Trieka came in, he swiveled his head slightly toward her. His eyes looked dead, as if he hid pain behind them.

"Captain," he said in a voice just as emotionless.

"Mr. Fairfax." Trieka paused, not sure what to say. "I heard you called medical. I just wanted to see how you were doing."

"I'm fine." He almost snapped the words, then his lips pressed tightly together and he blinked rapidly a few times. Trieka waited.

After a moment, he sat up in the bed and looked at her. His eyes were red-rimmed. Startled, Trieka realized he'd been crying.

"I'm sorry," he said, more gently. "The hyperspace jump had some side effects I didn't expect, that's all."

Trieka nodded. "Hallucinations?"

He merely looked at her without answering, then said, "What causes that?"

"Nobody knows. Theory has it that some people are more sensitive to the probability intersections than others. So the hallucinations are actually glimpses into other probabilities."

He absorbed her words in silence. His jaw clenched, a muscle bulging along his jaw line, then relaxing. He looked away from her. "I saw my wife."

"Oh," Trieka said, because she could think of nothing else. She could only imagine what it must have felt like. "I'm sorry."

"The doctor gave me a shot. She said it should make me feel better." There was a bitter twinge in his voice. Trieka moved toward the door.

"If there's anything I can do for you, please let me know—"

He looked at her then, and she froze in the intensity of his gaze. There were too many emotions in his eyes to count: fear, anger, heart-rending sorrow. Then a quick flash across his face: determination, decision.

"There is something you can do for me. No matter what happens, no matter what you find out, I want you to trust me."

Trieka swallowed. Her throat was utterly dry. "I don't understand."

He shook his head once, sharply. "No. Not understanding. Trust." He moistened his lips, still holding her in his gaze. "Will you?"

Her head moved a little to one side, as if in negation. She felt weak with him staring at her, as if she'd lost control of all faculties, mental and physical.

And suddenly she realized she wanted him. More than just casually, or out of curiosity. She wanted to cradle him with her body and make him forget the tears he'd just shed and whatever had caused them. And then she wanted to peel him out of his clothes and crush him naked against the wall by the narrow berth.

Control came back to her only because she fought for it. Still his eyes held her, and somehow she knew something fundamental was about to change. Within her, around her. Outside, hyperspace divided possibilities, probabilities, wide and narrow paths.

Tentatively, Trieka set her feet on one.

"I'll see what I can do."

GREAT CHEAP FUN

Discover eBooks!

THE FASTEST WAY TO GET THE HOTTEST NAMES

Get your favorite authors on your favorite reader, long before they're out in print! Ebooks from Samhain go wherever you go, and work with whatever you carry—Palm, PDF, Mobi, and more.

Samhain
Publishing
LTD

Printed in the United States
137798LV00002B/156/P